Island
Blues

Also by Wendy Howell Mills
Island Intrigue

Island
Blues

Wendy Howell Mills

Poisoned Pen Press

First Edition 2007

10 9 8 7 6 5 4 3 2 1

Library of Congress Catalog Card Number: 2006936947

ISBN: 978-1-59058-396-8 (1-59058-396-5) Hardcover

Poisoned Pen Press
6962 E. First Ave., Ste. 103
Scottsdale, AZ 85251
www.poisonedpenpress.com
info@poisonedpenpress.com

Printed in the United States of America

For my little gem in the rough

Chapter One

It was a nice day to toss a mullet on Comico Island.

The noon ferry was backing into its spot with great roars of engines and spurts of water, and the spring sun was drenching the air with exuberant light. Sabrina paused at the edge of the public beach to savor the view of the harbor, feeling the pleasant punch deep inside her stomach at the realization that she lived in this marvelous place.

As she approached the throng of people standing on the beach, an object flew high in the air and landed with a thump in the sand, accompanied by cheering and clapping.

"One hundred and five feet! Not bad, Jimmy!"

Sabrina made her way through the crowd to a spot where she could see the proceedings. A large rectangle had been staked off in the sand. At one end of the rectangle stood a man in a robe with a microphone, and at the other end lay a large dead fish. Every other available inch of sand was crowded with people and their beach chairs, coolers, and umbrellas. As Sabrina watched, Sergeant Jimmy McCall reached into a blue cooler and brought out a dead mullet. He hefted its weight in his palms and squinted down the beach. Several young boys who had crowded the end of the course nimbly moved out of the way.

Jimmy took the fish by the tail and swung it back and forth before letting it fly high into the air. It landed with a puff of sand, and several people ran out with a tape measure.

"One hundred and twenty-six feet! It's a record, Jimmy!"

"Jimmy always wins," a voice said in Sabrina's ear. "Course, if I was to throw one of them mullet, there's no telling how far it would go. Clear over to the mainland, I'd guess."

"Hello, Lima." Sabrina turned to greet her friend. Lima was older than he cared to admit, with the quirky temperament of a blue-eyed redhead, though his hair had long since faded to cinnamon and sugar. He wore ragged pants, a red flannel shirt, and white rubber boots up to his knees, and his face was creviced with sun and age, but lively with humor. He shook his head as he peered over Sabrina's shoulder at the next person who was stepping up to throw a fish.

"Poor Mickey couldn't throw himself away if he tried, but he just won't quit trying." Lima turned away from the young man hefting his fish and stared at Sabrina with sharp eyes honed by years and experience. "I heard you've been a busy little bee today."

"Hmmm." Sabrina never stopped marveling at the speed of the island gossip train.

"I heard about that tourist woman you helped save from the evil clutches of Vicki Carroway."

"Did you?"

"Someone needs to shoot Vicki Carroway and put her out of our misery. Nasty piece of work, that one."

Sabrina nodded. Vicki Carroway was the newest, hottest property manager in town. While her success at bringing people to the island was phenomenal, her people skills left much to be desired.

A gasp of horrified titillation rose from the crowd, and Sabrina turned to see that Mickey had thrown his mullet high into the air. It was immediately apparent that it was not going where it was supposed to, and everyone stared in fascination as the fish sailed off course and landed in the front seat of a BMW convertible.

"Isn't that—" Sabrina got up on tiptoes to try to see over the crowd.

"That's the best I've ever seen Mickey throw." Lima nodded with satisfaction.

"Lima! That's Vicki Carroway's car! She'll never get the smell out."

"Ooops." Lima smiled. "Anyway, I don't know why she felt the need to drive her car the two blocks from her office down to here. People don't know how to walk anymore. Our roads are so crowded it took me twenty minutes to walk down to the general store this morning. I feel like I'm living in the big city."

Sabrina suppressed a smile, because Comico Island, surrounded by water and mainly designated as a wildlife preserve, was about as far from the big city as one could get. But it was true that the traffic was increasing as of late, and their small patch of paradise was beginning to feel crowded.

"What do you think about these break-ins?" Lima spoke over the cheering crowd as the next thrower chose his fish.

Sabrina frowned. "I'd only heard about the one over at the Seas the Day Cottage."

"Good lawd, don't call it that! You sound like a tourist."

It was the worst kind of reprimand, and Sabrina nodded in solemn recognition of her error. "What other break-ins?"

"Weeell" Lima rocked back on his heels and tugged his hat low over his eyes. "Somebody broke into Hill Mitchell's house Friday night. Didn't take anything, just moved some furniture around. 'Bout drove poor Hill over the edge, and he's already standing there on one foot with his eyes closed just waiting for a strong breeze. He didn't call the police about it, since nothing was stolen, but I bet the same person's responsible."

"A rather ineffectual burglar, don't you think? To go to all that trouble and not take anything."

Lima shrugged. "In case you hadn't noticed, some people got brains God gave a toilet plunger. My great-nephew Kealy, for example, I'm sorry to say, falls in that very category. Some misguided soul sent Kealy an envelope full of cash, addressed to him and everything, but with no return address. So what does Kealy want to do? Turn it over to the police! Why, I ask you? Is it a crime to send a body money by mail?"

"No, of course not. At least, I don't think so, though nowadays there's no telling what might be illegal. But why would someone send Kealy cash anonymously?"

Raised voices on the other side of the crowd were growing louder and they turned to see that Mickey McCall and the owner of the BMW, Vicki Carroway, had squared off. From this distance it was difficult to hear what they were saying, but the pugnacious chins and red faces were evidence enough that tempers were heated.

"I wonder what kind citizen showed that Vicki Carroway where to park her fancy con-vert-i-bell."

"Oh, Lima, you didn't!"

"Maybe I did, maybe I didn't."

With a cackling Lima in tow, Sabrina made her way over to the convertible, where things were getting ugly.

"I s-s-s-s-said I was s-s-s-orry," Micky McCall was saying, his young face shining with angry sweat.

"'S-s-s-sorry' isn't good enough, you dumb hick," Vicki Carroway said. "You need to pay to have my leather cleaned. Capeesh?"

"C-c-c-ca-what?"

"C-c-c-a-what?" Vicki was not a beautiful woman, though her hair, a long, shimmering wave of silver, projected a beautiful person aura. That was until you noticed her churlish eyes and parsimonious mouth. She was tall, and instead of hunching her shoulders so she blended in with the smaller women with whom she shared the world, she wore heels and stood with a chest proud stance, the better to intimidate those around her. Right now she stood staring implacably down at poor, sweating, stuttering Mickey McCall, like a cat with every intention of squashing a bug, though only after she had wrung every last ounce of enjoyment from him.

"Hello, Vicki, what's going on?"

Vicki swung around and fixed Sabrina with an irate glare. "None of your business. Get lost."

"Well, I thought you should know something, but if you don't want to hear it—"

"I don't." Vicki turned away.

"Well, it's your call," Sabrina said cheerfully.

"Wait a minute," Vicki said, turning back around. "You're Sabrina Dunsweeney. You're the one who helped that dumb tourist woman this morning, aren't you? Next time you decide to stick your nose in my business, don't forget you're staying in one of my apartments. I could have you evicted so quick you won't know what hit you."

"Vicki," Sabrina said, "you might want to step out of the way. You, too, Mickey."

"What?" Vicki turned around to see a tow truck backing slowly through the crowd. Bright spring sunlight cascaded from the sky and ignited her hair into a nimbus of silver and gold, and it crackled and burned as she began to shake her head. "Don't you dare tow my car!"

"That's what I was trying to tell you earlier. Not only did you park at the finish line for the mullet toss, but it's also a tow away zone."

Chapter Two

"Hill Mitchell, you better get your butt over there and toss this fish or we'll have a riot on our hands."

Hill looked up from his magazine just in time to have a very dead, stinking mullet thrust into his hands. He flinched, though the rotund woman with impossibly red hair was too busy tapping her spotless white tennis shoe to notice.

"Mary, I don't—" He tried to give the fish back to Mary Garrison Tubbs, but she wasn't having any of it, the bossy old biddy. His skin crawled and he wished with all his heart he had never gotten out of bed today. It was something Hill often wished, but in fact this morning he was exhausted, as he'd spent the last two days disinfecting his house after the break-in. He was afraid his couch might never be the same after he hosed it down, and he'd had heart palpitations when he realized he hadn't replaced his toothbrush. Who knew what the burglar had done with it?

"Hill, we need a distraction!" Mary hissed, propelling him to the front of the crowd. "You're the mayor, do your job."

"Nobody told me throwing a dead fish was part of my job description!" But Hill did as he was told and paid his five bucks for the privilege of throwing a fish, though he wanted nothing more than to dive for the nearest sink to scrub his hands until they were red and sanitary. A good soak in bleach might even be in order.

"Folks, we have a surprise!" Pastor Josh said into the microphone. "I know you're not going to believe it, but Hill Mitchell has graciously agreed to toss a mullet to help raise money for our elementary school. I know you haven't forgotten, people, that every dime we raise today at the Mullet Toss Festival will go to buy our kids new dustless erasers, so get up here, I say, and do your part to help our schools, can I hear an amen! If Hill Mitchell can do it, any one of you can."

Mary's ruse seemed to be working as people, distracted by the sight of the fussy mayor holding a dead fish, turned away from the contretemps over the glossy BMW.

"I never thought I'd see the day," whispered someone, and another lady said, "You know, Hill won't even touch his own mailbox." Other islanders were yelling encouragement as Hill stood with his eyes closed, trying to pretend none of this was happening.

"Let's give Hill a little encouragement, friends and neighbors!" Pastor Josh said, as Hill continued to stand motionless. Pastor Josh started the crowd on a rousing rendition of Queen's "We Will Rock You," and while they were chanting about Buddy boy making a big noise and stomping their feet, the pastor took a surreptitious sip of a flask and then poured some in Hill's unresisting mouth.

When the chant wound down from lyric ignorance—there were only so many times you can sing "we will rock you" without feeling silly—Pastor Josh took the microphone again. "Okay, folks, Hill's going to throw now. And remember, if you're looking for a slightly dented, early model Buick, come on down to God's Grace Car Lot after we're done throwing fish. Okay, Hill, are you ready?"

Hill was thinking about his bed, longing for his thick plaid comforter and his soft, hypoallergenic pillow. If only he'd slept in today, he never would have seen the magazine article, heard about the new burglary, or be standing here with a germ-ridden mullet in his hands.

"Come on, Hill, make Comico proud!" somebody yelled.

"Hill's the man!"

Pastor Josh rubbed Hill's shoulders, loosening him up as he leaned his forehead against Hill's. "Keep focused, Hill, don't worry about the crowd. Remember, you're a winner!"

With one final pat on his backside, Pastor Josh pushed Hill to the starting line.

Hill took a deep breath, regretting it immediately as he inhaled rotting flesh—was it possible to *drink* bleach?—and threw the fish.

The cheers fell silent as the fish landed with a puff of sand. A tourist snickered, and a few islanders turned to glare, never mind that they had been hiding snickers of their own.

"Well, dang, Hill, my two-year-old can throw farther than that," someone said.

"Hill, my son, would you like to try again?" Pastor Josh asked.

"No, thank you. I think I'm going to throw up."

The crowd parted as Hill ran for the nearest restroom.

"Mary, that was pure meanness making Hill throw that fish," Lima Lowry said. "I have new respect for you."

"Hill is the most ineffectual man I ever did meet." Mary looked with satisfaction over the now peaceful crowd. Vicki Carroway had left without further incident and, at the moment, vacationers and islanders seemed to be getting along as they cheered a throw by Grandma Jill.

"If Hill's so ineffectual, why did you fight so hard to get him elected?" Lima scratched his grizzled cheek. "I swear, you must have something on him, to control him like you do. What, does he dress up in his grandma's underwear or something?"

"Lima, you're so full of it I'm surprised it's not coming out your ears." Mary caught sight of Harry Garrison and raised her voice. "Harry, I brought your mama some chowder this morning, but you better go over there this afternoon and check on her, or I'll want to know why!"

Lima clapped his hands over his ears. "Mary, you never should have given up your pompoms."

"As I recall, you liked my pompoms, now didn't you, Lima?"

"Ah, well, did you hear what Sabrina did this morning?" Lima's face was red, Mary noted with satisfaction.

She was loathe to admit that anything happened on the island of which she was unaware, so she was silent for a moment as she reviewed what she *had* heard today. The burglaries, the magazine article, the group staying over at Shell Lodge with their strange demands...

Mary looked over to where Sabrina Dunsweeney stood, her lemon-colored curls blowing free in the breeze, saucy blue eyes snapping as she laughed merrily. The sound grated on Mary's nerves. As usual, the woman was dressed in one of her neon dresses, this one pink and full-skirted. Where did she think she was, Hollywood?

"Well, you might as well tell me what she did today. I have nothing better to do at the moment," Mary said, giving up. "Did she find a pearl in her oyster? Win a Pulitzer prize? Lucy Garrison said Sabrina isn't selling conch shells anymore, so what in the world is she going to do next? I heard Missy could use another cab driver, maybe I should—"

"What I was saying, before you wouldn't shut up and listen, is that this morning Sabrina ran into the tourist whose cottage got itself burglarized last night. The tourist didn't want to stay at that cottage anymore, and Vicki Carroway absolutely refused to move her anywhere else. So Sabrina fixed her up with Gale Teasley, who you know had to turn her place into a rental cottage when she couldn't pay the property taxes anymore. But Gale hasn't been able to find anyone to stay at the house and she was getting desperate. Sabrina hooked up the tourist and Gale, and the tourist was so happy she didn't even mind paying Gale for the rest of the week, even though she'd already paid for the other place. And Gale, now, she's plain ecstatic to have some money coming in. Wasn't that just peaches of Sabrina?"

"Just peaches." Sabrina Victoria Dunsweeney was a colossal pain in Mary's backside. Some people thought the woman was as adorable as a bag of kittens, but Mary knew her for what she was: a buttinsky of the highest order who tried too hard to make people like her. "What's she doing running around helping people when she should be out looking for a job? Why does she keep quitting them anyway?"

"She's just trying to find her place here on Comico Island. She only moved here six months ago, you know. After her mother dying like that, and that spot of women's trouble she had, Sabrina is just going through a—what do you call it?—an adjustment period."

Lima's loyalty to the newcomer was sandpaper on Mary's nerves. "Maybe she should go on back to Cincinnati, if she's having so much trouble adjusting here."

"Mary Tubbs, you don't need to stick your nose into every living soul's business. And by the way, what's with your hair? You look like you dipped your head in a bucket of red paint."

Mary put her hand to her hair while she considered belting Lima one in the head with her purse. "The hair stylist over on the mainland swore this was the color I picked. I told her if I planned to look like a clown I'd have asked her to put in some purple and yellow as well, but she plain refused to change it without me paying her again. And of course I wasn't going to do that." Mary was still so angry about the whole thing she could spit nails. But darned if she was going to pay any more money to that lying, pert-bosomed stylist.

"You should have called the corporate office and seen if they had one of them um-bus-men. I was watching CNN the other night, and they said all the big companies have them now. They're having so many complaints about stuff, they have these um-bus-men to kind of negotiate between the customers and the company."

"Lima, you very well may be the most ignorant man I ever met." Mary said the words without heat, however, because an idea was forming. It could be the answer to all their problems.

She saw Hill emerging from the bathroom, looking pale and well-scrubbed. Mary made a beeline for him, leaving Lima sputtering in her wake, and she plain enjoyed the look of fright on Hill's face as she approached. He looked around for a hiding place, but she was coming too fast.

"Something needs to be done, Hill," she called when she was still fifteen feet away. "After that horrible article, and all these complaints we've been getting from the tourists, something has *got* to be done. And if you're not man enough to figure out a solution, I am. That is to say—well, never mind that. Did you hear what Sabrina Dunsweeney did this morning?"

Hill looked like he wished he could escape back into the restroom, perhaps hang out by the soap dispenser for the rest of the afternoon.

"No? Well, I'll tell you about it later. What's important is that Sabrina needs a job, right? And if the woman is good at anything, it's sticking her nose in other people's business. I think we should make her—"

Chapter Three

"Island Ombudsman?" Sabrina was pretty sure she must have heard wrong, so she repeated the phrase with a different inflection to see if a word was hidden in the midst of the unintelligible syllables. She still remembered Chris Robinson in the fifth grade telling her "immature" was pronounced "eye-ma-turd" and getting her to repeat it to all his friends to their hilarious delight. "Is*land* Om*bud*sman. "

It didn't help. The five smiling faces continued to smile, and now they were nodding too.

Sabrina knew the best way to deal with this type of situation was to nod along and look intelligent.

"Ah! What an interesting idea!" She was happy to see that this answer pleased her audience.

"We knew you'd agree, Sabrina." Sondra Lane of Sweet Island Music pushed back her veil of long dark hair. "You're the perfect person for this job. A former schoolteacher who is great with people, what more could we ask for? I knew it the minute Mary came up with you as a possible candidate."

Sabrina narrowed her eyes a bit as she looked over at Mary Garrison Tubbs, who sat smug and satisfied at the end of the table. Mary's idea? That put a different spin on things. Sabrina would have to be sure to look for the floating surprise in the punch bowl.

"And everyone knows you're between jobs, Sabrina, so this works out perfectly. Can you start right away?" Nettie Wrightly, small, round, and twinkly, was the newest member of the council. As Sanitary Concessionary, in charge of distributing the highly sought-after septic permits, she was arguably one of the most powerful people on Comico Island. Without her say-so, nobody could build a new house or add on to their existing one.

"Please? Oh, um…I would like to hear a bit more about what the job would entail, if you wouldn't mind."

Sabrina squirmed in the child-size desk, but no matter which direction she turned, there was no way to avoid having her thigh squeezed or her rump pinched. She suspected Mary had had a hand in the set up for this meeting. The five town council members were lined up in a row of adult-sized chairs at the head of Mrs. Lowry's third grade classroom, while Sabrina's tiny desk was positioned in front of them. She felt like a prisoner in front of a parole board.

"We only have ten more minutes before the children return from recess, so we need to make this expeditious," Bill Large said, frowning at his fellow board members. "I want to note for the record that I still think this whole idea is ridiculous." Bill was a very important man—to Bill. He represented the Lighthouse Estates contingent of Comico Islanders, recent transplants who lived in their expensive mansions in a gated community by the sea.

"We really don't care what you think, Bill," Mary announced. "Hill, are you going to conduct this meeting anytime soon?"

"Ah, yes," Hill said, on cue. It was the first time the mayor had spoken since Sabrina arrived, in a curious frenzy to know why the town council wanted to see her at ten o'clock on a sunny Monday morning. "You've seen the article, I suppose?" He asked the question vaguely to the back of the room, and Sabrina resisted the urge to turn around and see if there was someone standing behind her.

"I'm afraid not. What article?"

"But even *you* have noticed that relations between islanders and our visitors have been strained?" Mary asked, though her tone made it clear she was not at all certain of Sabrina's powers of observation or even her ability to butter bread without help.

"Of course. There's been a lot of them lately, and so many seem miserable. How can you be unhappy when you're vacationing on such a beautiful island?" Sabrina beamed at the group, but only Sondra smiled back.

"Oh, they have plenty of reasons to be unhappy if Vicki Carroway is booking their vacation. And she's booking more than half of the rooms and houses on the island now," Nettie said, her face crinkling so it resembled a crumpled paper bag. "She's making it almost impossible for anyone to book their own rooms without going through her. And her customer service stinks! You know Sabrina, I've started a new religion based on the joyous rewards of providing good customer service. What happened to a nice smile delivered along with your cheeseburger? Why can't—"

"Look, old woman, I don't want to hear anything more about your religion of the month—" Bill Large cut in.

"Vicki Carroway doesn't care what groups she books," Sondra Lane said loudly over their squabbling. "Like the 'Maximum Security Prison Reunion' group last month. And she'll tell people almost anything to get them to reserve a room or cottage. Then they're disappointed when they get here and don't have an Olympic-sized pool or their own golf course. They can't sue, because they sign these iron-clad contracts." Sondra shook her head, her hair swishing like a length of midnight blue silk. "And it's not like we can complain to her boss, because she's the president and owner of Paradise Vacations. Every time we try to pass an ordinance to stop her, she's one step ahead of us."

"She's bringing money onto the island, people, are you forgetting that?" Bill asked with disgust. "Don't you think that's more important than a couple of whining tourists?"

"Some things are more important than money, Mr. Large." Mary was frosty with a chill nip of scorn. "You may be happy with a dung heap in your front yard if someone paid you to store it there, but the rest of us—"

"I've seen your front yard, Mary, and while the sixty-seven Airstream certainly adds a touch of elegance to your flower bed and your urinal birdbath personifies class—"

"Why, you—"

"Please." Hill clasped his hands over his ears. "Please stop."

"I still don't understand what this all has to do with me." Sabrina knew she sounded plaintive, but she couldn't help it. She was as unhappy as the next islander by the influx of disgruntled vacationers, but what did the town council expect *her* to do?

"Why, Sabrina," Sondra said in surprise, making Sabrina feel like a dimwit, "we need someone to listen to their complaints and try to make things right. We need an ombudsman to act as a non-biased mediator between the visitors and the islanders."

"But I've never heard of an island having its own ombudsman. Isn't there supposed to be someone responsible for these type of complaints, like, like…the Better Business Bureau or the Visitors Bureau?"

"We don't have either of one of those. The only thing we have is a welcome center." Sondra looked uncomfortable.

"Comico Island has a welcome center?"

"We're getting off subject, dear." Nettie's tiny cinnamon eyes were earnest. "We really we need an ombudsman."

"Before it's too late!" Mary stood and began pacing in the space between Sabrina and the council members. Sabrina noticed that Hill flinched every time Mary got too close to him.

"If our tourists continue to leave unhappy, before too long no one will come back. Sure we may not always like the tourists, but we darn sure need their money." Mary avoided looking at Bill Large as she said this. "If they all stop coming, none of us will be able to afford to live here. We need to make sure they leave happy, and that's your job, Sabrina."

"But Vicki realizes this as well, doesn't she? If all of the people she books leave unhappy, soon she will be out of business."

"And then she'll move on to the next place," Sondra said grimly. "She's done it time and time again. She'll make as much money here as she can, and then move on, leaving us with her mess. I talked to a couple of people at the Small Island Association meeting last week, and several of their islands have already been victimized by Vicki Carroway and Paradise

Vacations. They said there's nothing you can legally do, just wait until *she* decides to leave, and that's not until she's sucked you dry and ruined your reputation."

"This is what she's doing to us." Mary tossed a magazine to Sabrina. "She's already made a start at ruining our good reputation."

Sabrina caught the glossy magazine. It was a popular coastal magazine, featuring a beautiful picture of Hurricane Harbor on the cover. Sabrina began to smile until she noticed the caption: "Comico Island: Paradise Destination or Hell on Earth?"

"The reporter booked a house through Vicki," Mary said, "and he records the entire horrendous experience. This magazine is read by thousands and thousands of people. If we don't do something fast, we may lose all of our vacationers."

A chorus of high-pitched voices began to echo through the halls. Mrs. Lowry's third grade class would soon be back to claim their room.

"Will you do it, Sabrina? We need to know right away, or we'll have to find someone else."

Sabrina pretended to study the cover of the magazine to hide her agitation. Could she do this?

"I don't think—" she began, her heart heavy with disappointment.

"Please, Sabrina, you have such a rapport with people," Nettie implored. "We heard what you did for that poor tourist woman yesterday, and look how much you helped my family last fall. You're wonderful with people, and you *like* to fix things for them. If you're doing it for fun anyway, why not get paid at the same time? We wouldn't know who else to turn to if you said no."

Sabrina frowned and looked back down at the magazine. She *was* between jobs again, with no better idea of what she wanted to do than when she came to Comico Island six months ago. After her mother's death and her breast cancer scare, she had wanted to start over, to experience all of the zesty life she had been missing. That's why she gave up everything she knew in Cincinnati to move to Comico Island, with no plan except to start over, to try something different. But different didn't always equal better, and life was no easier to figure out on Comico Island than it had been in Cincinnati. The reality was that she gave up a comfortable home—languishing on the market in Cincinnati—and a good job with benefits to move to a vacation island with a limited job supply. So far, none of them had worked out. Would this one be any different?

She wished she could go home and think about this for a week or so, talk to her friend Sally, and Calvin, and figure out the best course of action. But they needed an answer now, and what in the world should she do?

"I'll do it," she heard herself say, and stopped in surprise. "But only on a provisional basis," she added quickly, before her rebel tongue could get away from her again. "I'm not sure—well, anyway, let's see how I do, and then we'll decide whether I'll stay on in this position." They'll want to fire me in a week, she thought. I'll quit before that to save them the trouble.

"Wonderful!" Hill said, and everyone turned to him in surprise. He hurriedly looked down at his hands.

"I'll warn you," Sabrina said. "I'm all thumbs when I first start a job. It takes me a little while to get the hang of it."

"We've heard," someone muttered. The door opened and children erupted into the room, their happy shouting and swinging ponytails swirling and eddying around Sabrina and the council members.

"Ms. Sabrina! Have you come to read to us again?" one child shouted, and another one asked, "When are you going to do another play for the kids? I want to be in it!"

In the hall, she listened as Hill, with loud prompting from Mary, administered the Ombudsman Oath, which bound Sabrina to confidentiality and impartiality. She was still dazed and assimilating what she had just sworn to do as Mary ran through some additional information.

"…we still need to hammer out some details, like your pay—Health insurance? I don't know about health benefits, Sabrina, but we'll get to that. Right now, though, here are the most recent letters of complaint. I would suggest getting over to the Shell Lodge right away, that seems the most pressing."

A paper sack bulging with reams of paper was dropped into Sabrina's arms, and she staggered under the weight of the complaint letters.

"We're counting on you, Sabrina!" Sondra called as the council members left with expressions of relief, leaving Sabrina holding the bag.

Chapter Four

Hundreds of islands dotted the brilliant waters of the sound, clustered around Comico Island's belly for protection from the ferocious summer hurricanes. Most were uninhabited, though some held a single house or even small communities, and almost all were unreachable except by boat.

Shell Island was unusual in that a narrow causeway had been built eighty years ago, linking Comico and the smaller island. Shell Island was very private, and was only big enough for a single hotel, so officially it was considered part of Comico Island.

The causeway was lined with splashy flowers, and Sabrina drove slowly to enjoy the view of clear, swift-moving water framed by colorful blossoms. She had never been out to Shell Island, though she had heard about the island's hotel, the Shell Lodge. It was reputed to be breathtaking.

The hotel appeared at the end of a long, curving shell driveway, surrounded by lavish vegetation. She stopped the car, enchanted by the sight.

White shells covered every square inch of the outside of the large lodge, reminding her of the fancy gingerbread houses her grandmother used to painstakingly construct when Sabrina was small. Set point-end first into concrete, the whelk shells also decorated numerous walkways and the steps leading up to the lodge's massive front doors. It looked magical, unreal, like a castle out of a fairy tale.

Sabrina followed the driveway around to the side of the hotel where she found a parking lot filled with cars and trucks, as well as two Jeeps emblazoned with the Shell Lodge's logo. From this angle, she saw that walkways wound through riotous, gaudy bushes, stopping at several miniature cottages, each adorned with thousands of ivory shells, before meandering down to a small beach.

Sabrina followed the fanciful walkway up to the back entrance of the hotel and stepped through the screen door into a deserted dining room. It was mid-afternoon, but already she could smell delectable scents floating from the kitchen, promising a savory dinner to accompany the expansive water views.

"Larry, make sure you set out water pitchers and the coffee stations in the meeting room, they don't want us disturbing them once they start—"

The young man, dressed in a maroon Shell Lodge shirt and crisp khakis, stopped upon seeing Sabrina and smiled with professional charm.

"We've got light appetizers at the pool if you're hungry," he said with cheerful enthusiasm. "I'm afraid the dining room doesn't open until five, though. To get to the pool, you follow that hall all the way down past the lobby and presto, like magic, the door will open onto the pool."

"No, I'm not looking for food, though the smells coming from that kitchen might make me change my mind!"

The young man laughed, and stepped forward to offer his hand. His sandy hair was receding, and his nose was too pointy, but his laugh was infectious and his intelligent face attractive despite its flaws.

"I'm Matt Fredericks. Were you looking for a room, then? We've got a group in and we're all booked up. That's pretty unusual, so if you want to call back another time, I'm sure we'll be able to accommodate you. It's great that we're booked this week, but I don't like having to turn guests away. You hate to disappoint people, you know?"

Sabrina was having trouble getting a word in edgewise, so she waited until Matt took a breath and spoke before he could get started again.

"I'm Sabrina Dunsweeney, Matt. Do you own the Shell Lodge? It's captivating."

"Isn't it? It's a family business, has been since my great-grandfather, Kenneth Fredericks, built the lodge back in the twenties to take advantage of prohibition." He laughed at Sabrina's surprised expression. "There was a lot of money to be made during prohibition, if you weren't too scrupulous how you made it. And great-granddad was unscrupulous *and* ruthless, from what I've heard.

"A lot of high rollers came here on fishing and hunting trips back in the twenties, and my great-grandfather thought a hunting club where they could indulge in gaming and drink would make him a mint. He was right. John Barrymore, Ernest Hemingway, Errol Flynn, among others, all made their way to the Shell Lodge."

"During prohibition? How could he get away with that? Didn't the police know what was going on?" Sabrina was interested despite herself.

Matt laughed. "Bribing the police became very popular during prohibition, along with designer flasks and adding mixers to drinks to hide the taste of inferior liquor. The sheriff of Teach County, Fitz Mitchell, was often here gambling and drinking along with the society swells. But just in case the Feds got too interested, there were drop-down walls in the gaming room that could be closed if they showed up, and baseboards along the walls pulled out to make a hiding place for the bootlegged liquor."

"How in the world did they get all that liquor out here? Your grandfather wasn't making it himself, I'm sure."

"Oh, no. Only the real McCoy would do. As a matter of fact, sometimes Bill McCoy himself would bring ships full of liquor and set up a rum row off shore—it was vital to be outside the territorial waters of the United States, you understand—and every night, entrepreneurial islanders in small boats would risk the Coast Guard to go bring back boatloads of fine liquor. And, of course, since it was supplied by Bill McCoy, people knew it was high quality and not watered down."

"I suppose that's where we got the phrase 'the real McCoy.'"

"Exactly! Anyway, after prohibition ended, Kenneth—my great-grandfather—kept the lodge open, though it would never again do quite as well. It was my great-grandmother who insisted on the shells. She didn't like the liquor, so she would spend a lot of her time making the shell walkways and shell fences. It was a labor of love, let me tell you, who else would have had the patience? Grandpa Guy, Kenneth's son, is still around, though mostly he just feels like staying in his room and playing Battleship. But anyway, enough about me, how can I help you, Sabrina?"

Sabrina felt the need to take a deep breath, but she knew she needed to speak fast or forever keep her peace.

"Matt, I'm looking for Gilbert Kane. I understand that he's staying here."

"You're with the Hummers?" The politeness did not falter a bit, but Sabrina noticed a discernible cooling in Matt's expression. "Let's see, it's almost two o'clock. They got back from their morning, um—expedition, and went to lunch around twelve. They've been on their own since then, but they're due to meet at two-thirty. Shall I show you to the meeting room?"

Without waiting for her to answer, he turned and led Sabrina out of the dining room and down a bright hallway. Sabrina saw that some of the interior walls were adorned with shells as well.

"What did you call them…Hummers?" The hasty explanation Mary delivered outside the classroom was that a group headed by a man named Gilbert Kane was staying at the Shell Lodge and were very unhappy for some undisclosed reason. Nothing more.

"Yes, the Hummers. You're not one of them?" Matt slowed and peeked back over his shoulder.

"No, I'm the, uh, Comico Island Ombudsman." Sabrina blushed as she said the title, and Matt's blank expression did not help matters. "I've been hired by the town council to try to improve relations between tourists and locals. I understand Mr. Kane has a complaint, and I'm hoping I can help."

"I don't know what Vicki Carroway was thinking when she booked them, but there's no way we can accommodate—Hello, how are you enjoying your stay?" Matt nodded at a wrinkled couple, wrapped in bathrobes, who beamed at him in near-sighted delight.

"Off to get our massages! So nice that they do it down by the water," the woman chirped. "But, dear, I have an itsby-bitsy little question for you…"

Sabrina waited a few minutes, but Matt was not one to use three words when he could use five hundred instead. She waved her thanks at him and moved off down the hall. She had some time to kill, and she figured she could find the meeting room by herself in that time.

She itched to go introduce herself to the chefs in the kitchen and find out what delicious concoction they were preparing—perhaps she could share her new recipe for tilapia and sweet corn potpie—but she knew from experience that they would be unlikely to appreciate the interruption. Her hand went to her head as she remembered a particular incident with a French chef and a copper saucepan.

And she was here to work, after all, not gossip with fellow gastronomists. She went through the main lobby, dominated by a large shell-encrusted fireplace, and peeked into the lounge, which was adorned with dollar bills instead of shells. Thousands of dollars' worth, she saw, noting that many of the bills were signed. Shaking her head in wonderment at the delicious bizarreness of the place, she went out to the pool where several people were lazing in the warm sun or eating scrumptious-looking appetizers.

"This is too much for a person to bear," she said and promptly sat down at one of the poolside tables and ordered the grilled honey-and-orange-marinated prawns. When the waiter brought her food and iced tea, she asked him where the meeting room was located. She wanted to talk to him further about Gilbert Kane and his group of Hummers, but he was busy, so she contented herself with enjoying the delicious appetizer.

"How lovely," she murmured, though she herself couldn't say whether it was the food or the beautiful view which inspired her remark.

She contemplated the sun-splashed scenery and browsed through the conversations at neighboring tables.

"I don't know if I can do this, Patti," a low, urgent voice said directly behind Sabrina. "I mean, this morning was—"

"Sophie, girl, I agree with you," a woman answered, her voice rich and creamy, despite being sprinkled with a tinge of anxiety. "It was plain ridiculous. But at this point, I'm willing to do about anything, aren't you?"

Sabrina snuck a look over her shoulder and found two women at the table behind her. One was young and cover-of-a-magazine beautiful, though she was skinny almost to the point of emaciation. The other woman was substantial with a glorious set of cornrows.

"Oh, Patti, it's just all so awful! I don't know if I can take this Hum any longer!"

With that, the pretty girl rushed out, her eyes streaming with tears.

Chapter Five

The woman with the cornrows stood up as her young friend left, and then subsided back into her seat, shaking her head. Her handsome face was drawn with lines of worry, and she fiddled with the polished wood beads around her neck.

"Is there anything I can do to help?" Sabrina asked, swiveling in her seat so she faced the other woman.

"I'm not sure anybody can help at this point," said the woman, and sighed. "But thank you for asking. I'm Patti Townsend, by the way."

She was about fifty, and wore a vivid crimson dress, splashed with black, gold, and green, and accented by an array of stylish hand-made jewelry. She looked like she was comfortable in her own skin, though this contentment may have been hard won. She wore the battle scars of hard work and sorrow around her eyes and mouth.

"I'm Sabrina Dunsweeney. It's nice to meet you, Patti. Where are you from?"

"Is it so obvious I'm a tourist?" Patti laughed and looked down ruefully at her outfit. "I suppose it is. I'm from Cincinnati."

"Cincinnati! Patti, *I'm* from Cincinnati. I live here now, but that's where I came from."

Patti looked delighted, and stood up to clasp Sabrina's hand. "I'm always happy to meet someone from home."

They chatted about Cincinnati for a few minutes, until Sabrina noticed it was nearing two-thirty.

"Oh! I wish I could stay to talk with you, Patti, but I'm supposed to be somewhere right about now."

Patti said she needed to be somewhere as well, and they agreed to try to get together later and talk. Feeling fortified with her nice prawn appetizer, and the smile on Patti's face, Sabrina went back inside the lodge in search of the meeting room.

A man, well-dressed and scruffily attractive, was speaking as she reached the doorway. "What is the matter with you, Gilbert? You're getting sloppy, you know that? You've been acting like a chicken with its head cut off ever since we got here. You need to get it together, man!"

There were three people inside the room, and two of them looked up as Sabrina came in. The third, older man, wearing a bright yellow dashiki and a long beard, did not seem to notice Sabrina's entrance.

"Yes, did you need something?" The scruffy, attractive man looked up at Sabrina.

"Didn't you see the do-not-disturb sign? This is a private meeting, miss!" snapped the man who had been acting like a chicken with its head cut off. At the moment, dressed in an unfortunate olive-green suit and squatting in his chair, he looked more like a disaffected toad than any type of poultry.

"I am looking for Gilbert Kane," said Sabrina in a clear, firm voice. "I presume that you are he." She fixed her stern gaze on the toad. It was not in a former schoolteacher's nature to tolerate rudeness, no matter how uncomfortable she felt.

"Yes? What did you need?" The toad, a.k.a. the headless chicken, a.k.a. Gilbert Kane readjusted his attitude and smiled with what looked like painful effort. It was not a very convincing smile. He would not be a handsome man at the best times, and right now large sweat stains were spreading under his meaty arms and his muddy eyes bulged behind thick glasses.

"I am Sabrina Dunsweeney, Comico Island's Ombudsman." No one laughed, for which Sabrina was grateful.

"And what does that mean, Sabrina?" This from the attractive man who was radiating puzzled charm. His dark blond hair was mousse-spiked and fashionable, and his square chin was adorned with a two or three day growth of hair, trimmed into the shape of a triangle.

"I was appointed to work as a liaison between Comico Island's visiting guests and the local islanders. I understand you're having a problem?"

"Yes, we have a problem! I've talked to every official on this island, including that woman at the welcome center." A whiff of distaste crossed his face. "Anyway, this after it was clear that nobody was going to do anything to address our concerns." Gilbert popped a few discreet pills into his mouth and as an afterthought offered his hand to Sabrina.

"I understand you booked through Vicki Carroway at Paradise Vacations." Taking his hand, Sabrina found it cool and squishy, and she resisted the urge to wipe her hand on her skirt.

"I can't believe how that woman talked to me!" Gilbert sounded truly flummoxed by Vicki's rudeness.

"Why don't we start from the beginning? Tell me about yourselves, and what brought you to Comico Island."

Gilbert seemed to be calculating whether brown-nosing or belligerence was in order. His glance took in the few people gathered around the doorway and he made his decision. "Please sit down, Sabrina." His attempt at a schmoozy smile was unconvincing, more suited to a prostate exam. "We have a few minutes before our meeting begins. We are the—"

"I'm Michael Siderius." The good-looking man thrust an aggressive hand at Sabrina, cutting off Gilbert's words. "I'm the president of Hummers International. Gilbert is our spokesman." This with a dismissive nod toward Gilbert, meant to put him in his place. Gilbert did not seem inclined to be put anywhere. "This is my father, Joseph." Michael nodded at the man in the yellow dashiki by the window. "You'll have to excuse him, he's been tapped into the Hum for a long time now."

Michael apparently deemed this explanation enough, and Sabrina nodded in befuddled acknowledgement as the older man turned his stare on her. She felt the irrational urge to back away from the force of his gaze. The color of his eyes was very ordinary, a nice, medium brown, but it was the *way* he looked at her that made Sabrina want to turn away with a nervous laugh. The stare was probing, personal, though impersonal at the same time, like a doctor who touches you in the most intimate manner while thinking about yesterday's golf game.

Joseph turned away to look back out the window, and Sabrina exhaled with relief. What a spooky man.

"Perhaps you can explain a bit more about your group," she managed to say. "I'm afraid I've never heard of you."

"Hummers International Incorporated was founded by my father to bring together those rare, special people who hear the Hum. Only a small percentage of people hear the Hum, so it's important that they have a forum in which to talk with other people who share their gift." Michael reeled off the speech with practiced ease.

Joseph rose to his feet and began moving about the room, trailing his fingers across the windowsill and the podium. As Joseph approached Gilbert, the stolid man stepped back, a strange expression crossing his face. Joseph brushed by him, and Gilbert visibly shuddered.

"Most people say the Hum sounds like a diesel motor idling right outside their window. It's louder for some than for others, of course. No one experiences it the same," Michael was saying. Joseph went back to his chair by the window.

"But what *is* the Hum?"

"The voice of the universe," Gilbert said.

A conversation stopper if ever there was one. What exactly does the universe have to say? *All this cosmic dust is starting to chafe my nether regions?* Sabrina thought about that for a moment and then asked, "Do you hear it?" She directed the question at both Michael and Gilbert.

"Good Lord, no," Michael burst out and then reddened. "What I meant to say—"

"He means only the very special hear the hum," Gilbert interjected smoothly. "Our meeting is about to start, so we need to hurry this along. We have come to Comico Island because of its isolation. Several times a year we do a retreat with a few of our most talented members, the ones who Master Joseph has agreed to train in the proper management of their gift. We were unhappy with our last location, so we decided to try Comico Island. Our most pressing need is privacy, which Vicki Carroway at Paradise Vacations promised us." Gilbert leaned forward and knocked his knuckles on the table. "We've only been here a couple days and already we've been disturbed at our rituals! This isn't acceptable, do you understand?"

"I understand." Sabrina nodded with what she hoped passed for competent professionalism. "I will see what I can do."

"Thank you, Sabrina, we appreciate your help. We have important work to do here, and we cannot be interrupted!" Gilbert said the words with force, but his attention was on the people filtering into the room. Michael had gone to stand by Joseph and was holding his father's wrist.

As Sabrina left the room, she saw that Michael's eyes were closed, his head tipped toward the ceiling as he mouthed silent words. Joseph continued to stare out the window, indifferent to the touch of his son's hand.

◇◇◇

"Short of setting guards around their meeting spot, I can't promise them privacy," Matt Fredericks said when Sabrina found him in the lobby at the front desk. "They say their meetings have to be held outside, but how am I supposed to guarantee complete privacy under those circumstances? I've done everything I can do to try to accommodate them." He looked pained, as if it physically hurt him not to be able to make a guest happy. "I could strangle Vicki for doing this to us. It's not the first time, either."

"Then why do you let Vicki book groups for you?"

"If I didn't, I wouldn't get any groups." Matt was morose. "It was much better before she got here. All the hotels, bed and breakfasts, and rental companies fended for themselves, and we did fine. But Vicki set up shop on the island and cornered the market on booking Comico Island vacations. Her company is in all the good magazines and when you search on Comico Island on the Internet, her company comes up in the first ten spots. Everybody is going to her, especially when she started promising discounted rates to the guests. Some of us held out for a while, but the bottom line made it necessary to pay her exorbitant commissions and give her the discounted rooms just to stay in business."

"How terrible!"

"You see, I can't even complain about what she's done with the Hummers. She's got me over a barrel."

"Where do the Hummers hold their sessions now?" Sabrina needed to be practical if she was going to accomplish anything.

"We have a picnic spot on the other side of the island. It's hard to find unless you know where it is, so we've been driving them there in golf carts. The first day they were there, a young couple stumbled in on them. Mr. Kane and Mr. Siderius have been yelling ever since." His frown turned automatically to a smile as a guest wandered through the lobby.

"Is there nowhere else you can think of that would be more private?"

"Short of dropping them off by boat on one of the spoil islands, no, I really can't think of anything."

Sabrina raised an eyebrow.

"Yes...we *could* do that. Why didn't I think of it?"

"You did," Sabrina pointed out.

"What a marvelous idea! We'll take them by boat to Goat Island and no one will disturb them. It's perfect! Thank you, Sabrina!" Matt picked up the phone and began punching numbers.

Sabrina headed for the door.

Her work here was done.

Chapter Six

"Lima, it was so easy! I talked to everyone involved, listened to what they had to say, and we came up with a solution that's going to make everyone happy. I think I might be able to do this! I have some ideas that should really help things around here."

Lima liked to see Sabrina radiant with excitement. It was a far cry from the way she had been looking the last couple of months. He couldn't help but worry just a tad, though. Sabrina always meant well, she did, but sometimes things just snowballed out of her control when she got enthusiastic.

"It sounds like you done good, Sabrina." Lima just hoped things worked out as well as Sabrina expected, though eighty years of hard living told him that things seldom did. And his young friend didn't need any more disappointments just now.

The front porch of Tubb's General Store was deserted as dusk began stalking through the streets of the island. From where they sat they could smell dinner cooking in various houses and restaurants down on the harbor front. Not ready to go home to his dark, empty house, Lima wondered how he could talk Sabrina into having dinner without her offering to cook for him. She did so love to cook.

Bicycle Bob, who had been dozing on the bottom step, sat up and looked around in fuzzy puzzlement. Bicycle looked like a twelve-year-old who had done a forty-year Rip Van Winkle on his way to a pick-up baseball game, and taken to drinking upon waking to drown his confusion. He adjusted his baseball cap, which had fallen back on his peppered brown hair, and wiped in absent disinterest at his dirty tee-shirt and shorts. He took a drink from his paper-bagged bottle, and got to his feet without looking at Sabrina and Lima.

"Bicycle, you look like a befuddled billy goat," Lima called, but Bicycle didn't respond as he mounted Trigger, his bright yellow beach bike, and pedaled off toward the harbor where a blanket of crimson and orange had been thrown across the water.

"Did you hear someone put in a bunch of old change at the change genie over on the mainland dock? Bunch of quarters from the nineteen twenties, Davey said. Clogged up the machine good and the man who changes it was hopping mad."

"Nineteen-twenties change? That's odd."

"Weeell, the nineteen twenties, that was the time to live on Comico Island, let me tell you." Lima sat back in his chair. "I don't remember much about it, of course, but I've heard the stories. There was so much liquor being run off our coast that some mornings the shores were littered with bottles from rumrunners who had hit an oyster bar in the dark at high speed. Every man, grandmother, and kid who had a boat went angling for burlap bags of liquor every chance they got.

"Kenneth Fredericks and his high-falutin' Shell Lodge were bringing in some of the biggest names of the day. The twenties were like the sixties in a way, you understand, people going through a rebellious phase and having a good time doing it. Of course, a lot of people died too, from drinking bad liquor, or at the very least they went blind.

"Here on the island, the islanders were loving it. They were so poor that their only entertainment was when the preacher came to town every month or so and saved their souls and cut their hair. So, they were happy to make some money off of Fredericks and his crony David Harrington, who had built a house on the island just to use for smuggling. And the police did well as long as they knew how to look the other way. Sheriff Fitz Mitchell had that down pat—Fredericks and Harrington helped get him elected Sheriff of Teach County, which was right difficult for somebody living on Comico Island, and he had to show his appreciation somehow."

Lima continued his reminiscing, until Sabrina said, "Lima, I'll cook you dinner to celebrate my day's success." She got to her feet and looked at him in invitation. Lima thought fast.

"You've worked hard today so why don't we go to Walk-the-Plank Pub for dinner? Of course, I wouldn't dream of insulting you by offering to pay," he added hastily, "but we can go French."

"Dutch?"

"Whatever."

Lava colors glimmered and glowed across the surface of the water as the sun sank in a fizzle of clouds. Across the darkening sky, uneven lines of birds headed toward their night roosts, a few stragglers struggling to catch up.

The ruthless pull of instinct to find a place to roost for the night was making the seagull uneasy. Anxious squawks betrayed his indecision, but he was unable to pull his attention away from the man on the beach below. He was hungry, and humans on the beach sometimes meant food. The man might throw bread high up into the air, and the seagull would swoop down and snatch i, right before it hit the water.

Feeling a gust of wind, he adjusted his wings, and then had to flap hard as his loose, useless leg upset his balance. No matter how hard he tried, the broken leg would not tuck up under his body like the other one. It was no longer easy to catch the small fish and skittering crabs that were his mainstay, and he was hungry.

With a plaintive, mewling cry, he circled closer to the beach, his beady eyes fixed on the man lying on the sand. The man lay very still, and the seagull swooped down even closer, seeing something glittering beside him. A fish? The man did not move as the seagull hovered, contemplating. Did he smell blood? The seagull was unsure, as his sense of smell was erratic.

Something rocketed toward him and the seagull flapped his wings to get out of the way, almost crashing into a tree in his awkward haste. He looked up and saw the osprey coming back toward him, screaming in a piercing voice that this was his, his, his, and the seagull pulled away from the beach without looking back. There was no arguing with an osprey.

The sun was down, and oily dark was spilling across the water. Leaving the dead man behind him on the beach, the hungry seagull flew off into the night.

Chapter Seven

The dishes had been carousing again. No matter how many Sabrina washed, when she returned home there was always a pile of them in the sink, passed out and dirty from their midday bash. The natural product of such behavior, of course, was that they propagated. The beaming plates presenting her with baby saucers, the proud glasses producing bouncing coffee cups. Was it a bad sign that her dishware had a more active social life than she did?

"I *have* a very active social life, Calvin." Sabrina stacked the last steaming plate in the dish rack and looked to see if any dishes were hiding behind the plant, just waiting for a chance to jump in the sink and throw a kegger. "I have lots of friends," she continued, and Calvin, who was sitting on the windowsill watching the soap bubbles, did not answer. "Well, I do, and just because Sally says I need to go out on a date, well, she also said bell bottoms would never come back in style, so why in the world should I listen to her?"

Calvin, her bright yellow parakeet, darted forward and stabbed an errant bubble, chattering in bloodthirsty glee as it burst with a wet pop.

"I shouldn't, that's why. I'm perfectly happy." Which was true. After her successful first day as Comico Island's Ombudsman, everything seemed rosier and brighter this morning. She woke early in a frenzy to clean her apartment, skipping her normal morning peruse through her massive medical book, and after two sustained hours of catharsis, she could walk from the tiny bedroom to the living room/kitchen without tripping over anything.

Her apartment was small, the furniture and appliances old and worn, the kitchen a mere afterthought against the back wall. But the view out the large window made the cramped, dingy space worthwhile. Hurricane Harbor was revealed in all its morning glory as the sun flashed off the tall masts of the sailboats and sparked the wind-restless waves. Buildings lined the edge of the harbor, some ramshackle and suicidal in their tilt toward the water, the newer buildings on high stilts painted in a rainbow of colors. A large brick hotel stood out like a rotten tooth on the smile of the waterfront.

Beyond the public beach was Houseboat Alley, a motley collection of aging houseboats rocking gently on their tethers at the old ferry dock. A rusted metal fence past the houseboats blocked off the rest of the dilapidated docks from public use, though several fisherman had made their way over or around the fence to use the crumbling quay as a fishing pier.

Sabrina had talked to her real estate agent in Cincinnati, but the prospects of selling her mother's house—well, it was her house now, of course—were bleak at the moment. That meant she would be staying in the apartment for the indefinite future, and as she looked around the diminutive, gleaming space, and at the generous view beyond, the prospect did not seem as daunting as it did at first.

"Are you ready to go, Calvin? It's time to go to work." It was almost eight-thirty, and Sabrina had big plans for the day. Now that she had sorted out the Hummer dilemma, it was time to get to work on the rest of the island's problems. She hoped to have them solved by dinner.

Last night she had gone through all the complaint letters in the bag the town council gave her. Many of them were emails and notes from phone calls, though the most mystifying were a few written in a sprawling hand saying things like "dumb jerk thinks someone should fix his hot tub" and "wants privacy and I told idiot he was crazier than a Mitchell's day fisherman." Who wrote these puzzling missives?

She had organized the letters into two piles, the larger one from vacationers who were long gone. Those she would have to track down by letter and phone and at least apologize for their difficulties and see if there was anything she could do. The smaller pile contained complaints received in the last couple of days, including several from Gilbert Kane from Hummers International. These were the most urgent, and now that she had cleared up the Hummers' problem, she would move on to the next most pressing issue, which was the two break-ins.

Donning a raspberry shawl, she lifted Calvin to her shoulder and went out onto the narrow outdoor walkway that ran the length of the building. Doors to three other apartments lined the walkway, and at the far end were stairs leading down to the restaurant below. The air was cool and crisp, the wind brisk as it sloshed up white caps on the harbor and filled the air with the music of ringing sailboat rigging.

As Sabrina emerged into the restaurant on the ground floor, the smell of bacon and eggs made her stomach growl, despite the fact that she had made Grand Marnier sweet potato French toast this morning. Which reminded her, she needed to remember to put the batteries back in the smoke alarm.

"Sabrina, would you like some breakfast?" May, blowzy and spare, looked up from taking an order. Never afraid of hard work, the owner of the Blue Cam didn't hesitate to fill in when her waitresses called in sick.

"No thanks, May, I already ate."

Sabrina looked around at the happy customers, the funky, nautical murals on the walls, and the colorful tables and chairs. Working as hostess at the Blue Cam was her first job when she arrived on the island. May had been on the verge of selling the restaurant, and Sabrina shuddered a little as she remembered the boring menu and the plastic checkered tablecloths on the tables.

"Well, you know you can eat on the house any time," May called as Sabrina headed for the front door. "And any time you want your job back, just let me know. If it wasn't for you, this place would be out of business. I'll never be able to thank you enough."

◇◇◇

"Sabrina, hello!" Maggie Fromlin put down the knife that she was using to slice oranges and limes and came toward Sabrina. The small, round-shouldered woman looked a lot happier than she had a few days ago when Sabrina encountered her on the beach, still reeling from the break-in that had disrupted her vacation. Maggie ignored the proffered hand and clasped Sabrina in a warm hug, recoiling when she encountered Calvin's warm body under Sabrina's hair.

"Oh, it's a little bird!"

"His name is Calvin, and he's a budgerigar, more commonly known as a parakeet. He's rare because he's all yellow, except for the bit of white on his forehead and underside."

Calvin chirped a greeting.

"I came by to see how you were settling in." Sabrina looked around at the handsome, large room and the up-to-date appliances. Gale Teasley had done a good job of turning her home into a rental cottage. The house wasn't new, but it had character, and judging from the gazebo and the hot tub she could see on the back deck, Gale had added the amenities that the tourists would expect in a rental house.

"It's perfect! Everyone loves it. At first my mother-in-law was making snide comments about not being on the beach, but I told her she was welcome to go back to the Seas the Day Cottage and wait for the burglar to come back. You should have seen the expression on her face! And then the kids found the kayaks, and she hasn't been able to say anything bad about the place since." Maggie grinned.

"That's wonderful." Sabrina hesitated, loathe to bring up an unpleasant subject, but duty called. "I'm working as Comico Island's Ombudsman and—"

"Oh...how nice for you!"

Sabrina wondered if she would ever be able to say her title without seeing that momentary look of blank puzzlement on her listener's face. "Thank you. Anyway, it looks like your burglary was not an isolated incident and I wanted to ask a few questions to try to get to the bottom of the whole thing before the burglar strikes again and upsets someone else."

"We already talked to the police, but…what did you want to know?"

"I understand nothing was stolen. Is that correct?"

"Well, none of *our* stuff was stolen. He may have taken something that belonged in the house, but we didn't notice anything obvious missing, like the TVs or DVD players. The police called the owner of the house, Sue Harrington, and she's going to come down and look the house over, just to be certain."

"You said you saw the burglar?"

Maggie shivered and went back around to her cutting board. She resumed cutting fruit as she talked. "It was awful. I really don't remember much."

"I know it's scary to think about. Why don't we pretend there was a secret surveillance camera in the room? Just tell me what it would have seen." It was a memory-enhancing technique Sabrina had run across in one of her medical journals.

"Well…," Maggie looked doubtful, but she closed her eyes and began talking. "Doug and I are lying in bed. I must have heard something while I was sleeping, because I woke all of a sudden, like you do when you wake up from a nightmare and you're scared to move. But this time it was real. He went into the closet and I could hear him moving around in there, real quiet. I was afraid to even breathe, much less wake up Doug. Then he came out of the closet and started patting the walls—"

"Patting the walls?"

"Yes. Kind of like the way a police officer pats down a suspect on TV. Then, I must have moved or something, because he looked over his shoulder and I don't know whether he could see that my eyes were open or what, but all of a sudden he was running out the door. I screamed, and everyone woke up, but by the time I could get Doug to understand what was going on, the burglar was long gone."

"Would you recognize this person again if you saw him?" Sabrina wondered if there was a way to do a lineup of all the men on the island. Perhaps she could throw together a men's beauty pageant with Maggie as one of the judges?

"Sure, I'd know him anywhere. He was big—at least, I think he was, but it may have been his shadow that seemed big, I'm not sure. He wore a black baseball cap and black clothes, so he kind of blended into the darkness. Let's see…I guess I really didn't get a look at his face, his hat was pulled down pretty low, but I'm sure I would recognize him again if I saw him."

Sabrina smiled. Of course she could. "Anything else? Anything else that will help us find him?"

"Well, there was the piece of paper…I didn't see that it was important, but the police took it away."

"Piece of paper? Did the burglar drop it?"

"I guess he might have, but who knows?"

"Was there writing on the paper?"

Maggie frowned. "Yes, but I can't remember what it said. I mean, it didn't make any sense."

"Pretend that surveillance camera is aimed right over your shoulder at the piece of paper. Can the camera see what it says?"

Maggie grimaced, but once again closed her eyes. "The writing is kind of round and curly, and there are three…no four words. One on each line. The first and last one I can see pretty clearly. 'Mit' and 'Fred.'"

"Mit and Fred?"

"Yes. The other two words, the ones in the middle…they rhyme, I remember that, and they made me think of someone laughing. Hardy-har-har, you know? Oh wait! That's the first word. 'Har.' And the second one was 'Gar.'"

"So, in order, we have 'Mit,' 'Har,' 'Gar,' and 'Fred.' Is that right?"

Maggie nodded. "I told you it didn't make sense."

And she was absolutely right. It didn't make sense. But Sabrina smiled gamely. "You never know what will help. Was there anything else?"

"No…oh, wait. Yes, there *was* something else."

Chapter Eight

Bicycle Bob was sitting on the first step and humming as Sabrina approached Tubb's General Store.

"Hello, Bicycle, how are you?" She paused and looked down at him, but he kept his eyes on the ground as he hummed. His paint-stained fingers clasped a bottle of beer with fierce need. "Have you been painting today? I would love to see some more of your work. Everyone comments on the murals you did at the Blue Cam."

It didn't matter that Bicycle never responded. One of these days she thought maybe he would. She put her hand on his sun-warmed shoulder, feeling the sharp bones through his shirt. She knew that his family and neighbors looked out for him, but they couldn't fix what a steady diet of alcohol did to the human body.

Sabrina mounted the steps and sat down in one of the rocking chairs under the chalkboard that read: "Funeral for Uncle Will on Friday."

Where was Lima? It was rare that she came by here during the day and didn't find him.

A young girl, tall and red-headed, came out of the store to shake out a rug. Her direct gaze met Sabrina's and she nodded in greeting.

"Hi, Marilee," Sabrina said, and Calvin added his own chirrupped greeting. "How do you like working here at the general store?"

"I like it fine, Miss Sabrina, though I'm looking to pick up another job if I can." Marilee Howard's voice was country soft and confident. She was about sixteen, lanky and freckled, her extravagant red hair pulled back in a messy ponytail.

"Another job?" Sabrina frowned. "Don't you want to go back to school now?" Marilee had dropped out of high school last year to take care of her aging great-grandfather. He had died about a month ago, and Marilee had insisted that she wanted to stay in the family house by herself. It was a situation that would never work in the big city, but here it did. Family and friends looked after the teenager, and a small trust paid the bills.

"I got my GED." The girl's voice was neutral but firm. It was none of Sabrina's business, her closed expression said, but she was too well brought up to say it aloud.

"I'm happy to hear that. Are you thinking about college, though?"

Marilee shrugged and moved toward the door to the store. Something made her pause and she looked back over her shoulder at Sabrina. "I always did want to be an FBI agent."

"An FBI agent? Me too! Well, any sort of secret agent would have worked. You need to go to college if you want to join the FBI." Sabrina pulled out a notebook and started jotting notes to herself. "Have you taken your SATs? We need to look into scholarships and grants. Maybe a fundraiser..." She muttered to herself as she mapped out Marilee's future.

"You really think it's possible?" Marilee stared at Sabrina with the instinctive awe reserved for schoolteachers and doctors. These people were capable of daily miracles, she knew.

"Of course! We need to get to work, though. We'll talk soon."

Marilee nodded, her young face bright with hope. She raised her hand in farewell and went back inside.

"Sabrina! Aren't you a vision in pink. And yellow. And green. And—" Lima said as he came out of the store a few minutes later holding a Styrofoam cup of fragrant, homemade Brunswick stew.

A strangled, creaking noise came from the bottom step, and they both looked down to see that Bicycle was laughing.

"Well, call me a butt and slap me silly. I don't think I've seen Bicycle laugh in the twenty years he's been back on the island. Hey, did you know today was Mitchell's Day? I hope you're not planning to go out on the water."

"Lima, that's an old wives' tale." After several months on the island, she'd finally persuaded Lima to tell her the story behind the islanders' cryptic references to Mitchell's Day.

Lima snorted. "You live here long enough, and then you tell me it's an old wives' tale. You'll see. What have you been doing today, Sabrina?"

Sabrina ran through her morning: her talk with Maggie Fromlin about the strange behavior of the burglar, and then her very unproductive conversation with Mayor Hill Mitchell, who couldn't, or wouldn't, explain how he had known someone had been in his house while he was gone Friday night.

"That man's got so many screws loose he rattles when he walks." Lima shook his head.

"You know, I wasn't going to say anything, but did you ever notice his yard doesn't have anything green in it? It's all rock. No grass, bushes, trees, not even a weed."

"Yeah, I've noticed. He did that right after he retired from being a florist for thirty years. I guess he got tired of plants."

"Hill said nothing was missing, and so did Maggie. She remembers a note that the burglar may have dropped, though, reading 'Mit,' 'Har,' 'Gar,' and 'Fred.' Ring any bells?"

"Yeah, the silent one that only dogs and loonies can hear."

"Maggie also remembered that the thief was barefoot. What kind of thief breaks into a house barefoot and doesn't take anything?"

"Someone with more screws loose than Hill."

"If only the bad ones *did* rattle when they walked, at least we would know they were coming."

They thought about that for a while in the sleepy warmth of the noonday sun.

"Hey, Marilee," Lima yelled through the window behind his rocking chair. "I'll take another cup of this here stew. Best thing old Tubbs ever did, hiring Marilee," he said to Sabrina. "Stacy Tubbs did a great job behind that counter, but I didn't think Tubbs was ever going to find someone after Stacy left to go to college this past semester."

"Well, don't get too attached to Marilee being here. I just talked to her about taking her SATs and going to college. Did you know she wanted to be an FBI agent?"

"No, but I'm not surprised. That girl has a lot of spunk, let me tell you. Never a word of complaint, as bad as it must have been taking care of that old bastard, her great-grandfather. Not that Booker was a bad fellow, but he got right religious in his old age, always wanting to shove the Bible down my throat."

"It's never pleasant when someone tries to impose their religious beliefs on you."

"No, I meant he actually tried to push the Bible down my throat. This is when he was into his nineties, you understand. We got in an argument one night after we'd both had a few—Booker liked his whiskey—and he came over the table with the book in his hand. Before I knew what was happening, he had my mouth open and was shoving that Bible into my mouth, doing his darnedest to get it past my teeth."

"Oh, Lima!"

The old man shrugged, his eyes gleaming.

"Booker was one strange bird. Everyone says he was helping the bootleggers when he was on the police force back in the twenties. Some say he even helped cover up a murder."

Sabrina leaned forward as Lima settled back into his chair in preparation for a nice, long story.

"Weeell, Booker was the one who found Gerry Lowry right after he shot himself. Booker was only seventeen, and looking for work. He was tired of fishing already, and what else was an island boy supposed to do to make a living? All around him, people were making it rich off the liquor that was flowing through this island like Shinola through a septic field.

"No one knows for sure what happened, but it's pretty common knowledge that Gerry Lowry ran afoul of the bigwig rumrunners on the island and was planning to take the run boat—that's the boat that ran between the islands and the mainland—off the island first thing in the morning. Then he decided to off himself that evening, after telling everybody he was leaving? It didn't make sense. Like I said before, it was Booker who found him, and his testimony was key at the inquest the sheriff held before Gerry's body was even cold. The sheriff was so deep in the rumrunners' pockets it's a wonder he didn't choke on pocket lint. If the rumrunners *were* involved, the sheriff sure wasn't going to call them on it. And Booker…well, Booker might have had his own reasons for not being entirely truthful about what he saw that morning. Soon after that, Booker was hired by the sheriff, and it's rumored Booker made hisself a fortune looking the other way. Who knows, but most people agreed that Gerry Lowry wasn't the type to kill himself, especially by shooting himself. You see, Gerry was shot by accident by his big brother when he was a kid, and after that he couldn't even look at a gun without getting squirrelly-eyed and sweaty."

Neither had noticed Mary Garrison Tubbs until she spoke.

"Sabrina Victoria Dunsweeney, we give you a simple job, something even *you* can do, and you manage to muck it up in a gigantic way. I should have known, should have known!"

"Mary, you're one nasty bat, have I mentioned that today? What are you going on about now?" Lima rocked his chair angrily.

Mary took a deep breath and let it out in a delicious rush. "Gilbert Kane was found murdered over on Goat Island, that's what, and it's all Sabrina's fault!"

Chapter Nine

Sabrina pressed down harder on the gas pedal of her old station wagon and watched the speedometer needle tremble at the edge of fifty. Sabrina was trembling as well, a fine tremor emanating from deep inside her that rippled along her skin and shivered her fingers and the edges of her mouth.

"It was your idea to send those poor people out to Goat Island, wasn't it?" Mary had said with accusatory glee. "That's what I heard, and if it wasn't for you, that poor man would never have been on that island, and never got killed. I had second thoughts as soon as I suggested you for this job. You're about as responsible as my dog Curly, and I haven't managed to house train him all these years!"

Long Road never seemed longer as Sabrina sped past the endless grass-covered dunes. This part of the island was designated a national park, and except for the occasional homesteaded house and road, there was no sign that man had ever dreamt of beach houses and fruity drinks in sleek restaurants beside the sea. The park was full of birds and small animals, and bigger ones in the shape of the shaggy island ponies. Sabrina usually enjoyed the solitude of the road, which ran down to the other end of the island to an old, defunct military base, but right now she couldn't enjoy the stark beauty.

After what seemed like forever, she saw the discreet sign that signaled the turnoff to Shell Island. She took the turn so fast the station wagon slid in the loose gravel of the private road and ended up with its nose touching a pine tree.

Her trembling had bloomed into full-blown shaking as she sat staring at the tree.

"I've got to get myself together," she said out loud, wishing Calvin was with her. Not only was he a comfort, he also made her feel less like a shoo-in candidate for the loony bin when she talked to herself. "I'm fine. I can get through this."

The shaking refused to abate. She thought about turning around and going back to town, finding Mary Tubbs and telling her she was quitting. "I. Am. Not. Going. To. Quit!" she said between clenched teeth. "If I can't hack this job, then it's time for me to go back to Cincinnati." She took a deep breath. "I am sitting on a beach and I can feel the warm sand between my toes and hear the surf washing back and forth. I can taste the salt of the air and hear a seagull call…" The shaking slowly subsided as she continued to visualize her happy place. That her mental sanctuary, the one she created long before ever coming to Comico, closely resembled the island did not occur to her.

"Now, like a knight before battle, I will don my armor." Sabrina pictured herself pulling on the sturdy armor that was featured in countless King Arthur movies. She had no clue how one would get the armor on in reality, so in her vision it slid on like a suit of clothes, even complete with a nice modern zipper. Once her vulnerable naked skin was covered, Sabrina added the last touch, the helmet. She surveyed herself in an imaginary mirror. Despite the heavy armor, she was pounds lighter than normal. Unlike TV, delusional fantasies subtracted pounds instead of adding them.

Satisfied that her loins were sufficiently girded, Sabrina opened her eyes. As her therapist had promised, she felt better. At least she didn't feel as if she was walking around with her skin freshly peeled. She used to go through this ritual every morning, so she supposed she should be happy she only had to garb herself in armor on occasion now. Unfortunately, those occasions had been coming with more frequency over the last couple of months.

"Let's try this again."

With that, Sabrina put the car in gear and continued on to Shell Lodge.

"It was horrible," Matt Fredericks said, and shuddered. For a moment it looked as if he might cry, and Sabrina patted his arm.

"There, there," she soothed.

"He was floating there, face down, and he looked so *white*. Sam, our dock master, said we needed to go call the police, but I had to check, make sure, even though I could see the crabs scrabbling about in his hair." Matt flinched. "*God.* But what if he was still alive, and I left him there? I turned him over, and that's when I saw his ear. It was mangled, like pulp. His eyes were open and bulging and it looked like he was staring at me, and his mouth was agape, and I thought I saw bubbles and then I realized it was tiny fish in his mouth swimming around." Matt closed his eyes. "I've never seen anything like that before. Sam was matter-of-fact, but then he always is, but I—I yelled, kind of, and dropped him back in the water with a big splash."

He stopped and Sabrina continued her patting. She wondered if he felt like a dog. The thought made her withdraw her hand, but he unconsciously leaned toward her so she resumed the patting.

"He was dead, there was no doubt about it. As near as I can figure, someone hit or stabbed him in the ear. We got out of there, and called Sergeant Jimmy, who called in a bunch of other police."

Sabrina had ample knowledge of how a murder investigation was run on Comico Island, as a pirate ghost—well, a man, really, though everybody thought he was the ghost of Walk-the-Plank Wrightly—was murdered in the rose garden of her rental cottage when she first arrived on the island.

She patted and thought. "Stabbed in the ear? With what?"

Matt shook his head and closed his eyes. "I have no idea. The only thing I saw lying there was an empty wine bottle. And *that* couldn't have done that kind of damage to his ear."

"But you think that's what killed him? This injury to his ear?"

"That's the only thing I saw wrong with him." Matt scrubbed his head with his hands and then looked around the lobby to make sure there were no guests in sight. But the large room was empty; the entire lodge was languid in the honeyed afternoon sunlight, and it was easy to believe they were the only two in the building.

"His car. Well, that's interesting, isn't it? So, a-hem." Sabrina coughed, and stopped. "What…what was Gilbert doing out on Goat Island?"

She fully expected Matt to jump up and shout, "Why it's your fault completely, Sabrina, you know that!" but the young hotel owner just looked down at his hands and shook his head.

"He wanted to check out the island, so I got Sam to take him over there yesterday afternoon. I saw Mr. Kane go into the lounge, and then he came through the lobby fussing over a camera, which he put in his duffel bag, and then he went out the front door and started down the path toward the marina. That was the last time I saw him. He didn't look very good, upset or something, and he ignored me when I said goodbye. Not that that was unusual." A brief flash of guilt crossed his face. "I'm sure he was under a lot of pressure," he added quickly.

"I'm sure." Sabrina's hand was getting tired from all the patting. She switched hands. "He went with…Sam, did you say? By boat, I take it?"

"Sam is our dock master and fishing guide. He takes care of all our boats. He took Mr. Kane over in our Mako and was supposed to drop him off for an hour or two, then come back and pick him up before sundown. But—"

"Sam couldn't wait for him on the island while Gilbert—Mr. Kane—looked around?"

Matt shrugged. "Mr. Kane said he needed to be alone so he could feel the vibes of the island." He said this with a straight face.

Sabrina kept hers straight too. "I suppose ah, vibes are hard to feel with other people around. Though it's probably a good thing they aren't louder, or we would all be bee-bopping around to our own personal vibes."

Matt nodded as if she'd said something intelligent. He was a good boy. "Sam left him on the island and came back to our dock. A while later Mr. Kane called Sam and told him he didn't have to come pick him up. Sam locked down the marina and went home."

"Gilbert never came back to the lodge last night? Didn't anyone notice?"

Matt looked defensive. "Sam didn't tell me any of this until this morning, and of course I assumed Mr. Kane came back to the lodge last night. None of the other Hummers said anything else about it, but then, they were on their own for dinner, so maybe they didn't notice either. Anyway, they all acted pretty surprised when he didn't show up at the dock this morning. Mr. Kane had arranged for Sam to take them all over to the island at eight o'clock this morning, but he never showed. When Mr. Kane didn't answer the phone in his room, Sam and I went over to the island in the boat, and that's when we found him."

"Why would Gilbert tell Sam that Sam didn't need to come back for him? Surely he wasn't planning on spending the night on the island. Though, you did say he had a duffel bag…" Sabrina looked up. "You didn't mention seeing the duffel bag on the beach. Where was it?"

Matt thought hard, his whole face screwed up like a six-year-old concentrating on not peeing his pants, and then shook his head. "I didn't see it. It wasn't there."

"So, the bag was gone. Unless you just didn't see it." Sabrina made a mental note to ask Sam if he saw the bag. She had a feeling ten circus elephants could have been performing a line dance on the beach beside Gilbert's body and Matt might not have noticed. "If it was gone, that implies someone came and took it. Which fits in with Gilbert calling and telling Sam not to pick him up. Someone came to the island, unexpectedly, or why would Gilbert have initially arranged for Sam to pick him up? And it probably was someone Gilbert knew or why else would he decide to catch a ride back with him? And whoever it was killed Gilbert and then took the duffel bag."

Sabrina nodded with satisfaction. It all fit. All they needed to do was find the person who went to the island and they would have the murderer. Case closed.

Who knew this detective stuff would be so easy? She felt better already.

"Mr. Fredericks?" Two uniformed policemen came through the front door and Matt smiled automatically, though not before flinching as if someone had just delivered a quick jab to his abdomen.

"Can I answer any more questions for you?" Matt was courteous, though he couldn't seem to stop running his hands through his short sandy hair. Sabrina wondered if this nervous habit contributed to the noticeable recession of his hairline. It couldn't help.

"We would like to see Mr. Kane's room. Can you let us in?"

"Yes, of course."

Matt plucked a large key ring labeled "Master" off a hook on the wall, next to several other keys labeled "Jeep 2," "Jeep 3" and "Jeep 5." He led the policemen out of the lobby and down a hallway, and Sabrina tagged along without anyone objecting.

"Some of these doors still have char marks from the fire that almost burnt the lodge down in the twenties. The Feds were making one of their obligatory raids, and in the rush to hide the liquor, someone dropped a cigar in the hallway." Matt stopped at a door at the end of the hall and traced his fingers along several dark marks on the highly polished wood. "Back then, there was a brand-new La France fire truck on the island, financed by my great-grandfather, but they didn't realize until they got it to the island that it was designed for the city, and could only go about eight blocks. After that, the freeze plugs would blow out. That meant when a fire call came in, everyone would jump aboard the fire truck and race toward the fire. After eight blocks the freeze plugs would blow and then someone would have to climb down, pour in water, and hammer in the plugs before they could drive another eight blocks. Needless to say, it took a while for the fire truck to make it out here, though finally it arrived and was able to put the fire out."

Talking about the lodge's history seemed to settle Matt, and with steady hands he inserted the key into the lock and pushed the door open.

The large, comfortable room was empty. Through the clear glass of the closed balcony doors, Sabrina could see white patio furniture and bright flowers set in large pots and beyond that, a glimpse of radiant water. She saw something else, too.

The room had been ransacked.

Chapter Ten

Michael Siderius stood barefoot on the railing of his second story terrace and flexed his toes around the warm concrete. He stepped along the rail with fluid, precise movements, reveling in the feel of his muscles rippling under his suit pants. One of his gymnastics coaches made him practice on a balance beam to strengthen his floor exercise routine, and while men did not compete on the balance beam, Michael liked the thrill it gave him.

He lay on his stomach on the rail and let his legs dangle on either side. Then he brought his legs upward, careful not to extend them above horizontal or to arch his back. He performed this in three repetitions of twenty-five. He was not thinking about Gilbert's death, or his father, or Hummers International Incorporated. He was thinking about a pivotal moment at an Olympic trial fifteen years ago when he had fallen on a back flip. Not even a full-out, just a single lousy back flip.

Winning Olympic gold was the one thing Michael thought could steal his father's attention away from the Hum. They were living in England when Joseph started hearing the Hum, but he soon quit his job as an engineer and moved his young family back to the United States. Joseph returned to school and earned a doctorate in physics so he could better understand his own symptoms. Nothing could tear his attention away from the Hum. No amount of fighting, bad grades, or recreational puppy kicking elicited more than a distracted scolding. Michael's mother gave him anything he wanted, but it was never enough. She even tried to bribe an official into changing his decision after the Olympic trial, to no avail, and Michael despised her for failing him.

Michael stood with quick grace and then stretched forward to do a handstand. Below his face was dizzying space, and the shell garden twenty feet below, and he smiled as he balanced himself on his hands.

Now everything was different. He no longer wanted or needed his father's approval, and now that Gilbert was gone, he could stop worrying about what that clever, fat man thought of him as well.

Michael had long dreamed of Gilbert's death. Brake failure on a long trip, the unfortunate use of a hairdryer in the bathtub, an injudicious step into a busy street. Any day could be dear Gilbert's last, and Michael planned for the time when he would be solely in control of Hummers International. No more jelly-belly standing behind him as Michael tried to talk to an investor, and no more pudgy, sweating face creased with that condescending smile as Michael talked about his ideas. It had been that way ever since Michael started working for Gilbert right out of college, and nothing had changed, even now that Gilbert was supposedly working for Michael.

Michael lowered his feet to the rail and stood up.

Gilbert was gone, and Michael was feeling determinedly happy. But the doubts were creeping in. He knew Gilbert would tell him he should be down comforting the nut cases, wiping away their tears while he promised a personal conversation with the universe. But...

Gilbert was dead.

Michael laughed and stretched his arms high over his head. Gilbert was dead, Gilbert was dead, *Gilbert was dead.* He felt free, and exhilarated, and...

He wouldn't admit he was scared. He could handle it on his own. He knew the way things worked. If it wasn't for him and his father, the whole thing would have fallen apart years ago.

He was the main act in this circus, and Gilbert had just been a roadie. Michael knew it all along, and now he would prove it.

Feeling better, he tensed his muscles in preparation for a back flip.

Chapter Eleven

"Do you think they will cancel the retreat?" asked a very tall young man.

"Where in the hell is Siderius, that's what I want to know. How are we supposed to know what's going on when he won't bother to tell us? For that matter, where's the old guy?" This from a man in a dark blue suit who looked like he would prefer *Fortune* over *National Geographic*, aged scotch over beer, and first class most definitely over coach. He wore a pair of wrap-around high-tech sunglasses and his face looked as if it were no stranger to masks and moisturizers.

Sabrina stood in the doorway of the meeting room, but the three Hummers inside were too involved in their conversation to notice her.

The tall young man had a tendency to duck, even sitting, as if he'd encountered one too many ceilings in his short life, and had an open, engaging face, despite the strain evident on it. Looking around the room, Sabrina saw that all three men showed signs of strain. Of course, Gilbert's death could account for some of it, but this tension had the look of longevity about it. It took weeks or even months of constant stress to tense muscles so tight that not even constant neck rolling and finger flexing would relieve them.

"I don't think we need any water." A grayish man in the back of the room said this in a quiet voice, and it took a moment for Sabrina to realize that the apropos-nothing statement was directed at her.

"Oh! No, I don't have any water, though I think I have half a Diet Pepsi in my purse if you need it…" There was silence, and Sabrina realized they all thought she was a deranged hotel employee. She rushed on. "I'm Sabrina Dunsweeney, Comico Island's Ombudsman. I've come to see how you are doing and offer any assistance I can provide. May I say that all of us on Comico Island are so sorry that you have experienced this loss?" The speech went exactly as practiced and Sabrina beamed.

"We've all been interviewed by the police, but we haven't seen Michael or Joseph since this morning. We want to know when our sessions are going to resume," said the man in the sunglasses.

"I, um, I'm not sure of that." Sabrina was a bit nonplused by their determination to continue with their retreat in the face of Gilbert's death. "I'll find out when your sessions will be resuming as soon as I can. Is there anything else I can do for you? I know this must be a very trying time for you, and I would be happy to do anything I can to make this easy experience difficult. That is to say, to ease your way through this difficult experience." It was another speech she had practiced on the way here, and this one didn't go quite as well. The men were looking skeptical, and Sabrina knew she needed to do something fast. The question was, what? Her "Annie Get Your Gun" tap dance routine from her fifth grade recital didn't seem appropriate in these circumstances, though it had worked in other tight spots.

"We don't need anything—" said the grayish man.

"Well, that's good. Please feel free to ask if you need anything. Doughnuts? A shoulder to cry on? An oil lube?" That just popped out because she knew Pastor Josh was running a special on them down at the car lot. She needed to stop talking. She always talked too much when she was nervous. "I need to take down all your names."

Sabrina whipped out her brand-new pad of paper, but then had to search her purse for a pen. She always had a pen, for goodness' sake, but where had it gone? She pawed through uplifting sticky notes—"stand up straight and don't forget to smile!"—a comb and lipstick, a half a Diet Pepsi, a screwdriver, a flattened Twinkie—ambrosia for the downhearted soul—little petrified clumps of tissue, and finally upended her purse on a nearby table. A brochure on kayaking slithered to the floor and Sabrina stooped to pick it up.

"Oh, look. Kayaking. I've always wanted to try it. Are any of you kayakers?" Sabrina smiled brightly around the room. Sergeant Jimmy McCall, who had just stepped to the doorway, winced and ducked back out of sight.

"What in the hell are you jabbering on about?" the man in the sunglasses asked, his buffed body tense with annoyance. "I certainly don't kayak."

"How about you two? Do you like to kayak?" Sabrina turned to the other two men.

There was no response, except for a horrified choke just outside the door.

"Oh, well. Let's see, now what was I doing?" She looked down at the purse detritus on the table.

"Ms. Dunsweeney," said the tall young man sitting in the first row. "There's a pen inside that pad of paper you pulled out first thing. Was that what you were looking for?" He didn't seem sure that she might not have felt the sudden urge to clean her purse.

"Ah, yes. There it is." Sabrina stuffed the junk back into her purse and looked at him expectantly, pen poised.

"What? Oh, my name is…well, Dennis Parker." He said the name in a rush without looking at her. Sabrina wrote it down carefully, checking with him on the spelling of Dennis. People were doing all sorts of interesting things to traditional names nowadays, and one never knew. "And your address?"

Dennis, who seemed relieved to have gotten the whole my-name-is issue behind him, recited his Chicago address easily. He was a handsome boy, with dark curly hair, a touch of freckles, and a thin frame on which his clothes hung precariously. His hands looked proportionally too large, however, like one of those pictures taken with your hand in the foreground so your fingers look like gigantic sausages.

"Have you ever been to Comico Island before?" Sabrina asked Dennis.

"No. I've never been on an island. I grew up on a farm in Illinois, and we never traveled much. Of course, now I—well, I've never been to an island, that's all." His ears turned red, and he reminded Sabrina of a twenty-something Richie Cunningham. Not the way he looked exactly—Dennis didn't look anything like Ron Howard—but just the boyish charm he exuded.

Dennis suddenly grimaced and clutched at his head. Sabrina patted his shoulder, and looked around to see if anyone else had observed his distress.

"Dennis? Are you feeling okay?"

He looked up, his eyes glazed with misery, and nodded.

"Do you need some Tylenol? I have aspirin as well, but at your age you need to be careful of Reye's Syndrome, you know, so you're better off sticking with acetaminophen."

"It doesn't help," Dennis said in a low voice. "Nothing does."

Sabrina sensed that he preferred to be alone so she moved over to the table where the man who looked like he was a businessman with a capital "B" was sitting. He made no effort to ask Dennis if he was okay.

"Mrs. Dunsweeney," began the important businessman in an important manner. The man oozed money. His sunglasses alone, which looked capable of x-ray vision, translating foreign languages, and cooking five-course meals, probably cost more than Sabrina's house in Cincinnati.

"It's Ms., actually. And what was your name?"

"I'm Walter Olgivie. And while I'm sure you are a very capable person, I'm afraid I must insist that we speak with your superior. Someone of…higher rank."

Sabrina read his meaning clearly. Substitute "higher rank" with "possessing male genitalia." Walter Olgivie was similar to many men of a certain generation who were accustomed to their women at home, waiting for them to return home from the office—or more probably the golf course—with congratulatory smiles and proffered drinks.

"I have been nominated by the mayor and the town council, so you can view me as their representative." Sabrina managed a cool smile while inwardly picturing her suit of armor.

"Well, then, I would like to know what in the world is going on around here." Walter's taut, expensive face looked irritated. Sabrina wondered if he had some type of surgery to remove the hair from his face. It was that smooth, and Walter did not look as if he were adverse to surgical enhancement. Most sixty-something men did not have body-builder physiques and faces as unlined as a five-year-old child's.

"That is something that I will endeavor to find out as soon as possible," Sabrina said in a cheery voice. "And what is your name?" As she turned to him, the grayish man in the back of the room jerked as if she had shouted in his face.

"I'm Lance Mayhew." Even his voice was grayish and indistinct. He was one of those unforgettable people who could walk naked down the street during rush hour and later no one would be able to describe him. He wore a gray sweat suit, and his thinning hair was an indistinct medium color that was shades of sandy blond, brown and, yes, gray. His nose was high and arched, but it wasn't enough to give his face any sort of character. In fact, his face was as dull and blank as an empty movie screen. Perhaps like a movie screen animated by the focus of the projector, emotion would brighten Lance Mayhew's face with expression and passion, but just now there was no sign of it.

Sabrina moved over to his side with her pen poised. "And your address?"

"I would prefer not to give that." The words were said without offense or affect.

Sabrina smiled forgivingly and looked around the room. "Is this the whole group?"

"No, Patti and Sophie left to go to the ladies' room. They should be back soon," Dennis offered, without removing his head from his hands.

Sabrina nodded. She had suspected that Patti Townsend and her beautiful friend were Hummers. "Tell me, for what reason are you here on the island?" She looked around the room, surprised at the warring emotions on their faces.

"It's because of the Hum," Walter snapped. "Why else?"

"All of you hear the Hum? How fascinating. What's it like?"

There was silence, and then Dennis burst out with, "It's absolutely horrible, that's what!"

"Why?"

No one would look at Sabrina. Lance finally said in his expressionless voice, "We would prefer not to talk about it, if you don't mind."

A small scuffle at the door was the only warning before Joseph Siderius glided in, his yellow dashiki flowing behind him as he went over to a window and sat down without looking at anyone.

Behind Joseph was his son, Michael. The young, handsome president of Hummers International Incorporated stood at the door and surveyed the people inside.

"Where are Patti and Sophie?"

"Right here!" Patti Townsend rushed into the room, followed by her gorgeous, dazed-looking friend. They took seats at the front of the room.

"Gilbert Kane's death is a tragedy, there's no doubt," Michael said with perfect showman's timing. "But I know he would want us to continue with our important work, to not let his death stand in the way of our vital mission." He crossed so he stood with his hand on his father's shoulder, the image of virility next to the frail older man. He looked around at the group, making eye contact with each of the Hummers, while ignoring Sabrina.

"Are you ready?" he asked. "Are you ready to communicate with the universe?"

Chapter Twelve

Michael turned to Sabrina, with a wide, white smile. He sported a fresh cut on his chin, and his hands looked scraped and raw.

"I would like to speak with you later, Michael." Sabrina stashed her pen and pad in her purse and headed for the door. She knew when she was not wanted.

"Certainly." Michael turned back to the group before Sabrina even left the room. "I think we should resume our sessions as soon as possible. I've spoken with management, and they are going to arrange a place for us to go tomorrow morning. Now, Master Joseph has something he wants to say—"

Sabrina turned back to see that Michael had put his hand on his father's shoulder once again. The old man stared straight ahead, his expression blank and benign.

"Master Joseph says that death is not forever...he wants you to never forget that..." Michael's voice had dropped into a sing-song rhythm as he closed his eyes and swayed. This was interrupted as Joseph suddenly snapped his head around to stare at Sabrina.

"Thank you, Sabrina, I'll speak with you later," Michael said in a normal voice as he crossed the room with a long stride and closed the door in Sabrina's face.

Sabrina stood for a moment, listening to the murmur of voices inside the meeting room and trying to sort out what she saw right before the door shut. Shades of awe, desperation, skepticism, and hope were painted with a lavish hand across the faces of the five Hummers. Hope was the most vivid: anguished, fervent hope. They wanted badly to believe, no matter what their rational minds told them about the staged theatrics.

As for Joseph in his ridiculous yellow outfit, it would be easy to dismiss him as a charlatan, a willing accomplice to his son's medium act. But there had been something in the man's eyes as he stared at Sabrina…She couldn't begin to define what it was, but she was left with a lingering feeling of sadness and hopelessness.

Sabrina looked around and was thankful to see that Sergeant Jimmy was gone. Give him a while to cool down, and he would realize that she was just doing her job.

When Sabrina ran into Sergeant Jimmy McCall in the lobby, he was surprised to learn that she had been hired as Comico Island's Ombudsman, and that she planned to offer her help to the Hummers. She wasn't sure if he was going to laugh or cry, but her hands started patting anyway, just in case.

With a little sweet-talking, Jimmy had shared some details about the investigation. He told her the police discovered a kayak was pulled ashore on Goat Island around high tide the night before. Gilbert Kane arrived on the island close to high tide, and, according to the estimated time of death, died not too long after that. Someone else was on Goat Island at the same time as Gilbert, most likely the killer.

And the killer came by kayak.

Matt Fredericks saw Sabrina coming and groaned inwardly. He still felt sick whenever he thought about the fish swimming in and out of Gilbert Kane's mouth, and he knew Sabrina would insist on asking more questions about what he had seen. She was very thorough. He had so many other things on his mind, like how he was going to attract more people to his lodge, or get the money to patch the perpetually leaking roof. But he was too professional to show his weariness, or to let his money problems spoil his customer-friendly smile. Even if Sabrina wasn't a customer. Word of mouth happened, he liked to tell his staff, you never knew who, when, why, or how.

"Miss Sabrina! Sergeant Jimmy said he wanted to talk to you immediately. He was called away but you're to call him first thing. Here's his cell phone number."

Sabrina accepted the piece of paper from him as if he was proffering raw squid with a dash of liver. "And…how did he seem?" she asked.

"Pretty steamed. The sergeant was muttering under his breath the whole time he wrote the note. Something about 'doesn't listen any better than a crab pot'."

"Hmmm." Sabrina put the piece of paper in her purse and looked at Matt with her big, blue eyes. "I understand the Hummers are going to resume their sessions tomorrow. Where are they going to go?"

Matt ran his fingers through his hair. "The only other island that will work is Dead Man's Island. I told Mr. Siderius that perhaps it might not be appropriate and offered the picnic area again, but he insisted on the island. He said members of the group are threatening to go home if they aren't assured of their privacy."

And if he lost this group, he was in serious trouble. People looked at the Shell Lodge and saw a thriving, successful business. Matt looked at it and saw hurricane damage, exorbitant taxes, and rising insurance. It was a money pit, but it was his money pit, and he would do anything to save it.

Sabrina was still watching him with an expectant expression and he quickly finished his thought. "Tomorrow morning Sam is taking them out to Rainbow Island."

"Rainbow Island?"

"Mr. Siderius requested that we refer to the island by some name other than Dead Man's Island. Sam came up with Rainbow Island." The dock master had also come up with a few other less appropriate names as well, like Fruitcake Island and Feel the Vibe Island. Matt decided to go with Rainbow Island.

"It seems strange that they want to get back to their sessions so soon after Gilbert's death," Sabrina mused.

"Well, they only have until Saturday to finish whatever they hoped to accomplish."

"Yes," Sabrina said thoughtfully, "but what exactly did they hope to accomplish?"

Matt waved as Sabrina went off, and then looked back down at his scrawled figures. No matter how he juggled the numbers, they still came up short.

It was time for desperate measures.

Sabrina made her way down one of the shell-encrusted walkways, stopping to marvel at the intricacy of the inlaid shells. So many thousands of shells, placed precisely into the concrete. It must have taken years to finish. What did Matt say? A labor of love. Sabrina could imagine Matt's great-grandmother, young and pretty in a flapper dress, on her hands and knees with a trowel, placing the shells in the precise pattern she wanted.

She thought about Sergeant Jimmy's evasive answer when she asked him about the weapon used to kill Gilbert Kane. It was missing, he said. Yes, but what was it? she persisted. Did the police know what type of murder weapon they were looking for? Jimmy looked uncomfortable as he admitted that they weren't sure yet what could cause that kind of trauma to the human ear.

Not a knife, Sabrina concluded. Surely the police would have known by now if it were a knife. So what kind of weapon could have inflicted the kind of brutal damage that Matt described?

The beach came into sight through the thick trees. A cozy cove cuddled a narrow strip of white sand and a small marina holding several boats. Sabrina could see two miniature sailboats—they couldn't be much bigger than bathtubs—struggling to tack in the still afternoon air. The sun was growing larger and redder as it sank toward the horizon, and long shadows brushed coldly across Sabrina's face as she hurried down the path.

"You must be Comico Island's illustrious ombudsman!" A man's voice said as she neared the dock.

"Please?" She looked around but saw no man to go with the voice.

"Sabrina Dunsweeney, if I'm not mistaken," the disembodied voice continued. "Blond and disheveled and wearing something pink, or purple, or possibly yellow. The sergeant couldn't remember what you were wearing, just that it was blinding and neon."

"Please!" Sabrina huffed in indignation, unsure of which slight to address first. It was disconcerting to speak to empty air. Even as she moved along the dock she did not encounter the impertinent speaker, though a pelican was watching her appraisingly. Surely not... "I'm not disheveled, and my clothes are—"

The pelican lifted its long beak and fluffed its pouch, making a gargling sound that sounded disturbingly like a laugh. Sabrina glared at the bird.

"Don't you dare laugh at me, you—"

"I wasn't laughing." A man stepped out from under the dock and looked up at Sabrina. "Who's laughing?"

Sabrina looked from the chortling pelican to the man and forgot her ire. "Are you okay? Where are you hurt? Please, sit down—" Sabrina ran along the dock and down the short flight of stairs to the beach. The man was staring at her dumbfounded as she flew up to him and began patting his arms and chest.

"Where are you hit? Smile, raise your arms and speak a simple sentence. Oh no, that's for a stroke. Drat. Well, are you feeling lightheaded, are you having trouble breathing, are you—"

"What—"

"Sit down, please sit down." Sabrina forced the man down onto a nearby cooler as she continued her inspection. No weapons that she could see or feel, that was reassuring.

"What are you going on about?" The words were said with some vigor, enough to make Sabrina pause and look down at the man's face. He was compact and sinewy, with thinning hair bleached colorless by many years of sun. Thick creases encased his bloodshot pale blue eyes, and golden stubble covered his sun-darkened face. He wore cut-off khaki shorts and dock shoes, as well as a white tee-shirt. This was the de rigueur island wear, except for the fact that—

"You've got blood all over you." Sabrina kept her voice calm. People in shock oftentimes did not realize the extent of their injuries. Perhaps the man didn't even know he was badly injured.

"It's not mine."

"Please?"

"I said, it's not mine. But thank you for your concern." The man removed Sabrina's restraining hands and rose to his feet. He offered his hand, but retracted it with a grimace when he noticed the blood on it.

"I'm Sam Myers. I run the Shell Lodge marina, such as it is." He gestured to the dock, encompassing with a short wave the fuel pump, the ramshackle shed, a compact sailboat, and several other boats painted with the Shell Lodge logo. "That sailboat at the end is my current abode, so you could say this dock is my whole universe."

Sabrina surveyed him, but he seemed lucid and unhurt. Perhaps he was not injured after all, though she would be vigilant in case he stumbled or fainted.

"You said the blood wasn't yours?" Sabrina ended the statement with a delicate question.

"Nope."

"Where did it come from, then?" She was beginning to feel some trepidation.

"Did you know that crows are the most creative birds in the world?" Sam pulled a knife from a scabbard at his side and began testing its edge for sharpness. Sabrina took an instinctive step back. "Some say they may be even more intelligent than chimpanzees when it comes to tool making. They probe logs for grubs with twigs and they've been spotted placing nuts they want cracked beneath the tires of cars stopped at red lights. It's very unusual for animals to make tools, and crows seem to be among the most skilled."

Sabrina looked around, but there were no crows in sight. "That's very interesting, I'm sure. Perhaps you didn't hear me when I asked where the blood came from." She was backing away now, her hand slipping inside her purse, though there was nothing more lethal in there than a Twinkie. Perhaps she could throw it at him as she ran away. Nobody could resist a Twinkie.

"My point was, they are intelligent creatures, wouldn't you agree?"

"It certainly sounds like it, though I'd never noticed it. In Cincinnati they were quite annoying, always cawing and strewing trash on my lawn."

Sam looked up from his knife and grinned, his small, pointed teeth very white in his tanned face. "Ah, Sabrina, but don't you think *I,* as unprepossessing as I may seem, am as intelligent as a loud, obnoxious crow?"

"Well…"

"And don't you think," Sam was quick to interrupt, "I would be smart enough to not be caught covered with blood if I just killed someone? I'm assuming you think I am a homicidal maniac who finished off the fat tourist last night and moved on to another one for lunch."

"That's a terrible thing to say!"

Sam shrugged. "I didn't know the man. What little I knew I didn't like. He talked to me like I was an idiot, and he kicked my cat. So, no, I'm not sorry he's dead."

"Are you always like this?"

"Like what?"

"So, so, *rude.*"

"Ah, but some people, my dear Sabrina, find me charming."

"Well, I don't!"

Sam grinned, not at all concerned. "Would you like to see my abattoir?"

"I don't think—" But curiosity won out, and as Sam disappeared behind a rickety shed, Sabrina followed to find a rough table and sink behind it, right at the edge of the water. "I still would like to know—" she began, but stopped in shock at the blood-soaked sight that confronted her.

Blood, lots of it. Unidentifiable body parts. An overflowing bucket of bloody gore. A full meat grinder.

It looked as if a massacre had taken place.

Chapter Thirteen

A few curious pelicans were sneaking in close to the gruesome table, and Sam picked up a hose. With aggrieved squawks, they waddled a few feet away before he could even turn it on.

"I'm making chum. See?" Sam offered her the bowl from the grinder with cheerful enthusiasm.

"I can see quite well from here." Sabrina kept her distance, as the fishy smell was overwhelming. Her stomach—strong by anyone's measure—grew queasy a bit at the sight. "I've heard of it, but never…" She gestured at the bloody mess in mute dismay.

"I'll make up buckets of this and freeze it. When I take the next bunch of people out fishing, I'll bring along a bucket and hang it off the stern of the boat. It'll bring the fish, the tourists will catch their limit, I'll look good, and everyone is happy." Sam dumped the contents of the bowl in the bucket, indifferent to the gory splash.

"It seems cruel, grinding up those poor little fish so somebody can catch a bigger fish. I think it's horrible."

"Even the smallest creature has a purpose."

"Are you going to get all enigmatic again?"

"If you knew me well enough, you'd know I always have a point." Sam stuffed several fish parts into the meat grinder and began grinding. "These fish were caught yesterday, and were the special last night at the Shell Lodge restaurant. Today, I'm grinding up the rest of them to use as chum. Very little of these fish went to waste."

Sabrina was quiet a moment, watching Sam's powerful muscles flex as he applied force to the grinder's handle and trying to ignore the unpleasant squishing and cracking noises. "I'm sorry. I jumped to an inaccurate conclusion." The admission was grudging but sincere.

Sam tossed her a breezy smile. "It's not the first time someone has jumped to the wrong conclusion about me. I work hard at giving the wrong impression. So, what am I supposed to confess to you? The sergeant—he's a big fellow, isn't he?—said you would be coming around asking questions."

"And did he tell you not to speak with me?"

"Oh, no. He said it didn't matter whether I wanted to talk to you or not, that you would have the truth out of me in seconds flat. He seemed to have a lot of confidence in your powers of persuasion. As someone who has great respect for the inevitable, I'm ready to be interrogated." Sam raised his hands in mock surrender and peeked around his fingers at her. "Be gentle, please."

"Give me a break." Sabrina couldn't remember ever being vexed by anyone quite so much. Every time she started to warm to him, he said something outrageous. In fact, he seemed to take positive enjoyment in being obnoxious. "Would you please just tell me about Gilbert Kane?"

"That's a relief. I was afraid you were going to grill me until I confessed that I cheated on a math test in the fourth grade and killed a man last year. That would have been a lot more painful. Gilbert Kane, now that's easy, since there's so little to tell. Matt told me to take him over to the island yesterday afternoon. Kane showed up and we took the Mako over to Goat Island. When we got there he told me he would call me when he was ready to be picked up. I gave him my cell phone number and he checked his phone to make sure he had service. He did. I got back here and had to run around looking for a missing kayak. I still hadn't found it when the fat—Gilbert Kane called me and told me to not bother picking him up."

"What were his exact words?"

Sam paused, thinking back. "I've thought about it. I'm not sure what he said exactly, but my assumption was that someone else had come by to pick him up. I couldn't fathom who it might be, since all the boats here, except for the one-seater kayak, were accounted for, but I didn't think it was any of my business."

Questions swirled through Sabrina's mind, but she wasn't sure where to start. "Gilbert didn't sound strange when he called? Like maybe he was being coerced?" Another thought popped into her mind. "Or perhaps it was someone else who called and pretended to be Gilbert?"

Sam dropped another fish into the grinder and began to turn the handle. "That's like asking someone what color the grass was yesterday. You just assume it was green. He said he was Gilbert Kane, so I assumed it was. The reception wasn't stellar and I was busy looking for the missing kayak. I wasn't paying close attention. It could have been Bette Midler for all I know. But my impression at the time was that it was him, and that he sounded…" He paused, staring into the bloody bowl before him.

"He sounded what?"

"I don't know. I guess he did sound different. Too friendly, or calmer, or something. Different. I'm not sure how." He frowned, and Sabrina's heart warmed to him. He *was* trying to help.

"It could have been someone else impersonating Gilbert, or even Gilbert himself, under coercion. That would account for the different tenor of his voice."

"Or it was Gilbert, and I just don't give a flying squirrel one way or the other." Sam looked up and smiled as Sabrina considered strangling him.

"But…there's a chance it wasn't him."

"And an equal chance it was him."

"But he could have been coerced."

"Or maybe he found his vibe on the island and everything was so copacetic he found himself in a good mood. He might not have known what one was."

Sabrina wondered if pounding her head against the nearby dock post would make her obviously eligible for the rubber room.

Perhaps if she pounded Sam's head against the post…Anyone who knew him would understand, and she suspected it would release the same frustrated energy as pounding her own head. A lot less painful as well. For her, anyway.

"Let's move on. Gilbert was carrying a duffel bag, wasn't he? Did you happen to see what was in it?"

"You mean like if he dumped everything out looking for his camera, I might have caught a glimpse of what was inside?"

"Yes!" She quivered with excitement. "What was inside?"

"I don't know. He never dumped it out. Too bad, huh? That would have been convenient. Actually, what he did was unzip it enough to reach inside and grab his camera and then he zipped it up so fast he caught his hand in the zipper. Shrieked pretty good."

"Gilbert shrieked?"

"Well, his hand *was* bleeding. Anyone would shriek."

"But you didn't see what else he had in the bag?"

"Isn't that what I said?" Sam turned innocent eyes on Sabrina, widening them as if he was worried about her mental stability, or at the very least, her hearing.

Sabrina took a deep breath. "You have no idea what was in the bag."

"Nope."

Sabrina started her Lamaze breathing. She had never been pregnant, but she'd once attended a Lamaze class for fun. She found the breathing routine very soothing. Sam watched with interest as she huffed and panted herself into calmness.

"You said you were looking for a missing kayak. What can you tell me about that?" she asked when she felt better.

Sam raised an eyebrow. "It was missing. I went looking for it."

"Yes, but *when* did it go missing?" She knew the police must have asked similar questions, so Sam's show of blithe ignorance was unconvincing. And irritating.

"While I took the fat man over to the island. When I got back, I noticed someone had taken the blue kayak without signing it out."

"Signing it out?"

"The kayaks are a courtesy to the guests, but we ask that they sign for them so we know who has what. Whoever took the blue kayak didn't bother signing it out. Didn't bother bringing it back either."

"While you were taking the fat—Gilbert over to the island where he died, someone came and took a kayak without signing it out. That's suspicious, isn't it?"

"The police thought so. Especially when they found blood on it."

"They found blood on the blue kayak?" Sabrina remembered that Sergeant Jimmy said the police found signs a kayak was on the island about the same time as Gilbert. Something about tides that made them certain of the timing...

"I found the kayak last night, over on the other side of the island. I brought it back here, but it was too dark to see anything. This morning when I told the police about it, they looked at it and the other two kayaks that were out at the same time, and they found blood on the blue one."

"What other two kayaks?"

"The two that were out when I left to take Kane over to the island. They were returned a little while after I got back from taking Kane."

"Who took them out? Would you recognize the people?"

"Well, there they are right now."

Sabrina turned to see Patti Townsend and her young friend coming down the shell path toward them.

Chapter Fourteen

"That lady," Sam nodded at Patti, who was concentrating on making her way down the steep path, "has gone out several times since they've been here. The pretty girl joined her last night, just before I took Kane over to the island."

Sam went to the nearest kayak and began dragging it down toward the water. Sabrina followed him, still trying to think of questions about Gilbert, but failing. Her mind was too wrapped up with the fact that Patti and her friend were out on kayaks at the approximate time Gilbert died. Was there some reason why they would *want* to kill him, though?

"I hear you've been involved in the break-ins in town." Sam looked up at her, squinting a bit in the dazzle of the setting sun.

"Please?"

"The. Break-ins. In. Town." Sam enunciated the words slowly and clearly for her. He looked as if he considered doing sign language to be on the safe side.

"I heard you the first time! I was just wondering if you were trying to accuse me of breaking into houses. That's what it sounded like."

"Me thinks she protests too much! Did you?"

"No! Of course not. Why would you say such a thing?"

"I didn't. When he left, the sergeant said he had to go follow up on some things from the break-ins, and mentioned something to the effect that you probably wouldn't be too far behind him there either."

"I see." Sabrina was pleased that Sergeant Jimmy recognized what a good job she was doing.

"He muttered something else too, but I couldn't catch most of what he said. Something about 'license to be nosy' and 'as if she needed any encouragement.'"

"Oh." Her bubble burst.

"So?"

"So what?" Sabrina was aware her voice was verging on nasty, but at the moment she couldn't care less.

"So, what do you know about the break-ins? Have you zeroed in on your villain, just waiting for the right moment to bring him down? Perhaps you plan to call together all your suspects and elegantly reveal the evidence until the blackguard has no choice but to confess?"

"You're being silly." Sabrina did not mention her plan to hold a male beauty pageant and parade all the eligible men on the island before her only eyewitness, Maggie Fromlin. Small-minded people like Sam would only scoff at such an innovative idea.

"No, silly—and gruesome—is the modern Chinese practice of cricket fighting. It's been around since the tenth century, and the crowds love betting on the tiny gladiators as they tear each other limb from limb. That's silly, I'd say. Hello, Ms. Patti, Ms. Sophie."

Sabrina found that her mouth was opening and closing like a fish. She slammed it shut and smiled at Patti, who was dressed in shorts and a windbreaker, her long dark hair wound on top of her head like a coronet.

"Sabrina! It's nice to see you again. This is my friend, Sophie Jacquette." Patti turned to her young friend, who was nodding her head even before Patti finished her introduction. Then Sabrina noticed the tiny white earplugs in her ears and realized the girl was bebopping to her iPod.

"Hello, Sophie, it's nice to meet you."

Sophie Jacquette was tall, but so fragile looking that she projected a little girl helplessness. The short white dress she wore, which showcased her long, long legs and bared her slender shoulders, added to the image of girlish innocence. She wore her hair in a shiny blond cap, swept far over to the right side in a style reminiscent of the sixties. In fact, as Sophie Jacquette looked at Sabrina and removed her earplugs, she could have been British super-model Twiggy's sister, a leggy, saucer-eyed waif oozing sixties chic.

"How do you do, Lisa?"

There was a brief silence while Sabrina looked around to see who had joined the group. No one had. Who was Lisa? She waited to see who would answer, but everyone was looking at *her.*

"Were you speaking to me? My name is Sabrina."

"I know!" Sophie giggled and looked apologetic. "I'm sorry. I forget that everyone isn't like me."

If everyone was like Sophie Jacquette, the world would look like one of those young, hip TV shows where everyone was incredibly attractive and sat around talking about the color of their toenails.

Sabrina knew she was being uncharitable, and kept a charming smile on her face while she waited for Sophie to explain. For all she knew, the girl was a perfectly lovely person inside.

"I give nicknames because I can never remember anyone's name." Sophie's ravishing face was earnest.

"Please?"

"You remind me of a girl I knew in high school, Lisa. I'll call you Lisa so I can remember your name."

"But Lisa is not my name," Sabrina pointed out logically.

"But at least I'll remember it."

Sabrina looked over at Patti and the older woman shrugged, her handsome face apologetic. She was used to her young friend's foibles, and seemed inclined to forgive. Sabrina decided to give the girl the benefit of doubt.

Sophie's cell phone rang, and her eyes widened in alarm. "Shane, you're not supposed to call me," she said upon answering the phone. She moved away from them, but her distressed voice was still audible. After a moment, she covered the mouthpiece of the phone and whispered, "Patti, go on without me. This might take a while."

Patti sighed and shook her head. "I'd like to say that love's shambles is harder to deal with when you're young, but I don't think it's true. It's never easy. Would you like to go kayaking with me, Sabrina?"

Sabrina wasn't sure what to say. Did she really think that Patti had cold-bloodedly murdered Gilbert Kane and was now turning lascivious eyes on her as the next victim? Of course it was ridiculous.

"That sounds fantastic!" Oops. Way too enthusiastic. She toned it down a bit. "I mean, that sounds like fun. I've never done it before, though. Are you up to teaching a novice?"

"It's easy. You'll love it." Patti beamed and Sabrina saw that the woman took genuine pleasure in introducing other people to her favorite sport. As this was a good opportunity to talk to Patti in private, Sabrina was feeling pretty pleased herself. Any niggling doubt she squashed without compunction, and when she found it still wriggling, she stomped on it repeatedly until it stopped bothering her.

"Let's go. We don't want to miss the sunset." Patti dragged her kayak farther into the water and proceeded to give Sabrina a quick and dirty lesson on kayaking. Once Patti pointed out how easily the kayaks could flip over, Sabrina concentrated hard on the pointers about keeping her balance.

"You may need a jacket. It gets a little chilly after the sun goes down." Patti looked at Sabrina's short sleeve aquamarine shirt and her bright tropical culottes and shook her head. They were standing in knee-deep water, and Sabrina was shivering as the cooling breeze nipped at her wet slacks.

"Here." Sam finished adjusting the footrests on her kayak and stripped off his windbreaker.

"I couldn't—"

"You can tip me later."

Sabrina bit her lip to prevent herself from saying she had a tip for him right here and now: take a long walk off the Shell Lodge's short pier and take his blasted windbreaker with him. But sheer self-preservation won out. She was cool, and the windbreaker looked warm. She put it on, noticing that the jacket smelled not-unpleasantly of sweaty man and fish guts. Or maybe there was something wrong with her, because that combination should not have been appealing.

After donning her life jacket, Sabrina climbed on top of the kayak and Sam gave her an enthusiastic push that set her to rocking in the shallow waves. She frantically put the paddle out to the side as Patti had shown her, trying to regain her balance. For a moment it was touch and go, but finally she got the craft under control. She threw a dirty look at an entirely-too-innocent-looking Sam before paddling after Patti, who was already headed for the mouth of the cove.

For the next twenty minutes, she concentrated on sitting upright, dipping her paddle in by her toes and bringing it up again by her hip, and using her torso, not her arms, to bear the brunt of the strokes. Oh, and staying afloat, that took a good bit of her attention as well. The waves were minute, but they still presented a challenge to her novice sense of balance, and paddling smoothly was a bigger challenge than she had expected. But soon she fell into a comfortable rhythm and began to enjoy herself.

"How are you doing?" Patti slowed to allow Sabrina to come up alongside her.

"I think I'm getting the hang of it. You're right, it's easy once you get used to it."

"I've been coming out here every night since we arrived to watch the sun set. Isn't it glorious?"

She was right. Glorious. The sky was a neon display of orange clouds touched with the dark shadows of the disappearing light, and the pinks and yellows of an Easter egg hunt. The water reflected back all that glory in softer tones, no less spectacular for being muted by the quicksilver shimmer of the waves.

They were close to a small hummock of an island, all white sand and waving green grass and bushes, and thick trees huddled

in the center. Several birds circled above, and a large nest dominated one of the pine trees.

"That's Goat Island, where Gilbert...died. I looked it up on
the map in the bar when Michael told us last night we would be
coming here for our sessions. Of course, after what happened to
Gilbert, they're planning to take us to another island tomorrow
morning."

"But it's so close!" Sabrina looked back over her shoulder at
the massive bulk of Comico Island, and the slender umbilical
of the causeway that linked Shell Island to its mother island.
They had only been paddling for twenty minutes, and Sabrina
could still see the Shell Lodge perched high up on the hill, its
white shells reflecting sunlight like a fiery opal.

An experienced kayaker could be here in less than twenty
minutes. A motor boat could be here in much less. Despite the
isolated feel to Goat Island, it had not been far enough away to
stop a determined killer.

"Sophie and I were at this very spot last night about the
time the police say Gilbert died." Patti appeared shaken by the
thought she had been so close to a murder.

"That's awful!" Sabrina dipped a paddle in the water, watching the small pastel galaxies radiating out into nothingness. "I
don't suppose you saw anything?"

"Sophie told the police she saw another kayak coming around
the back of Goat Island, but I didn't see it."

"You seem pretty close to Sophie. How long have you known
her?"

Patti smiled and adjusted her paddle across the front of her
kayak with a faint clunking sound that seemed to travel far
across the darkening water. "Girlfriend, I hear what you're not
saying. I know we make an odd pair, and it's hard for me to
believe I just met her a couple of days ago. But that little girl
needs someone to look after her, even if she is a big-shot model.
She must've always looked like that, so pretty you want to blink
twice to make sure you're really seeing her right. I think people
do things for her because of the way she looks. But people don't

really care about her, you know what I'm saying? She might be on the cover of magazines, but no one really gives a damn about what she thinks or feels. That little act she puts on, she does it because that's what people expect from her. Underneath, she's in a lot of pain and scared to death."

Sabrina was silent for a moment, watching the crimson sun slip beneath the surface, leaving a sanguinary pool in its wake. "I imagine you have quite a few stray animals at home."

"You have no idea!" Patti laughed her luscious, opulent laugh. With that type of laugh, a person could survive on humor alone.

"So…this Hum. Is it painful? You have to excuse my curiosity, but I've never heard of anything like it before."

"I know it sounds crazy and I usually don't tell people. When it first started for me, I couldn't figure out what was going on. My whole head was buzzing, and I couldn't concentrate on anything. I thought maybe it was stress, because I'd been having some problems with my coffee shop, but it went on for weeks and weeks. Sometimes it was worse than others, but it was always there, like a little refrigerator I carried around in my head. I went to several doctors, and first they thought it was tinnitus, which isn't uncommon, just a ringing in your ears. But they ruled that out, and tested for about everything else you can imagine. They even did a CAT scan of my head, but didn't find anything wrong. I think they finally decided I was a kook, because they sent me to a psychologist." Patti laughed, but it was a dark, self-derisive scrape of a noise this time. "I got on my nephew's computer and did some research. I was at my wit's end, let me tell you! That's when I heard about the Hummers. There's other groups out there that say they hear the Hum, but Hummers International is the only one that says they can fix it. This Joseph Siderius, he's been around for a long time, knows everything there is to know about the Hum. There were a lot of testimonials on the website from people that he helped. They had a retreat coming up in a month and I signed right up."

"Was it expensive?" Sabrina adjusted her balance as a vigorous wave rocked her kayak. She had no idea how deep the water was, and as the fiery exuberance leached from the sound, leaving only inky waves in its place, she was aware that she was bobbing about on the surface of an inhabited, very carnivorous world. It occurred to her for the first time that it was Mitchell's Day. Lima had told her to stay away from the water today.

Oh, but that's just an old wives' tale!

"You're asking if this is some big scam to take money from poor deluded souls who think they hear the voice of the universe? Well, it's nothing I couldn't afford, and I'm not rich. And I needed a vacation from my business, so this was worth it for that, if nothing else. You can't figure that doing these retreats with five or six people at a time with what we pay is going to make anyone rich. And I looked into it before I signed up. I tracked down some people who have done this before and asked 'em if they were cured. Every one said they were. Now, what they *didn't* tell me..." She trailed off and picked up her paddle. "We need to be heading back before it gets full dark."

Sabrina flexed her fingers, realizing that they were hurting from maintaining a death grip on the paddle. "What didn't they tell you?" This was no time to be subtle. She felt that she was getting close to something, but what?

"I didn't expect..." Patti waved her hand in a futile gesture, then shook her head and began paddling.

Sabrina paddled hard to catch up, her kayak swaying dangerously with her efforts. "Patti, I'm confused. I thought you all *wanted* to understand this voice of the universe. You say you just want it to go away."

Patti threw an unreadable look over her shoulder and then paddled harder, forcing Sabrina to concentrate to keep up.

"Patti—"

An explosion of noise and froth beside her sent Sabrina's kayak careening back and forth. She opened her mouth to scream as she lost her paddle, and then her balance.

Down she went into the opaque, avid water.

Chapter Fifteen

"It came up right beside my kayak. Before I knew what was happening, I lost my paddle, and then splash! Right into the water. I just knew something was going to eat me. Of course, it's Mitchell's Day, so I should have known better than to be out on the water." Sabrina picked up her glass of wine, noting in the reflection of the tawny liquid that her drying curls made her resemble Medusa. Since she was sitting in the Shell Lodge's swanky dining room in a fluffy white bathrobe, it probably didn't matter much what her hair looked like.

"It was a dolphin. He must have been chasing a fish or something, because he came up beside Sabrina's boat with a huge splash. It startled me too." Patti took a bite of her lobster cake, which was topped with an avocado relish and mustard cream sauce.

"If it wasn't for Patti, I don't think I'd ever have been able to get back on that kayak. Of course after I floundered around for a while I realized that I could stand up. The water was only four foot deep."

Dennis Parker laughed and reached over to fill Sabrina's wine glass, which had somehow become empty. The tall, country boy was more cosmopolitan this evening in his suave dinner coat and polite dinner manners, though he still looked as if he were too elongated for the dining chair in which he sat.

"Thank goodness you're all right, Lisa," said Sophie Jacquette, and tears welled in her beautiful eyes. "I would have been so scared!" The model was dressed in some sort of fluffy crimson concoction that would have looked ridiculous on anyone else, but with her blond cap pinned back with a baby barrette and her flawless skin bared strategically, she looked stunning.

Sabrina was feeling too mellow to care about Sophie's continued inability to remember her name. The girl did seem genuine in her concern.

When Patti invited Sabrina to dinner, she almost declined. All she wanted to do was go home and change out of her dripping clothes and look in the fridge for some comfort food. But duty called, and besides, the prospect of driving home soaking wet wasn't appealing.

So here she was, savoring her blue corn crusted chile relleno, chock full of prawns, scallops and Monterey Jack cheese, but thus far she had not been able to manipulate the conversation to Gilbert's murder or Hummers International Incorporated. She'd been plain enjoying herself, watching Dennis' tentative courtship moves, and Sophie blossoming under his attention. Sophie had even told a few funny stories about modeling, though they were more funny-ouch than funny-ha-ha.

"And what do you do again, Dennis? You said you're in sports?" Sabrina asked, but she was interrupted by the "Love Boat" theme song.

Patti grimaced. "I'm sorry, I know it's rude, but I'm expecting a very important phone call. I'll be just a minute." She retrieved her phone out of her purse and left the table.

"Do you follow sports at all?" Dennis asked, and looked relieved when Sabrina and Sophie shook their heads. "Well, in that case—"

"I think the food in this place is inedible, don't you agree?" Walter Olgivie stopped by their table and waved a disgusted hand around the restaurant. Buffed, polished and botoxed, the businessman was dressed in a suit that probably cost more than Sabrina's car.

"I think it's lovely!" Sabrina said in instinctive defense of the restaurant. Walter had spoken too loudly, and other patrons were turning to stare. As if they needed any more reason to stare with a cover model sitting at the table chatting with Medusa in a bathrobe.

"I'm sure you don't know the difference between good food and bad, but I can assure you that you are eating inferior fare." Walter covered a hiccup with his manicured fingers.

"In fact, I am quite conversant with fine dining—" Sabrina began but Walter waved off her comments.

"I think I'll go and find another drink," he continued. "It's the only thing that helps this noise in my head. If I drink enough I can go to sleep at night. Earplugs sure as hell don't work, and those sound machines helped some at first, but not anymore. You'd think that after seeing the best doctors in the country over the last six months I'd have a better remedy than good old Glenfiddich. I might even take a couple swigs tomorrow morning before they cart us off for another session. I'm not sure I can take another one sober." He staggered away toward the door.

"Is this Hum that bad, then, that he needs to drink it away?" Sabrina toyed with the remains of her marvelous relleno and hoped she sounded casual.

Dennis and Sophie did not look at one another. "It's the voice of the universe," Sophie said in sonorous tones at the same time Dennis said: "We have a special gift."

The party line, Sabrina noted. Michael and Joseph Siderius were nowhere in sight, but these two were maintaining the Hummer platform. Did they believe what they were saying? Their neutral expressions were unrevealing. Perhaps believing their hum was otherworldly gave them comfort.

Or perhaps what they were hearing *was* the voice of the universe. Who was she to say?

"How long have you two been hearing the Hum? It must be exciting to have such a rare gift." She was watching for reactions, and this time she was rewarded. Both grimaced.

"It's not very exciting," Sophie admitted. "Master Joseph says it is a cross we must bear for the rest of the world, and only when we understand what the universe is saying will it subside.

I've been hearing it for a couple of months, but hopefully after this retreat I will be able to control and understand it."

Dennis nodded. "I first heard the Hum about three months ago. It was in the middle of my season, so I didn't have time to pay much attention to it at first. It's gotten worse and worse, and finally I decided I had to do something about it. Nothing else worked, so Master Joseph must be right. If he's not right, I don't know what I'll do."

"It'll work," Sophie said in a bright voice tinctured with desperation. "I can already feel it working. The rituals *are* working."

"What rituals?" Sabrina was quick to ask when she saw the identical expressions of dismay on the young faces.

"Nothing—" Dennis began while Sophie sat in mute consternation.

"What did I miss?" Patti asked, arriving back at the table in a whirl of colorful skirts and perfume. She sat down, her face drawn and worried, and did not seem to notice the relieved expressions on Sophie and Dennis' faces.

"Is something wrong?" Sabrina asked, forgetting her mission for a moment in the face of Patti's obvious distress.

"I need to find Michael Siderius. I might have to leave early," she replied.

"But why?" Sophie cried. "No, Patti, you can't leave until we're done!"

"I don't want to," Patti answered, her face grim, "but I'm being sued. I've been in negotiations for months, but now the witch has decided to sue if I don't give in to her ridiculous demands. Have we seen Michael this evening? I need to talk to him."

"I think he eats with Master Joseph in their rooms," Sophie said. "I've never seen them down in the dining room, have you?"

"I saw Gilbert a time or two in here, but he always sat by himself except the one time I saw him talking to Lance," Dennis said. "They looked like they were arguing, so I didn't even stop to say hello."

Sabrina recalled Lance Mayhew, the withdrawn, forgettable Hummer she had met that morning. She couldn't imagine him arguing with anyone. He seemed too vague.

"Well, I'm sorry to have to run, but I need to go." Patti waved a distracted hand as she left the table.

"I hope everything's all right with her," Sophie said, her face echoing Patti's worried expression. "This lady that's suing her, she and Patti went to high school together and argued over some guy. I think they've hated each other since then. The woman's rich as anything, but she wants whatever Patti has. Patti doesn't need this on top of everything else."

"Poor thing," Sabrina said, and her hand was making little abortive patting motions on the table. "I wonder if there's anything we can do to help?"

"It's all so horrible," Sophie said. "What more can possibly go wrong?"

Sabrina made her way down the well-lit back steps of the lodge, enjoying the fresh, laundered smell of her clothes. Matt was an efficient manager. When she returned soaking wet from her kayak trip, he offered a hotel bathrobe and to have her clothes washed. She thanked him for his kindness and asked him a question that had been bothering her.

Who knew Gilbert was going to Goat Island yesterday afternoon? If the killer went by kayak, as looked to be the case, then he or she would have had to know that Gilbert was going to be on the island. Sabrina asked Dennis and Sophie if they knew Gilbert was going to the island, and they both agreed that he hadn't said a word about his plans at the meeting.

"I didn't even tell Mr. Kane about our idea until after their afternoon meeting was over," Matt replied when questioned. "He came back fifteen minutes later and asked if I could arrange for Sam to take him to the island in an hour. Most of that time he spent in the bar. You'll have to ask Pete—that's the daytime bartender—if Gilbert talked to anyone at the bar. He'll be back on at ten in the morning."

"Could someone have overheard you talking to Sam? Someone who overheard you say Gilbert would be on Goat Island?"

Matt ran his fingers through his hair. "Ah…Let's see. I called Sam right after Gilbert left. It's possible someone was standing in the lobby when I called, but I really don't remember anyone in particular."

That was all he could say.

She clutched Sam's clean windbreaker to her chest, deriving all the warmth she could from it without actually putting it on, and headed down the dim path toward the dock and the sailboat Sam indicated was his. From the top of the hill, she could see lights on it, so she assumed he was still awake. He was not around when she arrived back from her disastrous kayak trip, so she didn't have the chance to return the jacket. Which was good, since it gave her the opportunity to ask him a few questions.

She stepped onto the dock, glad for the small solar-powered lamps that trembled on top of the pilings. Even the shadowy flickers were better than nothing.

At the end of the dock floated Sam's sailboat, emanating soft music. Something brushed against her ankles and she looked down to see a small black cat butting its head against her shin.

"Hello, little guy." Sabrina stooped to rub the feline behind the ears. She missed the two cats who had kept her company during her first difficult month on the island. They came with the cottage she rented, and when her month at the idyllic place was over—as much as she would have loved to stay, the house was rented out for the rest of the year—the cats stayed behind, along with the wild pony who had made himself at home in the backyard. She stopped by every once in a while to say hello.

"Good kitty," she crooned, and stood back up to face the sailboat. She debated how to make her presence known. There was no doorbell to ring or front door upon which to knock. She crouched a bit and peered through a window, or whatever boat-speak was for the openings-through-which-one-saw-the-outside. Sam was sitting at a polished wooden booth, a box in front of him. He seemed to be lost in thought as he stared down at whatever he held in his hands. She could not see what it was, as the box blocked her vision.

"Sam! It's Sabrina!" she said, and then repeated herself louder when he did not look up. The second time he heard her. He looked toward the window and then hastily put something back in the box—was it a bottle?—and stashed the box under the table. He stood for a moment, and then leaned down and shoved the box farther underneath the booth and firmly out of sight.

Then he stood and headed for the door.

Chapter Sixteen

Sabrina hesitated a moment before accepting Sam's hand to help her step across onto the sailboat. He did not seem surprised to see her as he led the way to a small back deck, where he had a camp chair set up next to a cooler. A plant, a boisterous African violet, if Sabrina was not mistaken in the dim light, added a cozy touch to the scene.

"I wanted to bring your coat back," Sabrina said, which was the first thing she had said since Sam appeared on the deck of his boat. She wanted to ask him what was in the box he furtively stowed under his table, but good manners prevented her from asking. Better manners would be to manufacture some excuse to go down into the cabin and sneak a look.

"I'm not sure what I would do without it," Sam said, accepting the jacket. With the innate neatness of a seaman, he folded it and stowed it in a nearby compartment before pointing Sabrina to the chair and opening the cooler.

"Drink?"

"No, I'll only stay a minute."

Sam shrugged and pulled out a bottle of water. He was dressed in jeans and a dark long-sleeve cotton pullover, and his feet were bare. Somehow his bare feet were endearing, and Sabrina forced herself not to stare at them. They were very ordinary feet, after all, but they made him seem vulnerable. It was not a characteristic she was comfortable applying to Sam.

"How was your kayaking trip?" Sam asked, sitting down on the cooler and taking a long swig from the bottle.

"I fell in."

Sam sputtered, and water ran down his chin. "Did you really?"

"Yes."

Sam wiped his chin, leaned back against the rail, and stretched his feet out in front of him. The deck was small enough that this brought his legs within brushing distance of Sabrina's skirt.

"I wanted to ask you a question. When Matt called to ask you to take Gilbert over to Goat Island, was there anyone standing nearby when you took the call? Anyone who could have overheard you and known Gilbert was going to the island that afternoon?"

Sam was silent. He seemed to be staring at the sky, and after several moments of resisting the urge, she finally looked up. She once watched a reality show where an actor stood on a busy street and stared up at the sky. A camera rolled as person after person stopped and looked up as well. Soon a crowd gathered, pointing up at the sky and tall buildings, while telling each other knowledgeably what they were seeing.

This time, however, there was truly something to observe. The sky was a sheet of black onyx, smooth and shiny and flecked with the bright silver of stars. Sabrina felt she could reach up and pull the stars out of the sky one by one, stringing them into a cold, incandescent necklace.

"Did you know that they are training wasps to detect drugs and explosives? The wasps only take five minutes to train, and they're very good at finding contraband. The problem is they keep dying. They only live 12 to 22 days, you see, so you have to keep training a new bunch over and over again." Sam spoke to the glory of the heavens, his words so low that Sabrina had to strain to hear. She waited, accustomed to his obfuscatory ways by now.

"One person's exercise in futility is another's salvation, I suppose." He sighed and looked back over at Sabrina. She could barely see his eyes gleaming in the small string of Christmas lights strung up on the mast. "No, no one was around when Matt called about my taking Kane over to the island. If the killer had asked, I would gladly have divulged the information, but no one asked. I didn't tell a soul. Perhaps it was a fortuitous coincidence for his killer to be on the island at the same time as Kane. The universe works that way sometimes, you know."

The small black cat dropped down into Sam's lap and he rubbed its ears as it rumbled its pleasure.

"What's the cat's name?"

"I don't know. Cat, I suppose."

"Your cat doesn't have a name?"

"He showed up right after I got here. I wonder sometimes if he's going to leave the same way he arrived, but so far he seems content to stay around. When I leave, he may decide to come with me, he may not."

"How long have you been here?" The strange conversation with an almost impalpable man in the dark was making Sabrina feel light-headed.

"A couple of months. I'll probably be around a couple more. I like it here." He continued to rub the cat, and Sabrina sat with absolutely no urge to move. Sam didn't seem to find it strange that they should sit in silence in the near dark for a while.

After a while, Sabrina stirred and stretched. She felt alive and pleasantly numb. "I need to be going."

Sam nodded but didn't speak. The only sound she heard was the ragged purr of the small nameless cat as she left.

Sabrina steered her station wagon down the narrow causeway that linked Shell Island with Comico. Clouds covered the moon and stars and no lights shone from the bulk of Comico Island in front of her. That section of the island was national park land, and nobody was out and about at this time of night.

Sabrina drove slowly over the causeway, conscious of the large rocks that lined the road and the lightless water just beyond. It was still Mitchell's Day, after all, and she did not want another run-in with the waters of the sound. Once was quite enough for one day.

The night was dark and thick, and her headlights seemed to make no headway against it. She slowed down even further, glad that there was no one behind her to complain.

Suddenly, she heard the roar of a motor. When she looked in the rearview mirror, she saw headlights bearing down on her at a high rate of speed. Someone was in a hurry. Flustered, she sped up, and then swerved to the shoulder. Large rocks loomed, and Sabrina yanked the car back onto the road.

Behind her the car was almost upon her, and at first it didn't look as if it were going to slow down or even try to miss her. At the last minute, the approaching vehicle slowed and then skidded around her, but it went by so close that Sabrina would have had trouble sliding a piece of paper between their cars. She slammed on the brakes and instinctively veered toward the rocks again. Sparks flew as her bumper skimmed first one rock and then another. If the other car got any closer, it would push her onto the rocks and into the black water beyond.

For just a moment, it looked as if that very thing was going to happen, but then the other car sped up and roared off down the causeway.

Sabrina stared at the departing vehicle with shaky disbelief, noticing just before it disappeared out of the range of her headlights that it was a Shell Lodge rental Jeep.

Chapter Seventeen

By the next morning, Sabrina had convinced herself that the whole incident on the causeway the night before was an accident. Most likely, somebody had too much to drink and didn't notice her until the last minute. It was regrettable that people still drank and drove, but it happened.

Sabrina looked up to discover that she had no idea where she was. As she spent a good bit of time lost, this did not concern her unduly. She always managed to find her way back.

It was a fine morning for a bike ride, though most people would not have ventured down the trail that Sabrina had chosen. Paths ducked and dodged through the trees, and Sabrina had to be on the lookout for homicidal trees and bottomless potholes. Every once in a while she would encounter a larger path and she would turn onto it hopefully, and each time the path would dwindle and grow aimless. After a while, she heard the sound of a creek, and she headed for it as best she could on the uncooperative paths.

This morning she confronted her massive to-do list, and one item had jumped out at her. "Find the welcome center." It seemed ridiculous that Comico Island's Ombudsman did not know where the welcome center was located, and even sillier that she had not introduced herself to the people who manned the building. Surely they encountered people with problems all the time. It was imperative that they know to whom to refer those problems.

It was perhaps not the most urgent thing on her list, but Sabrina wanted to tie up a nagging loose end.

Sabrina rang the little bell on her bicycle, enjoying the cheerful jingle. She was close, she thought, but she was so hopelessly turned around now that she had no idea if she was pedaling toward or away from her destination. It had been more difficult than she thought to find the welcome center on a map. In fact, after perusing several maps of the island this morning, she still had not found it. It was only after looking through an old travel guide to the island, one of several that she had collected, that she found mention of its location.

She passed the first sign. Painted in faded black on weathered plywood, the sign read: "Comico Island Welcome Center" and below that "Enter at your own risk."

Sabrina sped up, looking forward to free cookies and paper cups of lemonade. The "enter at your own risk" part of the sign was puzzling, but she knew whoever was there would be happy to talk to her.

The next sign read: "You've been warned." As Sabrina accelerated past, she saw what looked like bullet holes peppering the wood of the sign, though of course they couldn't be bullet holes.

There was a clearing ahead and the burbling sound of the creek was increasing when she came to the final sign: "Are you stupid?"

This time she didn't even slow down. There was a building up ahead, and Sabrina pedaled faster.

Until the first shot buzzed by her ear.

Sabrina ducked and swerved into the woods as a second shot rang out. A thorny bush saved her from running headlong into a tree, but inflicted painful scratches to her arms.

"Hello!" Sabrina called. "My name is Sabrina Dunsweeney. Please stop shooting!"

"Dunsweeney? Any relation to Leah?" The voice was that of a woman, thickened with age and nicotine, tainted by virulent paranoia.

"Yes!" This wasn't strictly true, but the falsehood seemed harmless in the face of a shotgun. Sabrina had met Leah Dunsweeney, long-time inhabitant of Comico Island, and after exchanging extensive family histories, they concluded that their ancestors might have been kilt-wearing neighbors several hundred years ago.

"I don't like Leah. She used to steal my tomatoes when she thought I wasn't looking." Another shot whizzed by.

"Surely not!" Sabrina could not imagine the staid, sedate Leah Dunsweeney stealing anything in her life.

"Are you calling me a liar? I said the woman is a thief!" This time the shot exploded in the tree above Sabrina's head, and wood fragments rained down on her head. Sabrina pulled herself farther into the bushes and decided that Leah Dunsweeney wasn't such a close friend, after all.

"You know, now that I think about it, she might have once stolen a pot holder from me," Sabrina yelled at her unseen assailant.

There was silence. "What do you want?" The voice was closer. Sabrina peered through the bushes and saw a skinny figure holding a shotgun.

"I'm Comico Island's Ombudsman. I must have gotten lost. I was looking for the welcome center."

The tall woman was in sight now, shuffling along in slippers topped with grinning rabbit heads. She wore a blue bandanna around her head and looked as if she hadn't missed a day of Jerry Springer in her life.

"Comico Island's Ombudsman?" The woman threw back her head and roared with laughter, the sound surprisingly robust coming from her gaunt frame. "You're the poor schmuck! Come on out, I want to take a look at you."

Since her bush wasn't offering any protection, Sabrina had little choice but to obey. Leaving the bike in the embrace of the bristling branches, Sabrina backed out on her hands and knees.

"I'm Sabrina Dunsweeney," she said, after climbing to her feet.

"Lizzie Garrison." The woman stood with her hips thrust forward in a wide-legged aggressive stance. She held the gun down at her side as she surveyed Sabrina from head to toe. Then she laughed again, a hoarse, barking sound, and said, "Seems we're fellow civil servants. I run the welcome center. Come on up to my office."

She was talking as she strode up the road, her torso floating back like a helpless kite as her hips led the way. They rounded the last curve and a one-roomed hut, crouched on the edge of a small creek, came into view. A sign, almost as large as the house, read: "You Have Reached the Comico Island Welcome Center. Now Go Away!" One rocking chair stood on the porch, which Lizzie claimed without even looking at Sabrina.

"They came by and told me they'd hired someone, and to send anyone who came by with a problem to you. I forgot your name as soon as they said it, though."

"Sabrina Dunsweeney."

"Any relation to Leah?"

"No."

"She's a thief, you know."

"I know."

Sabrina cast around for a place to sit, and then settled for standing at the foot of the stairs. "How long have you been doing this?" Sabrina looked around at the bare dirt yard and the shack, which looked as if it were one board away from a pile of scrap wood. It was about the most uninviting place she'd ever seen.

"Thirty years. They decided they needed a welcome center about the same time I was in that accident that cost my Jarvis his life, and left me in a coma for six weeks. After that, I couldn't work so good, so they hired me to run the welcome center, and I've been doing it ever since." Lizzie ran an appreciative eye around her yard and nodded with satisfaction. "The people who make it out here, I listen to their whinging, and send them on their way. I even write up reports and send 'em to the town council if I think it's necessary."

Sabrina remembered the several scrawled notes in her pile of complaints. They must have been from Lizzie. One of them, she remembered, was dated this week. What did it say? Something about a crazy man complaining about privacy. That would jibe with what she already suspected.

"Did you have anybody out here this week?"

Lizzie nodded, and took a bag out of her pocket. Using two fingers, she stuffed a wad of chaw inside her lip, giving her mouth a pugnacious, bulldog sneer. After a moment, she spit a stream of brown liquid through her teeth, narrowly missing Sabrina's feet.

"Man came by at the beginning of the week. Mad as a wet hen right off the bat, complaining about some damn-fool thing." Lizzie picked up a jar that stood on the table beside her chair and took a long draw of the brown liquid it contained. "Want some?"

"No, thank you."

"I still make it the way my grandpappy, Foster Garrison, used to do it, even using an old felt hat to strain it, and if it doesn't have the right color," Lizzie leaned forward, and horribly, winked, "I spit some of this here tobaccy juice in it." Sabrina was profoundly grateful she had refused the drink. "Course, Grandpappy Garrison was stupider than a fisherman out on Mitchell's Day. During prohibition, he got rich bringing in liquor from rum row for the guys who ran the rum-running on the island, Kenneth Fredericks, the one who built the Shell Inn, and his buddy, David Harrington. Then Grandpappy gambled it all away. After prohibition, he was so poor that when he lost a bar of soap in a hurricane he complained about it until the day he died." Lizzie snorted in disgust and raised the jar in remembrance of poor, stupid Grandpappy Garrison.

"This man who came by." Sabrina refused to be distracted. "Was he a stout man, with glasses? Did he say he was the spokesman for Hummers International Incorporated?" Gilbert had mentioned going to the island's welcome center at Sabrina's first and only meeting with him.

"Yeah, I reckon that was him."

"What did he say?"

"You expect me to remember every complaining tourist who wanders across my doorstep, then you're stupider than a blade of grass. Matter of fact, didn't you say you were related to Leah?" A hand went out to the shotgun standing beside her against the wall.

"Leah, the thief? No, absolutely not." Sabrina was sweating, and she flinched as the next string of spit hit her shoe. She kept on, though. "Do you remember anything odd about him? Somebody killed him, you know."

"I thought he was crazy as a loon, is what I thought. After he got off the phone, he started talking to himself, and walking in circles. Reminded me of a rabid dog I had once; had to shoot him to put him out of his misery." Lizzie was caressing the shotgun now.

"Wait a minute," Sabrina said, trying to blink the sweat out of her eyes, "you said 'after he got off the phone.' Did you hear who he was talking to?"

Lizzie snorted. "Like I cared. But he seemed agitated enough afterward that I offered him some of this here 'shine. I was afraid he was going to blow a gasket right in my front yard. He must have been well on his way already, because it didn't take much for him to start babbling away. 'Fore I knew it, he was sitting on my stairs telling me his life story."

"His life story? What did he say?"

Lizzie waved a hand and took another long swig. "Like I listened."

"You must have heard *something.*"

Lizzie shrugged. "He was talking about a snake, I remember that."

"A snake?"

"Yeah. He said he was holding onto a slippery snake, and he was losing his grip on it, and he was afraid if he gripped it too hard it would turn around and bite him."

"Did he say anything else?"

"Oh, he said he was tired of his partner, that he was like a big stupid puppy he had to keep on a leash." Lizzie paused and took a guzzle from her jar. "He also said death was stalking him. He said he was amazed every morning that he'd survived the night."

Sabrina was just finishing up her research at the library when she heard someone say, "Hey, Mrs. Hillkins, someone said they saw Miss Sabrina come in here. Is she here?" It was Lou Beth Tubbs, one of Mary Garrison Tubbs' numerous grandchildren. The woman had strong genes as well as a strong personality, because every one of her children and grandchildren bore a striking resemblance to the short, plump woman. Poor things.

Sabrina grimaced and pushed back from the computer. Thankfully, she was done. After leaving the welcome center, she had come straight to the library, intent on discovering as much as she could about the Hummers and Gilbert Kane. She ran into Marilee Howard, however, and spent an hour poring through college admissions books with the lanky, young redhead before turning to her own research.

Sabrina braced herself as Lou Beth came around the corner of the computer station. Any missive from Mary Garrison Tubbs was bound to be unpleasant.

"Miss Sabrina," the portly girl said loudly, "Grandmama Tubbs says you better quit loafing around and get to work. Missy Garrison's house got broken into last night, and everybody knows it was some tourist, because no right-minded person would mess with Missy's world-famous driftwood collection. Grandmama Tubbs wants to know what you're going to do about it!"

Chapter Eighteen

Missy Garrison, a plump, dark-haired woman who favored blue jeans and dangly earrings, opened the door wearing a tee-shirt that said: "Save the planet. Stop breeding."

"Sabrina! Did you hear what happened? I'm going to kill the little bugger when I catch him."

"I'm sorry, Missy. I wanted to ask you a few questions, if you have the time?"

"Sure." Missy opened the door and joined Sabrina on the porch. On the island, front and back porches often served as extra living rooms. Being shown to the wicker furniture on the porch didn't mean your host thought you smelled, or found you otherwise offensive. It just meant that a cool breeze off the water made that location more pleasant than inside. And this spot was very pleasant, overlooking acres of greening marsh grass undulating under the soft caress of the wind. Calvin murmured in contentment and settled onto the arm of the chair.

"First of all, have the police been here yet?"

"I called Sergeant Jimmy last night." Missy pulled a soda out of a small refrigerator and offered one to Sabrina.

"Did you see the burglar?" Sabrina held her pen and notepad at the ready, prepared for the onslaught of words. Calvin pecked at the top of her soda can.

Missy scowled. "I couldn't pick him out of a lineup of one, Sabrina. Actually, I didn't even see him. I heard him run out the back door, but by the time I got there, he had disappeared into the marsh. But let me tell you something, it's not going to stop me from finding him and peeling his—"

"You keep saying 'him,'" Sabrina interrupted, not at all anxious to hear what Missy had planned for the crook. After a full night of stewing, it was bound to be inventive. Her first impression of Missy had been that of a good-natured Jane-of-all-trades—Missy waited tables, drove a cab and was the town's registrar—who liked to wear provocative tee-shirts. Since living on the island, she'd heard stories about Missy's legendary temper. "Why do you think it was a man? Why not a woman?"

Missy snorted. "What woman would be stupid enough to do something like this?"

"You're saying it was a man and a tourist? All this from the sound of his footsteps?"

Missy gave her a pitying look. "Only a tourist would be stupid enough to think they could steal my collection and get away with it. It had to be a tourist."

"Why is that, Missy?"

"First of all, anyone on the island knows I won't rest until I find this…person. And second, what would someone on the island do with my collection? They couldn't very well put it on their wall at home, you know. People would recognize it as mine."

"But surely, driftwood is driftwood, how could anyone know for sure?"

Missy stared at her in amazement. "How could they not? You haven't heard about my driftwood exhibit?"

Sabrina felt as if she had admitted to not noticing that the sky was frequently blue. "Well, no, but—"

"Believe me, my driftwood is unique."

A pony wandered into Missy's yard and fell to nipping at the grass. His coat was a crazy quilt of brown and white and his mane and tail were shaggy and long. He did not seem to notice or care about the women on the porch, though Missy clucked at him in recognition.

"So, this person stole some of your driftwood display. What—"

"No. He didn't steal anything."

"But I thought you said—"

"I never said he stole anything. I chased him off before he could steal them or worse. I found a handsaw lying on the table. I'm wondering if he wasn't planning on desecrating the pieces instead of stealing them. Sometimes the tourists find the display offensive."

"Desecrating? Offensive?" Sabrina felt as if she'd wandered into a tea party where all the participants were speaking pig Latin.

"Sure. Not everybody understands what I'm trying to do with the display. I'm showing the beauty and grace of nature in my pieces, in all its primitive shapes and forms. Some people just don't get it."

What in the world was so difficult to understand about a driftwood display? "Nothing was taken, but you found a handsaw near your display."

"Yes, and all of the pieces on the wall were removed and were lying on the table next to the saw. He was planning something, the sneaky little—"

"Let's go back to the beginning. You said this took place right after dark last night. That's pretty early for a burglar to be rummaging through someone's house. How did he know you wouldn't be home?"

"The jerk set me up. I thought he was a legitimate fare. He called me to come pick him up from the mainland, and while I was over there, he broke in. So busy doing God-knows-what," Missy's dark expression spoke volumes about her suspicions, "he didn't hear me until I was in the kitchen. Then he ran like a scared rabbit."

"It wasn't a crime of convenience." A breeze born of fragrant mud and briny pools laden with squirming life riffed through the marsh grass and brushed pungently across Sabrina's face. "Your house was targeted. I wonder why?"

"It's because of my collection!" Missy was exasperated at Sabrina's denseness. "On Sundays, on my days off, I do tours of the driftwood. Tourists come out and pay to go through the display. A lot of them come back year after year, and some locals even bring guests by. I had quite a crowd on Sunday. I serve tea and cookies on the porch, and I even ran out of cookies, there were so many people here that day. Some days I don't get anyone, and some days it's a crowd. You never know."

"People pay money to come see your driftwood. Hmmm." Missy was an enterprising woman. She could probably convince people to pay money to inspect the contents of her refrigerator, so Sabrina shouldn't be surprised they would pay money to look at driftwood.

"I told Sergeant Jimmy I couldn't describe who was here on Sunday. There was a family—I wish parents wouldn't bring the rug rats if they're just going to come running out and demand their money back—and several couples, and a man who came in one of the hotel rental Jeeps. The tourists all look alike, you know? All squinty eyed and sunburnt. I visually tune them out after a while."

Sabrina tapped her fingers on the arm of her wicker chair and scrawled a note in her pad. "I suppose Sergeant Jimmy took the handsaw for fingerprints."

"I wanted to keep it. I thought of a perfect way to use it when I catch up with that guy."

Sabrina didn't ask. She'd have to talk with Sergeant Jimmy and ask his opinion of this newest break-in. She was a little disappointed he didn't call to tell her about it last night. She would have to impress on him how vital it was to keep each other in the loop.

"What time did you do the tours?"

"I run them from noon to four every Sunday. It's my only day off from the Tittletott House. I'm surprised you haven't ever come by. Though some people are not intelligent enough to understand the concept." Missy smiled sweetly.

"I've never heard about it, Missy." Sabrina was pretty sure she was intelligent enough to understand the concept. Well, reasonably sure, anyway. How hard could it be to grasp the cosmic meaning of a driftwood display?

"Oh, I'm sure you'd get it, you being a schoolteacher and all. Well, come on, I'll give you a free tour. You probably want to see the scene of the crime anyway."

Sabrina followed Missy into the house.

"Watch your step. My great-grandfather Garrison built this house in the twenties, and he did a haphazard job at best. I never knew him, but my Aunt Lizzie said he was always drunk more than he was sober, so I guess that explains a lot."

Missy opened a door leading into the back room. The walls, including the windows, were draped with swaths of black velvet, and black glossy tables lined the room. On top of the tables and attached to the walls were the driftwood pieces.

"It's very nice," Sabrina began as Missy hit the switch that illuminated the spotlights.

It took Sabrina a moment to absorb what she was seeing. Then she gasped, but tried to swallow the sound into a cough so as not to offend. Calvin imitated her, sounding like a consumptive washing machine.

"Well, what do you think?" Missy gazed proudly around the room.

"It's certainly…interesting," Sabrina managed, trying not to stare overlong at any one piece. Each of the driftwood pieces was polished and carved into various animal and human forms. They were beautifully done, if you could get past Missy's selection of subject.

Sabrina smiled weakly as she gazed around at the collection of reproductive organs Missy had carved.

Chapter Nineteen

"Will you get out of my way? I'm in a hurry." Vicki Carroway elbowed her way to the front of the line. She ignored the grumbling of the people who had been standing in line for ten minutes or more to receive their cups full of foaming keg beer.

"Dern tourists think they own the place" and "go back up north where you're wanted" followed Vicki as she pointedly ignored the tip jar and strode away with beer in hand. She didn't usually drink beer, but it was the only alcohol available. She pushed her way through the crowd, at one point jabbing someone in the ankle with the tip of her high heel, until she stood at a prime spot on the bulkhead of the small public beach beside the ferry docks. It was the Wednesday sunset celebration, and Vicki made a habit of attending such events to gauge the local barometer.

"Hey, lady, you about pushed my kid over the bulkhead. We were here first, you know. What's your problem?"

Vicki turned and looked the man in the eye. After a moment, the man backed away, muttering, "oughta ban you folks, they should" under his breath. Men were intimidated by a woman who was their size and who didn't back down. Vicki was used to getting her way.

The sun was sinking down toward the water, and the sound of bongo drums was becoming louder and more vigorous. Vicki debated going over and slapping the dirty, dreadlocked young man who was ecstatically pounding on the drums, but it wasn't worth the struggle through the excited audience. Vicki sipped her beer and surveyed the sun, which was huge and bloated as it rested its weary bulk on the water. The crowd around her was cheering.

Vicki tried to tune the idiots out. She thought about the newest group she was wooing to the island, and her mouth salivated at the money signs they represented. The locals would really *love* this group, but there was nothing they could do about it. She knew they were getting restless, but she thought she had a while longer before she exhausted this market. Comico Island was proving to be a gold mine of untapped possibilities, and she was loathe to leave before every last penny was extracted.

It was an art, what she did, and she prided herself at being the best at it. She moved into a tourist area, dominated the market with advertising, and bullied the locals into cooperating with her. Then she used her considerable marketing skills to book the biggest groups she could, reaping monstrous commissions. Eventually, the market would tap out and she would move on to her next prospect. Paradise Vacations, of which she was the owner and president, was a guaranteed moneymaker.

Vicki chuckled. It was like stealing baby's binky. The locals never knew what hit them and she could just imagine them staggering about trying to pick up the pieces in her wake.

Around her, the crowd was cheering as the sun finally dropped out of sight. Vicki turned to leave and caught sight of that obnoxious busybody, Sabrina Dunsweeney. Vicki had a good laugh when she heard the town council bumpkins had appointed her as island ombudsman. Island ombudsman, for God's sake, who had heard of such a thing?

But Vicki would keep an eye on the woman. People like her, the ones who asked questions until they got answers, who didn't look the other way when something bad was going down, those were the ones who tended to kink up Vicki's plans.

If Sabrina kicked up too much of a fuss, Vicki could always evict her from her apartment. That should keep her occupied for a while.

Vicki was too smart not to take Sabrina Dunsweeney seriously.

The mood of the crowd was uneasy. Sabrina could feel the tension and simmering anger as she made her way through the throng of people. It was just after sunset and the bongo drums had stopped, replaced by a band playing Caribbean tunes. Nearby, at Houseboat Alley, beer flowed freely as people congregated on the front porches of the dilapidated boats. A few people had already started to dance on the square, and that number would increase as the night wore on.

The smell of crab cakes and fried shrimp was making her mouth water. Normally, she loved the island's weekly sunset celebration. It was a chance to get out and see people and have some fun. But tonight, the atmosphere was different, which was why she was here. Tonight she wasn't having fun, she was working.

"Lima!"

The old man was sitting on a bench, Bicycle Bob next to him on the ground. Bicycle Bob preferred to stay close to the ground.

"I'm glad you made it, Sabrina. Do you see what I mean? Everybody is all bent out of shape." Lima was the reason she was here. After seeing Missy, she was on her way to talk with Sergeant Jimmy when Lima waved her down to tell her that emotions were starting to run high. The locals were convinced that a tourist was behind the break-ins, and their tempers were up.

"I wanted to come to see for myself. But you're right. I saw Bill Large cuss out a tourist for stepping on his toe, and a tourist yelling at someone for jostling him. Even Nettie Wrightly was rude to a customer who accused her of shortchanging him, and you know how sweet Nettie is. The visitors are on edge, and now the locals are too. It's starting to get to everybody. I need to do something!"

That was why she was here, to see if she could calm the escalating tempers. But what could she do? Nothing she had done in the past three days seemed to be working. She tried to help the Hummers, and their spokesperson ended up dead. The break-ins continued, despite her best efforts, and now the locals and tourists were at each others' throats. If anything, she had made things worse.

"Everybody knows that a tourist was responsible for breaking into Missy's house," Lima said. "And probably all the rest of them break-ins as well. That on top of everything else is making people itchy."

"There's no proof that it was a tourist. It could have been anyone."

Lima shook his head. "Nobody on this island would mess with Missy's driftwood pieces. It had to be a tourist, either wanting to carry them off to the mainland or cut them up with a handsaw. Everybody knows that."

Sabrina blushed as she thought about Missy's X-rated collection. Who would want to mess with it? "But what about Hill's break-in, and the one at the rental cottage? Those don't have anything to do with Missy's collection."

Lima sipped his beer and surveyed her with one fluffy, ill-kempt eyebrow raised. "He's a thief. It doesn't matter if it's Missy's driftwood collection, or a DVD player, he's a thief plain and simple."

"But he hasn't stolen anything! Not a single thing."

"Give him time. He will."

That's exactly what they didn't have, Sabrina thought as she watched a frowning vacationing couple walk by, followed by muttered imprecations from the locals standing nearby. She had to do something, and fast, but what?

"If I prove that a tourist wasn't responsible for Missy's break-in, that should ease the tensions some," she mused out loud. She noticed that Bicycle Bob was humming "The Impossible Dream" and gave the back of his head a dirty look. "But then the tourists are still going to be unhappy, because Vicki Carroway will be booking their vacations. We need to stop her, Lima."

"There she is right there, talking to Bill Large. I'll hold her down if you want to give her titty twisters until she agrees to go away."

"Lima!"

Bicycle Bob creaked at their feet, and they both looked down at him.

"He's laughing again," Lima said in wonder. "That's twice in the last couple of days. I wonder what's got into him."

"I think it's wonderful. You need something to laugh about, don't you, Bicycle?"

Bicycle didn't acknowledge her.

"He used to laugh all the time," Lima said wistfully. "Before he went away to the mainland and became a big shot lawyer. He was a fun kid, always pulling pranks and making people smile."

"Bicycle was a big shot lawyer?" Sabrina felt as if her jaw was resting on the ground.

"Sure. He—"

"Sabrina! I don't know what we're paying you for, you're always sitting around and jawing with this old reprobate." Mary Garrison Tubbs stood in front of them holding out a cell phone to Sabrina. "This call just came in for you. I hear you haven't bothered to go out to the Shell Lodge today. I swear, I don't know what you're good for."

Sabrina put the phone to her ear. "Hello?"

"Thank God. I didn't think I was ever going to track you down. Where have you been today?" It was Matt Fredericks, and Sabrina pressed the phone tighter to her ear so she could hear over the Jimmy Buffett tune.

"I've been busy with other pressing matters, Matt," she said. "What's going on?"

"The police are on their way, but she's been asking for you. You've got to come quick, Sabrina. Sophie Jacquette was just attacked in her room!"

Chapter Twenty

Sabrina stepped on the accelerator and sped down Long Road toward Shell Island. First Gilbert's murder, and now this attack on Sophie. Did someone have a grudge against the Hummers?

Through her research at the library this morning, she learned quite a bit about the Hum. Thousands of people around the globe experienced the Hum—a sound like a large diesel engine idling nearby—and it was blamed for blurred vision, dizziness, fatigue, nosebleeds, insomnia and headaches. Long-term exposure to the Hum reportedly caused marital strife, paranoia and even suicide.

A significant percentage of people in Taos, New Mexico, experienced the Hum, and in the early 1990's they persuaded their congressman, Representative Bill Richardson, to initiate an investigation. Richardson named three weapons projects which he thought were likely sources of the phenomenon, and wrote a letter to Defense Secretary Les Aspin asking him to "make the necessary changes" to end the problem. The Pentagon denied involvement, however, and a thorough investigation, utilizing scientists from Los Alamos and the Phillips Air Force Laboratory, among others, turned up no clear source of the Hum.

Those seemed to be the only definitive facts about the Hum, however. It was not known whether the noise was acoustic in nature, or a low-frequency pulsed electrical signal. Nobody knew for sure what caused it. Theories ranged from military com-

munications, to industrial machinery, singing fish, geological
activity and even aliens from outer space.

Hummers International Incorporated was not a mainstream
group. In fact, many of the other Hummers, or Hearers as some
called themselves, thought that Hummers International and
their belief that the Hum was the voice of the universe were a
bunch of quacks.

There were several articles about Joseph Siderius, and it
appeared that he was a well-respected scientist in the early days
of the Hum. He gave several interviews to newspapers and
was part of the 1993 government-funded investigation into
the phenomenon. Sometime in the past ten years, however, he
developed his belief that the Hum was the voice of the universe
and his views lost favor. Despite Hummers International's loss
of prestige in the Hummer community, it had grown in national
prominence. It was certainly the group with the most impressive
web presence and the slickest website.

Sabrina slowed down as she reached the turn off to Shell
Island, so as not to repeat her close call with the tree. A makeshift
barrier had been set up across the road and a man was standing
there with a powerful flashlight.

"Do you have reason to be here, Miss?" he asked, shining the
light into Sabrina's eyes.

"Yes. Matt Fredericks called me to come over. Lincoln, is
that you?"

"Hi, Miss Sabrina. I recognized you, but I thought it'd be
more professional if I didn't mention it." The young man backed
away, spoke into a radio, and then smiled as he waved Sabrina
forward.

Bemused—since when did the Shell Lodge need security?—
Sabrina waved and drove onto the causeway. It was hard to concentrate when she was feeling so frazzled. She hadn't managed to
do anything at the sunset celebration to stem the rising animosity
between vacationers and locals, and now she was rushing off to
help the Hummers with no idea of how she could help.

She wasn't even sure what she thought about them. Were they quacks? She certainly didn't get that impression from Patti, Sophie, or Dennis. They were saner than she was, she suspected. And though she might not like Walter, the self-centered business-man was sharp. No mental deficiencies there. The only one she did not have a handle on was the grayish, mysterious Lance, but he had not given her any reason to doubt his mental stability. So what brought them all to a retreat to hear the voice of the universe? They were completely different people, from all walks of life. The only thing they shared was the disabling Hum…and a look of quiet desperation.

Sabrina frowned. Had Gilbert, Michael, and Joseph taken advantage of that desperation? To what end? Money didn't seem to be a motive, unless Patti was lying about how much she was paying to attend the retreat. And if money was the motive, would Joseph be a party to such a scheme? He had been involved in Hum research for thirty years. Would he really ruin his reputa-tion, and very likely the credibility of the Hummers, on some sort of scam?

But if there was anybody who seemed iffy in the mental clarity department, it was Joseph Siderius. He had not spoken once that Sabrina had heard, and he seemed as unconnected to reality as a balloon in the grasp of a two-year-old.

And as for Michael and Gilbert, Sabrina was pretty sure she could believe them capable of almost anything.

"Sabrina!" Matt Fredericks was in the lobby talking to a police officer. "Where have you been all day? Things are terrible."

Guilt engulfed her. What *had* she been doing all day? It felt like a lot, but clearly she hadn't been doing her job.

"I'm sorry, Matt, but I'm here now. What's going on? What's with the guards?"

"That's because of what's happening with the media. I've been trying to reach you all day, you know. The media has caught onto Mr. Kane's murder and it must seem pretty juicy to them."

"I suppose it must, considering that a pretty model like Sophie is involved."

Matt gave her a strange look. "They've been trying to sneak onto the island all day. The Hummers are in an uproar. And now with what happened tonight…"

"What happened? Where's Sophie?"

Matt gestured for her to follow him. "It happened right after dinner. Ms. Jacquette returned to her room to find someone inside. Thankfully, Mr. Dennis Parker was just outside. He heard the commotion and was able to drive the intruder out."

They were outside now, passing by the pool, and plunging down one of the shell walkways lit only by small, solar-powered lamps. Bushes rustled in the darkness and Sabrina shivered. "Was she hurt?"

"It looks that way to me, but she refuses to let me call an ambulance. She didn't want me to call the police either, but I felt I had to do that. I also called Doc Hailey to come see her."

"That man's never in his office," Sabrina said disapprovingly. She'd been hearing about Doc Hailey since she arrived on the island, but had yet to set eyes on the man, and this after numerous visits to his office.

"I'm sure Ms. Jacquette will agree to let him check her over. No one says no to Doc Hailey."

"What was the motive? Do we know? Was it burglary, or—or something else?"

"We don't know." Matt's voice was grim. "It doesn't look like anything was taken, but Ms. Jacquette hasn't been back into her room to verify it."

Another burglary with nothing stolen, Sabrina mused. And this one violent. Was this the work of their serial burglar?

"Did she see her attacker?"

"No one has been able to talk to her, but Mr. Parker said the man was dressed all in black and wore a mask. Also, when Mr. Parker went into Ms. Jacquette's cottage, the lights were out, so I don't think there's any chance she saw his face."

They had reached a small cottage, and Matt knocked on the door. After a minute, the door opened a crack and Patti peered out.

"Sabrina! Thank goodness you're here!" Patti opened the door and pulled Sabrina inside. "Sophie just told me who did this. It was her ex-boyfriend, the famous actor Shane Ludrow!"

Chapter Twenty-one

"He says he'll do anything, absolutely anything, to get me back," Sophie said in a low voice, drawing the blanket up until it was almost touching her chin. Patti rubbed her hand and murmured reassuring words.

Sabrina, who sat on the edge of the bed, nodded without speaking. So far, Sophie had revealed that she had been in a two-year relationship with Shane Ludrow, who was apparently some young heartthrob. Sabrina did not watch a lot of TV and wasn't surprised she had never heard of him, though she kept this to herself. Sophie seemed to assume she would know who he was. Patti did, that was clear.

"Sophie, are you sure I can't look at your stomach? I'm worried that you may have some sort of internal injury." Where in the world was Doc Hailey? The man was never where he was supposed to be.

"No, Shane has done much worse. I'll be fine." Sophie struggled upright and her beautiful face hardened a bit. Even with her hair mussed and a black eye, she still managed to look stunning. "I told Shane three months ago that it was over. This was after he slapped me in a restaurant and broke my arm when we got home. I was afraid he would kill me if I didn't get away from him."

"Good for you!" Patti's cheerful tone belied her grim expression. When Sabrina arrived, she revealed that she was the one who had requested that Matt call Sabrina. Patti said she thought an ombudsman was just what Sophie needed to keep the police from pushing her around.

"He wouldn't take no for an answer," Sophie murmured. "He kept calling, and coming around, and he's threatened to kill me several times. I was hoping he wouldn't find out I was here. He doesn't know anything about the Hum, so I thought I would be safe on the retreat. But somehow he found out!" She drew the blanket across her knees.

"Tell me what happened," Sabrina urged as someone knocked on the door and Patti went to answer it.

"I came back from dinner, and the cottage was dark. Before I could turn the lights on, he tackled me. He slapped me and threw me on the bed and when I tried to scream, he punched me in the stomach. Dennis walked me back from dinner, and he must have heard something, because he came charging in the room. Shane saw him and ran." Sophie looked toward the windows, which were covered with drapes. "He's still out there, somewhere, waiting for everybody to leave me alone."

"How do you know it was Shane? Matt said he was wearing a mask. Did he say something?"

"No, he never said anything. But who else could it be?"

"And how are we feeling?" The smooth, buttery voice invited confidence. "I'm Doctor Jeremiah Hailey, but everybody calls me Doc Hailey. You must be Sophie. I've heard how brave you were tonight." The man limping toward them was not young, and his face could only be described as homely. In the way of older men, his nose appeared too large for his face, and his hair was a distant memory except for a cotton-candy nimbus around the perimeter of his head. His eyes were the only part of him that matched his marvelous voice—they were cobalt blue like a serene autumn sky.

Sophie had tensed at his approach, but now she gazed up at him in wonder. "Me? Brave?"

"Beautiful and brave, what a wonderful combination. You remind me of one of the Roman goddesses, Diana, perhaps." In his warm, resonant voice, the words seemed real and true.

"Oh," Sophie breathed, her eyes starry.

"Do you mind if I take a look at you? A quick one, I promise."

Sophie stiffened, remembering her objections to medical attention, but not wanting to shatter this man's illusions of her as a Roman goddess.

"I'll wait outside." Sabrina stood and offered her hand to the man. "I'm Sabrina Dunsweeney, Doc Hailey. I've been trying to get an appointment with you for ages."

"I've been traveling. It's nice to meet you, Sabrina. I've heard a lot about you." His direct blue eyes twinkled with humor and intelligence.

"You have?"

"No, Patti, don't leave!" Sophie was almost in tears, and it was soon established that Patti would stay for the examination. Sabrina took her leave, promising to come back as soon as the doctor was finished.

"I think you've been avoiding me, Sabrina," a voice said from the darkness as she closed the door behind her. She jumped, and stifled a scream. Then the familiarity of the voice overrode the image of a man in a ski mask.

"Jimmy, you scared the life out of me!"

"Good. You need to be scared." Jimmy came into the light cast from the porch lamp, and Sabrina saw that his broad face was tense with weariness and strain. "How is Ms. Jacquette? She hasn't let me speak with her. We need to, you know, if we're going to find her attacker."

"Didn't Matt tell you that she recognized him? He was supposed to. It was her ex-boyfriend Shane Ludrow." Sabrina sat down on a chair and Jimmy followed suit, the wood straining a bit under his bulk. He was the most grounded, imperturbable man Sabrina knew. On an island where everything was fickle and changing, including the water, the sky, and the ground they stood on, Jimmy McCall was the stoic and enduring live oak.

"That's a start, but we need to talk to her personally. Can you try to talk her into it?"

"Well, if anyone can talk her into something, it's that Doc Hailey." Sabrina was feeling a little put out with the man. *She* was supposed to be the soother, the one everybody turned to in their time of need, though why this was so, she wasn't sure.

Jimmy chuckled. "So you've met the good doctor. I didn't know he was back in town until tonight. Yes, they say he could charm the scales off a fish."

"I noticed."

The door opened and Doc Hailey appeared.

"Oh, good, Sergeant Jimmy, you're here. Ms. Jacquette would like to talk to you now. She has some things to tell you. She'll be fine, by the way, just some nasty bruises." Doc Hailey removed his glasses and smiled.

"It's good to see you, doc. Where were you this time, was it Egypt? Nigeria? I've forgotten."

"Myanmar, kayaking on the Irrawaddy River, actually. It was a wonderful trip, but I am glad to be back." He stepped aside so Jimmy could go into the cottage.

Sabrina watched the sergeant go, aware of the unasked questions dancing in her head like sugar plums. Did the police have new leads into Gilbert Kane's murder? Was there anything new to report on the string of burglaries?

"Miss Dunsweeney, may I walk you back to the safety of the lodge? I think they will be a while."

"Thank you, that would be nice."

They started back along the rocky path. "I am only seeing a few patients nowadays," Doc Hailey said, "but if you would like to call my office, I would be happy to see you."

"Thank you. I have these persistent headaches, and my elbow twinges when I bend it, and I might have rabies, though that's a long story. I could probably use a check up."

As they reached the hotel, the door opened and Michael and Joseph Siderius appeared. Joseph was as serene as usual, but Michael seemed twitchy as Sabrina introduced the doctor to them, and explained that they had come from seeing Sophie.

"I just heard about her attack," Michael said, and his voice sounded tight with tension. "My father and I have been meditating in my room. When I plugged the phone back in, I got the messages. How is she?"

Joseph stood in his yellow dashiki with a pleasant, vacant look on his face. He seemed unaware of their conversation.

"Shaken up, of course, but she will be fine. Joseph Siderius, did you say? I heard you speak, sir, about fifteen years ago at a medical convention. You spoke eloquently on the Hum, and how it presents differently than tinnitus. I found it very interesting data."

"You did?" Sabrina swallowed and tried to moderate the disbelief in her voice. "I mean, what a coincidence that you two have met."

Joseph Siderius turned his head slowly and looked at Doc Hailey. Then he nodded in recognition of the compliment, and placed his hand on the doctor's arm.

"Father wants to see Sophie as soon as possible," Michael said and tugged at his father's sleeve. "He says the universe is telling him that Sophie is very disturbed at this hour."

"How very perceptive." Doc Hailey's voice was dry as he watched Michael hurry his father down the path.

"What do you think about all of this Hummer business, Doctor?" Sabrina asked, as they made their way down the hall.

"I think, given the right provocation, the human animal is capable of more viciousness on a day to day basis than most of us would like to admit." His voice was resigned.

"Do you think the fact that Gilbert Kane was stabbed in the ear has any significance?"

Doc Hailey stopped and turned to Sabrina. Despite his age, there was a confident, erect tilt to his shoulders, and his eyes were bright and agile. "I'm going to tell you something I think you need to know. I trust that you will keep the information to yourself, as I, myself, have obtained it from a friend in confidence."

"Yes?" Sabrina tried not to sound too eager, but it was difficult.

"I think it quite probable that Gilbert Kane's death is connected to his role as spokesperson of Hummers International. Stabbing him in the ear seems very symbolic, does it not? Furthermore, this person, whoever it may be, is desperate, about as desperate as a person gets."

"Why do you say that?"

"You know the police haven't found the murder weapon, don't you? However, they have come to a conclusion on what type of weapon they are seeking."

"Really?"

"It's not unusual, unfortunately, to murder someone. But murdering someone by jamming a corkscrew into his ear strikes me as the act of either a very angry, or very desperate, individual."

Chapter Twenty-two

The sound of an acoustic guitar, enthusiastically if not expertly played, drifted down the hall as Sabrina approached the lounge. She was obscurely disappointed when Doc Hailey said goodbye in the lobby, but her disappointment was soon overcome by the rumbling in her stomach. She had not eaten since lunch, and in Sabrina's world, that was just not acceptable.

As she neared the doors to the lounge—the only source of food at the Shell Lodge this time of night—she saw a man in a gray tee-shirt standing in the hall with his back to her.

"Mona, I don't care what you say, you're not going to get those kids. You don't even want them! You're just trying to get back at me and I'll do anything to keep them away from you!"

The man clicked his phone shut and stood for a moment, his shoulders heaving with emotion. As Sabrina came closer she saw that the imperturbable Hummer, Lance Mayhew, had been perturbed.

He looked up, and his eyes widened when he saw Sabrina.

"Lance. Are you okay?"

Lance stared at her a moment longer, and then shook his head like a dog shaking off a flea. "Fine, thanks." His voice was brusque.

"I overheard some of your conversation and it sounds like you're going through a nasty divorce. I was about to go into the lounge, and I would be happy to buy you a drink. It looks like you may need one."

Lance hesitated, and then nodded. Sabrina didn't miss the calculating look he leveled on her before accepting. Whatever his reasons for agreeing to her offer, it was not because he wanted her company. There was some other motive lying behind his cool, gray eyes.

Lance led her into the bar and to a table. She was still shaken by Doc Hailey's revelation that the weapon used to kill Gilbert was a corkscrew. How horrible! And what a strange choice of weapons for a murderer to choose. Was there some significance?

The lounge was dim and warm, the guitarist playing to a small, lethargic crowd. A large colorful map covered one wall, a stylized rendition of Comico and its satellite islands. As she sat down, Sabrina looked at the dollar bills, all autographed, that covered the walls.

"There must be thousands of them," Sabrina exclaimed to the bartender when he approached.

"Over sixty thousand, actually," the bartender said amiably.

"I bet you lose a few every night." Lance's voice was wanly cynical, all emotion once more leached from it.

"Most people add to the wealth, not subtract. Though, a lot of times in the morning when I come in there's a pile on the floor. I sweep it up and the owner gives it to charity."

"That's wonderful!" Sabrina would have to congratulate Matt on his generosity.

"Can I get you something?"

Sabrina ordered the grilled asparagus, wrapped with prosciutto and topped with a béarnaise sauce, and Lance ordered a plain Coke.

Sabrina studied him for a moment, debating the right way to approach him. His expression was closed down again, leaving him as unapproachable as a boarded-up shop.

"How long were you married?"

"Fourteen fun-filled years."

"You have children, I take it?"

"Two. Melinda is twelve, Kobie eight."

"I take it you're going through a custody battle." Sabrina wondered how long he would allow her to go on. Her questions were disturbing him, but he was still answering them. Why?

"My ex-wife is trying to get back at me. She never wanted those kids in the first place, and they sure don't fit in with her new lifestyle. She says she never got a chance to have fun when she was young—my fault, apparently, for marrying her when she was eighteen—so now she's intent on doing all those fun things she missed out on when she was a teenager. The kids are just a reminder of all that she missed. Of course, she'll feed you some line of bull crap about how much she loves them, and how she can't stand to be away from them. *I've* been their primary caregiver for years, and that was while I was working and she was at home with them!" The emotion was back, surging red and hot across his face. He swallowed and visibly tried to calm himself.

"Custody battles can be very unpleasant," Sabrina said. "It must have been hard to leave the kids and come to this retreat." Time to get this boat to shore.

He was back in control and watching her with careful eyes. "At the time, I felt I had to. The Hum was about to drive me insane. My patience with the kids was nil, and I couldn't concentrate on my work. I'm a computer programmer, and if I can't concentrate, I can't work. Now, though, I wish I'd never..." He stopped.

"You wish you'd never come? Why is that? You don't think the retreat is working?"

"No, no, I think it'll work. It's just all this drama with Gilbert's death and the media circus today." The answer seemed quick and glib and Sabrina narrowed her eyes.

"I understand you had an argument with Gilbert."

Lance drew back. "Who told you that?"

"You were in the restaurant. A lot of people saw you." Sabrina did not see any reason to tell him that it was Dennis who told her about the argument.

The bartender brought their order, and Lance did not answer for a few moments as he unhurriedly stripped his straw of its paper sleeve. Sabrina's mouth watered at the delicious aroma of her appetizer, but she kept her gaze on Lance.

"What?" He looked up. "Oh, my so-called argument with Gilbert. We disagreed over whether or not I had paid the full amount for the retreat. I knew I had, and he was mistaken."

"And things got pretty heated over this large sum of money?" It was clumsy, but she was still curious about how much the Hummers were paying for the retreat.

"It wasn't such a large sum of money, and we worked it out. It was no big deal." Lance sipped his drink and watched the guitarist who was trying to elicit names from the audience so he could work them into a rhyming song. Nobody seemed interested.

"Well, that's good. I'm sure the police agreed."

By Lance's reaction, Sabrina saw that she was right in her surmise. No one had told the police about the argument, and she resolved to do this as soon as she saw Sergeant Jimmy again.

"I've got to get some sleep." Lance stood, throwing money down on the table. He left without another word.

There goes a very unhappy man, Sabrina mused. But was he a guilty man?

Twenty minutes later, Sabrina had finished her asparagus and was standing at the bar trying to get the bartender's attention so she could pay. He was much more interested in the young ladies at the end of the bar.

"Good luck," she said to the big, bald-headed gentleman in a leather jacket who slid into the seat beside her. "I think you have to be cute and about twenty-one to get any service right now."

The man threw her a look and did not comment.

"How are you enjoying your stay? Isn't the hotel wonderful?"

The man turned his shoulder so his back was angled toward her.

Sabrina always enjoyed a challenge, and besides, she was bored. "I've seen you around. Where are you from?"

The man waved a twenty-dollar bill in the direction of the bartender. "Can I get some service over here?"

This caught the bartender's attention, and Sabrina watched as the man ordered a shot, and with a harried look over his shoulder at Sabrina, downed it. He turned to leave.

"Well, I hope you enjoy your vacation. It was wonderful chatting with you." Sabrina smiled at the man as he hurried out the door. She turned back to the bartender who was drifting back toward the young women. She handed him her money and asked for a receipt. She wasn't sure if she had an expense account or not, but it never hurt to be prepared.

"I don't suppose you're Pete," she said when the bartender returned with her change.

"No, Pete works during the day."

"I guess I'll have to try back tomorrow." On her mental list was to talk to the bartender who served Gilbert right before he left for Goat Island.

"If you just want to talk, you're in luck. He's sitting over there having a drink."

Sabrina made her way over to the table the bartender indicated. A young man with short blond hair and a lot of bright white forehead was sitting by himself near the guitarist, who had just taken a break.

"Are you Pete?"

"Last time I checked. Though if you're going to complain about the screwdrivers this morning, all I can say is that my name is Rob."

He was flying high on a beer buzz, but wasn't yet drunk, Sabrina decided. "No, no, I'm sure the drinks were fine. I wanted to ask you about something else."

She sat down and explained who she was and that Matt said he was the bartender who served Gilbert Kane just before he left on his fateful trip to the island.

"Sure. Me and Lynwood were his favorite people, I can tell you that." He nodded to indicate the other bartender, who was back flirting with the ladies.

"Gilbert liked to drink?"

"Like a fish. Held it pretty well, not that we worry too much about that on the island, since there's nowhere much for them to drive. Though, I heard somewhere they've started giving people breathalyzers on their barstools. If they start that here we might have problems. Lots of these folks aren't licensed to drive barstools." He laughed long and hard at this. Sabrina waited with some semblance of patience until he stopped finding himself amusing.

"Did you notice anything unusual about Gilbert Kane that last afternoon? How drunk was he?"

Pete was still chuckling at his own wit. "He had three shots. That wasn't unusual. I think the night before he might have had four or five, and that's besides a bottle of wine. He liked his wine. That afternoon, he was still capable of driving his barstool, if you get my drift." This set him off again, and Sabrina waited through his gales of laughter.

"Did he talk to you? Did you notice anything about him?"

"He didn't look so hot, now that you mention it. He was sweating a lot, shaking, and kind of clutching his head. He knocked over a glass and almost soaked his camera, and he cussed about that for a while, though the camera was fine. And then he got pretty agitated over a phone call."

"Do you remember anything about the phone call?" Sabrina leaned forward. Who was talking to Gilbert a mere hour or two before he was killed?

"I didn't hear much. Something about somebody being on the island. He seemed pretty pissed about it, maybe even worried, but that's all I can remember."

"Do you remember if he talked to anybody else? Did he tell anyone that he was going to Goat Island that afternoon?"

"Nah, he didn't talk to anyone else." Pete waved at the bartender. "Hey, Lynwood, tell Bud he needs to get back up here and sing!"

She was losing him. "Gilbert didn't say anything else?"

"Not that afternoon. He just ordered a bottle of our best wine, asked for a corkscrew, and left. Not much of a tipper, I can tell you that."

Sabrina shivered as she thought about how the corkscrew had been used. Was this a spur-of-the-moment crime, and the killer used whatever weapon was handy? "You said he didn't say anything else that last afternoon. Did he talk to you other than that?"

"Yeah, that first night he was here. He got pretty drunk, and was kind of hunched over, holding his head. I asked if he was all right, and he said, let me think, how did he put it...?" Pete scrunched up his white forehead.

"What did he say?"

"Something along the lines of...as long as people stayed dumb and gullible, he was fine. It was when they got smart that he had problems."

Chapter Twenty-three

"Oof!"

The impact knocked Sabrina back into the bushes and she had just enough time to worry about poison ivy before hitting the ground. Later, it would occur to her that her priorities might be a tad skewed if poison ivy was her biggest worry upon being knocked to her backside on a dark, deserted path mere hours after another woman was attacked.

The man who had run into her spared her a brief, unreadable glance, and then went off down the path without apologizing. It was the bald, burly man from the bar, and he obviously wasn't feeling any more kindly to her now than he had before.

"What are you doing?" Michael Siderius loomed, staring down at her in puzzlement.

"Could you help me up?"

"Oh. Yeah. I'm sorry. Sure."

He extended a hand and Sabrina used it to struggle to her feet. She took stock, and decided that she was probably fine, barring a fracture to her tailbone, an unfortunate encounter with a poisonous plant, or a bite from some unseen insect. Perhaps she would go ahead and make that appointment with Doc Hailey tomorrow.

"Do you know that man? The one in the leather coat? I saw you talking to him, right before he turned around and ran into me. He seemed to be in a hurry."

"That man? No, I don't know him. I was asking him if he'd seen my father. How about you, have you seen him?"

"Joseph? No, I haven't seen him. You've lost your father?"

It was hard to read his expression in the dim light, but his shrug was impatient. "Ever since we got to this island he's been going off by himself. After we saw Sophie, he took off and I've been looking for him ever since."

"I'm sure he just decided to take a walk for some fresh air. I *have* been wanting to talk with you, Michael."

"Yeah? Well, I'm sorry, but I'm kind of busy right now. I need to go look for Dad."

"I'll go with you." As soon as she made the offer, Sabrina felt the little angel on her shoulder shake his head in disapproval. It was late, it was dark, there was both a killer and a possible rapist on the loose tonight.

"Whatever." It was grudging, but it was permission. Sabrina followed after Michael as he turned down another path, strong aftershave trailing behind him like a noxious cape.

"I was wondering if you had any thoughts on who killed Gilbert. Did he have any enemies?" Sabrina tripped over a loose shell and almost fell, but Michael didn't even pause to look over his shoulder.

"The police already asked me that."

"I'm sure they did. Now I'm asking." She was getting tired, and plunging into the dark after a man who might well be a murderer was not her idea of fun.

"Gilbert was a business man. I'm sure he made some enemies, but I can't think of anyone angry enough to kill him." Michael's voice was clipped and short as he headed farther away from the lodge into the darkness.

"I understand he quarreled with Lance Mayhew. Do you know anything about that?"

This at least slowed him a little. He looked back over his shoulder. "Lance? Why do you say that?"

"They were seen arguing." At least he had stopped so she could catch her breath, though they stood in a patch of shadow so it was hard to read Michael's expression.

"Well, I don't know anything about an argument between Lance and Gilbert. I'm sure it wasn't anything important since Gilbert didn't mention it. Gilbert reported to me, you know." The words were peevish, as if he was tired of having to remind everyone who was in charge of Hummers International.

"I understand it was over money. Do the people who sign up for your retreat often complain about the amount of money you charge?"

"Never. All of them feel that it is money well spent. My father is a very important man, you know, and some people would pay a lot more money than we charge to spend a week in his company." Michael felt comfortable enough with this subject to resume his journey down the winding path.

Since nothing the Hummers had said contradicted this statement, Sabrina couldn't argue as she stumbled after him. Her implication that the Hummers charged too much for their retreat was getting her nowhere. She tried another tack.

"Gilbert didn't seem to think the people who signed up for your retreat are very intelligent. He called them dumb and gullible." She was desperate for some type of reaction from him.

Another pause, and Michael turned back to her. "He called them what?"

"Dumb and gullible."

Michael shook his head. "That doesn't sound right. It does not reflect how we, at Hummers International, regard our members at all. We think they are very special and unique."

"Then why would he say something like that?"

"I have no idea."

"Do any of the Hummers on the island have reason to want to kill Gilbert?"

"Why would they? Our only goal is to help them harness their amazing gift."

"And how do you do that? What goes on at your sessions? I've heard several people refer to them as 'rituals.' What kind of rituals are you performing that you need so much privacy?"

This was shouted after Michael's retreating back. He didn't even slow down as he disappeared around a curve.

Sabrina shook her head. She had run out of questions and the stomach for hurtling down an unstable path through the dark night.

She turned back up the path, thinking back over their conversation. Her impression of Michael remained unchanged. He reminded her of a six-year-old put in charge of a toy factory. Here he was charging around at all hours of the night searching for his father. Where was Joseph, anyway?

As if her thoughts conjured him, she saw Joseph descending an adjoining path. He moved silently, as if under his long flowing pants his feet were pedaling along on air, instead of the hard shells and rock that Sabrina was traversing.

"Joseph!" she called, but he did not pause. Father and son shared a knack for ignoring her, Sabrina reflected, as she hurried after yet another Siderius.

"Joseph, could I speak with you a moment?" She caught up enough to catch the edge of his sleeve and tug. He slowed and looked back over his shoulder at her. She drew back, astonished by what the watery light of the moon revealed.

The old man was crying. Tears streamed down a face ravaged by grief, his eyes twin cavities of despair and misery.

"What's wrong? Joseph, are you all right? Are you looking for your son? He went down that way looking for you. Stay here and I'll go get him for you." His grief was catching and Sabrina felt a sob catch in her own throat as she patted his arm with desperate sympathy.

He turned his head to look down the path and then looked back into her face. His mouth opened, but no sound emerged. Shaking his head, he patted her on the hand, a gesture of acknowledgment, of affinity, that sent tingles up her arm. Then he turned and continued up the path.

◇◇◇

By the time she arrived at Patti's cottage, Sabrina was dirty and exhausted, and her head was buzzing. After running into Joseph Siderius, she had gotten lost. This was no great surprise, but if she hadn't run into a police officer with a flashlight, she thought she might still be out there wandering the dark, sinuous paths.

Sergeant Jimmy and Patti were talking outside the cottage and, forgetting her weariness, she rushed toward them.

"Is Sophie okay?"

"Sabrina, where have you been? I've been looking all over for you." Sergeant Jimmy's comprehensive look took in her disheveled appearance.

"I was—I'm here now. What's going on?"

"Sophie is fine. Between Doc Hailey and Master Joseph, she calmed right down, enough to fall asleep. Though she wouldn't do that until Dennis was sitting next to her holding her hand." Patti's smile was maternal and a bit conniving, the proud mama seeing her chick safely mated up. "I don't know what to think, Sabrina. Sergeant Jimmy just told me that they tracked down Shane Ludrow."

"Already? That's wonderful!"

"They tracked him down in London. It's been verified and everything. There's no way he could have been here tonight in Sophie's room. So who attacked her?"

Sabrina wasn't entirely surprised. She'd thought all along that Sophie's naming of her ex-boyfriend as her attacker was based on fear and assumption, rather than a clear-headed identification. "Now the question is," she said, "was the person who attacked Sophie our serial burglar or Gilbert's killer?"

Patti gasped. "Do you think someone is trying to kill us Hummers? Are we all in danger?"

"We don't know what's going on, ma'am," Sergeant Jimmy said. "I think you should all be careful until we figure this thing out. Right now, why don't you try to get some sleep? I'm sure we'll want to talk to you in the morning, but we're done for the evening."

"There's no possible way I'll sleep tonight," Patti declared. "What if he comes back?"

Jimmy waved his hand, a meaningless gesture into the darkness until Sabrina saw a uniformed man step out from under a nearby tree.

"He'll be here all night. You can sleep in peace, ma'am."

"What about the media? They've been a nuisance today. We couldn't even have our session today, and we're leaving on Saturday. That only leaves us two days of sessions!"

"While we are here, we'll keep out anybody who doesn't belong, including the media."

"That'll be a relief to Sophie, I'm sure," Sabrina said.

"I'm sure she'll appreciate it too," Patti said, with a curious look at Sabrina. "Sabrina, you'll be here tomorrow, won't you? With all that's going on, I really feel like we need you around. We'll be going to Rainbow Island at ten, but it would be wonderful if you could be here after that."

"I'd be happy to go with you to Rainbow Island if that would make you feel better." Sabrina felt warmed by a flicker of appreciation. It was a cold and lonely flame that promptly went out with Patti's next words.

"Goodness, no! I mean, thank you for the offer, but our sessions are private." Patti said her goodnights and went inside, leaving Sabrina and Jimmy alone.

"What do you think goes on at those sessions?" The words were thoughtful, and not directed at Jimmy, though he could be excused for thinking they were.

"What I'd like to know is what in the world you've been doing tonight."

Sabrina filled him in on her various conversations, touching on Lance's argument with Gilbert, Gilbert's comment about dumb and gullible people, and her run-in with a distraught Joseph Siderius. She left out the fact that her arm still tingled from his touch, and that she was hearing a crackling noise that reminded her of the sound of Rice Krispies, just doused with milk.

"I'll pass this along." Jimmy put away his notebook.

"Have the detectives checked Gilbert's phone records to see who called him at the bar? Maybe that person knows what Gilbert planned to do on the island. Or maybe he or she followed him to the island and killed him. It doesn't appear too many people knew he was going to the island."

"I do know he talked to several people on his cell that day. Most of them were in New York, from the Hummers International headquarters, but he also talked to Michael and Lance Mayhew. His last call was to Sam Myers, however."

"That makes sense. Gilbert called to tell Sam not to pick him up from the island."

Jimmy nodded. "All three have been questioned about the conversations, and they maintain they were routine conversations, nothing important."

"Hmmm." This raised all sorts of interesting possibilities, but Sabrina was too tired to contemplate any of them.

"Gilbert buying a bottle of wine fits right in with another piece of evidence. We found the bottle near his body, and his blood alcohol was triple the legal limit. He was very drunk when he was on that island."

Sabrina yawned. She was too exhausted to think of any more questions, though she knew this chance at a cooperative Jimmy shouldn't be passed up.

"Let me walk you back to your car. I need to be getting home, too. Darlene called an hour ago to tell me that the meatloaf was starting to resemble a charred football." Jimmy steered her toward the path that led to the hotel and Sabrina didn't argue.

"What did Michael say about the scratches on his hands?" she asked through a yawn when they were almost back to her car. It was the only intelligent question she could think to ask.

"He said he fell off his room's balcony rail. There was blood there to confirm his story."

"What in the world was he doing on his balcony rail?" The question fell on deaf ears as Jimmy answered a call on his radio.

He sighed as he clipped the radio back onto his belt. "Darlene is going to kill me, but it looks like I need to go finish some paperwork. You should be fine from here." Jimmy opened her car door and watched until she was safely inside with doors locked and engine started. He knocked on the window, and she rolled it down.

"I wanted to tell you that I appreciate the job you're doing, Sabrina," he said. "I wish you'd be a little more careful, but I do appreciate what you're trying to do."

Sabrina stared at Jimmy in astonishment.

Raising a hand, he disappeared into the darkness.

Sabrina sat and smiled for a moment. Then she realized she had to use the restroom. Badly. The two glasses of water she drank with her prosciutto asparagus were clamoring to be released, and she didn't think she could last until she got home.

"If you gotta go, you gotta go." She turned off the car and got out.

It only took her a moment to ascertain that the back door she was accustomed to using was locked. She headed for the massive front lobby doors, her bladder protesting enough that she didn't hesitate.

A woman she had not seen before manned the desk, and she was happy to point Sabrina in the direction of the restroom.

A few minutes later, feeling considerably relieved, Sabrina went back out into the night. As she walked around the side of the hotel, she was alert for any noise or movement, which was why she heard the faint sound of arguing voices.

She stopped and strained to hear, but the voices were indistinct. Somebody was arguing, though, there was no doubt about that. Sabrina hesitated only a moment before plunging back down the dark path away from her car. She comforted herself with the thought that she had been wandering these walkways all evening without ill-effects. A few more minutes couldn't hurt.

The voices became louder as she moved down the path, and she tried to keep her footsteps as noiseless as possible.

Just then she heard Michael Siderius' voice as clear as if he was standing next to her.

"Did you do it?" The words were not very loud, but angry, falling somewhere between a hissing whisper and an irate yell. "You did, didn't you?"

There was a response, but Sabrina could not make out the words, or even the gender of the speaker. As she continued on toward Michael and his unseen companion, she heard more words, but nothing she could distinguish. She wasn't even sure if it was Michael or the other person speaking. Then came the unmistakable sound of flesh hitting flesh.

By the time Sabrina rushed around the last curve of the path, Michael was standing in the clearing by himself, blood streaming down his face.

Chapter Twenty-four

The fact that Patti Townsend was not a morning person did not prevent her from opening a coffee shop. She always wanted to run her own business, ever since she was a little girl and sat in the corner of the shop where her mother cut hair. She swore then that one day she would be the boss, and that no one would tell her what to do and make her cry when she got home after a hard day's work.

Day after day spent selling shoes in a shop on Beechmont Avenue and watching people bring their own coffee cups from home convinced her that the stretch of street needed a coffee shop. When the storefront next to the shoe store went up for lease, she was ready to go to her bank with a business plan.

She was ecstatic when they approved the loan for a fun, quirky coffee shop that specialized in friendly, quick service.

Still, not having to get up at four in the morning was a rare luxury she was determined to enjoy. She had not been on a vacation in the five years since she opened the store, and she still felt guilty about being away. But her manager was her sister, with her mother as backup, and there were not two more competent people on the face of this earth. And she needed this time away, needed it badly. If she didn't get this Hum thing straightened out, she was afraid she might lose the shop. It was so hard to concentrate! Sometimes it felt like her head was going to explode, and it was enough to drive a person crazy. She couldn't focus, couldn't sleep, and she'd actually snapped at a few of her regulars. She apologized immediately, of course, but it was still not acceptable. She needed to get this thing taken care of, and fast. Lucille's lawsuit was just icing on the cake. Patti had thought about leaving the retreat when her sister called to tell her about the lawsuit, but there wasn't anything she could do right away. It was far more important to get rid of this Hum in her head than talk to a jealous maniac who was determined to get even with her for a long-ago high school feud. For God's sake, get over it, Patti wanted to tell the woman, but there was no reasoning with Lucille. Thus, the lawsuit.

Patti glanced at the clock and groaned. She should be feeling decadent and well-rested; after all, she'd slept in until almost nine o'clock. Instead, she felt gritty and exhausted. It's hard to sleep when it feels like your pillow is vibrating all night long, and even tranquilizers didn't help. She'd taken so many of them one night that she got scared and made herself vomit, afraid she was going to overdose.

But it was time to get up. They were meeting at ten to take a boat over to some island for this morning's session. She was dreading it, as usual. The whole thing was horrible, but she comforted herself with the knowledge that at the end of this week she would be rid of the Hum forever. So if she had to go to these sessions, and pretend that she believed in a voice of the universe, so be it. Anything was worth getting rid of this Hum.

Patti swung her feet over the side of the bed, and stood. She needed to check on Sophie. She'd offered to stay with her last night, but the girl had shown surprising backbone and insisted that she would not let the attack affect her life. Patti knew taking on a stray puppy when she had so much else going on in her life was ludicrous, but she couldn't seem to help herself. Sophie seemed so needy, and Patti had never been good at saying no to needy people. No matter how bad things were, Patti reminded herself, her mother used to keep quarters in her pockets to drop in the cups of the homeless people. Patti could do no less.

She reached the bathroom and stared at herself in the mirror, once again astonished at the depths she had reached. She heard somewhere that aluminum foil might block electromagnetic noise, and it seemed reasonable, didn't it? At this point, Patti was willing to try anything.

She reached up and removed the aluminum foil hat and placed it carefully on the bathroom counter.

She might need it again tonight.

Sophie hung up the phone and looked down at her toenails. They looked pretty, not too messy, and she felt proud of herself. She hadn't painted her own toenails since she was a kid, before her mother dragged her to New York for an interview with the talent agency. She tried to tell her mother she didn't want to miss her first year of high school, but her mother told her to stop whining, and smile for the camera. Didn't she want to make her father proud? Was she so selfish she was going to say no to a few extra bucks that their family could use to buy a new house and car?

So Sophie smiled. After a couple years, she smiled so much and so well that she had made it onto the covers of some of the nation's top fashion magazines. Her mother was there every step of the way, screaming at everyone on the set and bullying the photographers. Sophie didn't have to do anything but smile, and that's what she did, year after year, while her mother grew fatter. In direct inverse relation to her mother's enormous weight gain, Sophie grew skinnier. But that was great, because skinny was in, and Sophie only grew more popular. And Sophie found that no one really listened to what she said, so she soon found passive-aggressive pleasure in mangling people's names and saying outrageous things.

Sophie wiggled her toes and put the earplugs from her iPod back into her ears. Listening to the Dixie Chicks sing about a jerk named Earl went a little way toward blocking out the buzz in her head, though not by much. She wondered what her mother would say if she knew Sophie blew off a gig with *Glamour* magazine to come to Comico Island, and then felt a burst of joy at the traitorous realization that she really didn't care. The blow-up had come three months ago, when Sophie told her mother she was going to break up with Shane. Her mother was horrified. Was she crazy? Shane Ludrow was the most popular teen idol since Johnny Depp.

But Sophie was serious this time, and to both of their astonishment, she told her mother she could leave if she didn't like it. Her mother did, certain that Sophie would call the next day, begging her to return.

Sophie never did. She felt like a heavy, smothering mink coat had been removed from her shoulders, and she reveled in the feeling. Then the Hum started, and she hadn't been able to enjoy anything since.

Just thinking about Shane made Sophie sick to her stomach. Her eyes flew to the door and windows, which she knew were locked, since she had checked them herself twenty or thirty times. The images from her attack came rushing back from the cellar in her mind where she had banished them. She was good at not thinking about things, but the Hum made it harder to lock the memories in the safe room again.

After a moment, Sophie got up and went to look in her closet. It was almost time to go to the dock to meet for this morning's session. Sophie wasn't looking forward to the session, but she really, truly thought they were working. The Hum seemed to be lessening, and that was worth any price. She knew Patti thought Master Joseph and his voice of the universe were silly, but Sophie saw the sincerity in Master Joseph's eyes. He was a good person, and he was going to help her.

Patti was a good person, too. It was sweet of her to call to check on Sophie, and to offer to walk her down to the dock. She wished Patti were her mother. How differently things might have turned out for her!

Sophie pulled out a designer shirt and blue jeans, indifferent to the fact that the clothes she received free, on the off chance she might be photographed wearing them, were worth a small fortune. She wanted to look great today, for Dennis.

She turned up the music on her iPod and concentrated on not thinking about anything.

Lance Mayhew massaged his hand as he walked down the shell path toward the docks. He was early, but he was compulsively early for everything. It was one of the things that his ex-wife disliked about him most, which was funny, since Lance hated *her* for much more concrete reasons. She was a slob, a bad mother, and a drunk. That she was perpetually late for even the most important appointments was just another facet of her already badly flawed character.

But she'd given him Melinda and Kobie, and for that he was prepared to forgive a lot. Melinda was his sweet little girl, never mind that she'd switched out pink tutus and ballet shoes for the grungy jeans and tees that were so popular nowadays, and was prone to saying "Daaaddd" in that uniquely teenage tone that conveyed profound disgust. In rare moments she still smiled that radiant, beautiful smile and told him she loved him. And Kobie, Kobie was great. He hadn't gotten old enough yet to despise his old dad, and the two of them could talk for hours about the latest computer viruses and the hottest new processors.

Lance missed his two children. He had just got off the phone with them and could tell their mother was at it again. She did it every time she had the children, which was seldom enough, but still damaging. Little comments about him, and how stupid he was, and how much better things would be if they lived with her. Melinda could go out on dates with her new boyfriend, and Kobie could have the best computer on the market, the one his father couldn't afford. Little things, like barbed hooks in their souls. How cool was it to have a mother who had won the lottery? When they got back from their visits with her, they looked around his small house with disdain, and looked at him with suspicion, as if they now questioned every word out of his mouth.

He resisted the urge to smash his hand into a nearby tree. Now he had this noise in his head to contend with as well. When it first started, he unplugged every appliance in the house trying to discover the source of the annoying buzz. When that didn't stop it, he drove around town, trying to pinpoint where the noise was coming from. It was natural for him to turn to the Internet for help after that, and he found a plethora of information.

At first he resisted the Hummers International website, after an initial read-through revealed the group's belief that the Hum was the voice of the universe. It sounded so hokey. He cruised the other websites, discovering that the Hum had been reported as early as the nineteenth century, described as a "swarm of bees," and that incidents of the Hum appeared in the nineteen seventies in the UK, but not until the nineties in the United States. He learned about "electromagnetic radiation" and "TACAMO," which stood for "Take Charge and Move Out" and referred to aircraft that were used to relay messages to submarines. Could these aircraft be causing the Hum? No one knew.

He joined an online group of people claiming to hear the Hum, and experimented with many of their suggestions. He'd tried a water helmet, a Cathedral crypt, a cave deep underground, and, one desperate night, he'd even tried climbing in the refrigerator in his garage. Anything to shield himself from whatever was bombarding his head with ambient noise.

But nothing worked, and eventually he found himself drawn back to the Hummers International website. After all, they promised a cure for the Hum, which no one else did. Did he really care if they couched their promise in a lot of mumbo-jumbo? If it worked, it really didn't matter how it worked.

Now, of course, he knew better.

But regret couldn't extricate him from this situation. Nothing could.

As Walter Olgivie came down the path toward the dock, he saw Lance in front of him, but saw no reason to quicken his step to catch up with the sullen man. Walter didn't have any desire to deal with a morose Lance Mayhew. The man was like a constant downer. Walter spent a lot of money to look and feel great, and he saw no reason to expose himself to such constant negativity.

Of course, keeping a positive flow of energy was difficult lately. The Hum was one thing that money did not seem to alleviate. No matter how many doctors he consulted, the electro-therapy he endured, and psychics he consulted, nothing seemed to make a dent in the droning in his head. It was damn near unbearable. He'd taken to clipping a fan to his bed, finding that the constant noise helped relieve the worst of the symptoms. At home, he'd even bought an air mattress and slept in his kitchen next to the refrigerator when the noise got too bad.

But he was determined to use the trip to this godforsaken island to his advantage. Walter didn't see any reason not to use everything to his advantage, and it surprised him that other people did not see opportunities the way he did. While he was still in college, he bought his first apartment building. He fixed it up enough to avoid the building inspector's condemnation and rented it out to a bunch of numbnuts who were willing to pay good money to live in a roach-infested hellhole. He didn't stop there, and made his first million by the time he graduated college. He seemed to have a knack for seeing money signs where no one else did. Or maybe he just had the nerve to follow his instincts. He wasn't sure which, and he really didn't care. As long as he was making money hand over fist, he didn't care about all the poor shmucks who didn't share his gift.

He'd gotten a little bored of late, though. Money had somehow ceased to inspire him. Now it was the hunt, finding something special where nobody else saw value and snatching it up. The island had surprising possibilities, and Walter didn't see any reason not to pursue this game on the side.

Of course, now he had to get through another one of these highly unpleasant sessions. Speaking of unpleasant, there was Michael Siderius standing on the dock, wearing a pair of dark sunglasses and talking with Patti and the beautiful Sophie.

As Walter drew closer, he noticed that Michael was sporting a broken nose.

Walter smiled and quickened his pace.

Dennis Parker jogged up to the dock, trying to act like he wasn't watching Sophie smile wanly at something Michael Siderius was saying. He quelled an instant surge of jealousy. He didn't like the looks Michael sent Sophie's way, or the many opportunities the man found to touch her.

Dennis had no right to feel jealous, no matter how strong his feelings for Sophie. He had no idea if she reciprocated, and there was something fragile about her that made him hesitate. Not that he ever was a lady's man, like some of the guys he knew. They teased him about it sometimes, but he didn't care. His mom and dad had been together since they married at eighteen, and had shown five strong, independent boys how a marriage was supposed to work. Dennis had seen the real thing, and he didn't plan to settle for less.

He wondered if Sophie would be mad when she found out who he was. It was refreshing that she didn't seem to know, but he hated to deceive her. On the other hand, it was nice to leave all that behind him and just be Dennis Parker again, like he used to be back in his hometown. Some of the others knew, but Michael must have talked to them, because no one was saying anything. That was the condition he made before signing up for the retreat. Michael Siderius was happy to agree.

Dennis slowed as he reached the dock, disconcerted to see that he was the last to arrive. He started out planning to run to the dock, but when he saw he had more time, he decided to run the path by the water. He'd found that running helped the Hum, and he did it every chance he got. At home, he surrounded himself with thick insulation, TVs, fans, and indoor fountains. He'd even invested in a generator, after one hellish night spent without power. Without his appliances making white noise, he'd spent the night with pillows over his head.

Running also helped him forget for a while how much he wasn't looking forward to the upcoming session. But now he was late, and he jogged down and leaped onto the boat. The captain undid the lines as Dennis apologized for his tardiness. He was so busy pretending he wasn't noticing how great Sophie looked in her pair of jeans that it took him a moment to realize that Michael Siderius had a broken nose.

Now wasn't that strange?

After Dennis got himself settled in a seat, he looked back at the dock. A blond woman—was it Sabrina Dunsweeney, the nice island ombudsman?—was standing at the shore watching their boat leave. There was someone with her, and Dennis had to rub his eyes to make sure he was seeing clearly.

Chapter Twenty-five

Lima felt about as dumb as a floor rug for agreeing to this. He should have stayed on his rocking chair on the general store's porch, having a congenial conversation with Bicycle (the fact that Bicycle Bob did not participate in these chats did not bother Lima much) and pondering whether he would have sausage or country ham on his biscuit this morning. That's what he should be doing on a sunny Thursday morning, not standing on a beach on godforsaken Shell Island contemplating going for a boat ride on a banana peel.

"You can have the blue one, Lima." Sabrina had the air of a long-suffering mother appeasing her three-year-old. As if *he* were the one being unreasonable.

"Don't care if it's blue or yellow, still looks as slippery as a banana peel. How am I supposed to stay on?" The two of them exchanged one of those looks, like when Grandpa starts talking to the clothes hangers.

Like he hadn't been on boats since the day he was born, and that was long before either one of these two were even a wrinkle on the foreheads of their parents. Lima and boats were simpatico; Lima and banana peels were another story. It didn't help that he was feeling queerly again, a little light-headed and breathless, not that he would say anything to yonder hypocat. She'd have him strapped to a stretcher faster than he could blink, on his way to the mainland for some white-coated teenager to stab him with needles that they swore wouldn't hurt. Since when did sharp pointy things jabbed into your arm not hurt? What good did it do to lie to people when they'd know you were a liar within two seconds?

"What're you looking at?" Lima turned to the dock master and did his best James Cagney sneer. James Cagney was a putz, so Lima didn't mind stealing his sneer.

"That sailboat out on the water." The dock master didn't even flinch, which made Lima scowl even harder. He didn't like this lean, tanned whippet of a man, with his bright blue eyes and his smart comments. Shane, or Sal, that was his name. Sally, was more like it. Lima didn't trust him as far as he could see him.

"Lima, if you don't want to come, it's fine. Sam can take the kayak back up the beach and you can go to the lodge and get breakfast. I'll be back in a little while. You're really not dressed for this, you know." Sabrina in her sensible screaming orange miniskirt and ruffled pea-green silk shirt. And *he* wasn't dressed appropriately.

A little boy and his mother passed them on their way to a homestead of chairs, towels, coolers, and beach toys staked out on the beach. The boy stared in awe at Lima while the mother smiled in generous amusement. Lima did his Cagney Special to them as well and the boy shrieked.

"I'm going. And I don't need any help. Just get out of my way." This to the young dock master, who didn't look like any dock master Lima ever met, and he'd met a few in his day. In fact, the man looked about as untrustworthy as a four-dollar-bill as he helped Sabrina onto her kayak. He was copping a feel, was what he was doing. Lima hadn't missed the little looks and amusing banter between the two of them. The whole thing was about as cute as a coupla cats using a sandbox.

"Lima, be reasonable. You don't want to go, so why don't you stay here until I get back?" Sabrina asked in a rational voice, as if she was acting like the most rational person in the world. Which she wasn't, which was why he was coming along. The girl needed looking after. And if he couldn't talk her out of this whole thing, then he'd go along to keep her out of trouble.

It all started when he got back from seeing Mrs. Linler's second grade class this morning. He was just settling his tired bones in his accustomed rocking chair on Tubb's porch when here comes Sabrina flying up the stairs, almost stepping on Bicycle and having to turn back and apologize to the old boy. The whole time Calvin was just a screechin' on her shoulder, flapping his wings to keep his balance as Sabrina thrust a newspaper in Lima's face.

"Do you know who that is?" She stuck her finger at the paper, but since she had it practically shoved up his nose it was hard to see one way or another.

Lima removed the paper from his nasal cavity and stared at the picture of the young man caught in flight as he stuffed a basketball through a hoop.

"Sure. That's Dennis Parker, one of the best basketball players in the country. They say gravity and him never met, and you'd believe it when he goes flying up in the air to dunk a ball."

"Lima, what in the world are you wearing?" Sabrina stared at him in bemusement for a moment, and then shook her head. "Never mind. It's Dennis Parker, that's who it is. One of the best basketball players in the country." She said this in a voice like she was accusing the boy of routinely crapping in the flower beds.

"That's what I said. I've never seen anybody play like him."

"Dennis Parker, this famous basketball player who everyone knows about, is staying at the Shell Lodge, and no one told me. Did you hear me, Lima? *No one bothered to mention it.*"

"Sabrina, are you all right? You're looking a little high-strung there. Sit on down before Calvin blows a sprocket." The bird was feeding off his mistress' emotions and resembled nothing more than a howling swirl of buttercups.

"What else did they not bother to mention? How could they not tell me something like that? No one's been honest with me, and here I thought I was getting somewhere! They probably all know who the murderer is and are not bothering to mention it *to me!*"

Sabrina was shouting and Bicycle stood up to leave. He didn't like any type of strong emotion and was apt to go off and hide when someone started yelling or crying. Lima didn't blame him. He'd like to go off and hide right about now.

"Sabrina, would you sit down!"

She blinked like he'd struck her, and he felt guilty, like he'd kicked a kitten. Not that he liked cats, but he didn't make a practice of going around and kicking them. Cats got even.

Sabrina sat back down.

"I need to put in my notice. I need to tell them this whole thing was a mistake, and that they need to find another ombudsman. I should have done it days ago." Her voice was soft and trembly. Now Lima wished she was yelling.

"You were just hired a few days ago." Practical and matter-of-fact, that's what the situation called for.

"Well, I should have quit the first day, then. Then maybe Gilbert wouldn't have died, Missy's house wouldn't have been broken into, and islanders and locals wouldn't be walking around looking like they wished they had assault rifles hidden up their sleeves."

"You get a promotion when I wasn't looking? They're calling you God now?"

"Please?"

"I think you're giving yourself a lot of credit, thinking you could be responsible for this whole mess. You're doing the best you can to clear up a bad situation, but there are things outside your control, you got to accept that."

"No, I don't."

"What?"

"Accept that things are outside my control. If I were good at my job, I would be in complete control at all times." Sabrina was stroking Calvin, and the little bird was calmer, but danged if he didn't look sad now.

It was hard to stay practical and matter-of-fact in the face of blatant unreasonableness. "Stop feeling sorry for yourself, Sabrina! Do the best you can, that's all anyone asks."

"Doing your best isn't good enough if you fail and let people down. And if I couldn't even win the Hummers' confidence enough for them to tell me who Dennis Parker is, then I'm just a failure."

She went on and on like this, and Lima listened with as much patience as he could muster, which mostly consisted of disgusted stomps and irritated spits off the side of the porch. Finally he couldn't take any more. "Let me see if I understand: you think if you'd done a better job, these people would have confided in you more, and by now you'd have solved this murder." He said it to show her how post dumb she was being, but she nodded in pure miserable agreement.

"They won't even tell me what they're doing on the island. They go off for these private sessions, but none of them will talk about them. Maybe if I knew what happened in their meetings, I'd understand more about what was going on with them. Those sessions are the key to the Hummers, I just know it."

"There you go. You just need to find out what goes on in those sessions."

"Lima, that's it! You're absolutely right!"

Lima rocked his chair, feeling complacent and pleased with the world, and most especially the intelligence God had seen fit to bestow on him.

Until Sabrina outlined what she had in mind. Now, as he stared down at the kayak in front of him, he wondered why God hadn't seen fit to grant him a few more I's and Q's.

"I said I don't need no help," Lima snarled at the man named Shane or Sal, who had gotten Sabrina into her kayak and was now looking at him with a sardonic smile.

"You know, there's a tortoise in a zoo in Australia that's more than 170 years old. It's one of the tortoises Charles Darwin took from the Galapagos back in 1836, and it's still alive and kicking."

Lima stared at the man, and then shook his head in disgust. "If you ain't got nothing intelligent to say, keep your dang mouth shut." He turned to the kayak and sat down on it, balancing his weight to compensate for the rocking of the waves. It was just a boat, after all, and if there was something Lima knew about, it was boats. Well, that and a whole lot of other things too, but boats in particular.

He picked up his paddle, ignoring the small crowd that had gathered on the beach.

"Hey, look at the clown on the kayak!"

Lima didn't even glance back as he paddled away. Dern fools, that's what they were.

Chapter Twenty-six

Sabrina watched Lima paddle toward the entrance of the cove and tried to muffle a sigh.

"I don't know what's gotten in to him," she said to Sam as she dipped her paddle in the water. "He's not usually so rude—well, I guess that's not true, but, anyway, I'm sorry. I thought that story about the tortoise was very nice, even if he didn't."

"I don't know why he would have thought it was nice. I called him an ancient old turtle who moves slower than molasses."

"I thought you meant—" Sabrina gave up. "Well, that was rude!"

She tossed her head, and then regretted it when the kayak rocked alarmingly. Without another word she paddled after the clown, complete with white paint and bulb nose, who was weaving an erratic path in the wrong direction.

Lima did so love to dress up. When she found him on the porch at Tubb's General Store, he'd just gotten back from entertaining Mrs. Linler's second grade class and was still garbed in full clown regalia. He would remain in character most of the day, Sabrina knew from experience. He would grumble that now he was all dressed up he didn't feel like taking off the outfit, but in reality he loved the attention.

What she'd never expected was that Lima would insist that he accompany her to Rainbow Island to spy on the Hummers. Never in her wildest dreams. She told him she had to leave right away, thinking that the fact he was dressed like a clown would dissuade him. She should have known better. If anything, it had made the whole expedition more appealing to him.

So, here she was, on a covert expedition to Rainbow Island with a scared bird on her shoulder—Calvin didn't like big bodies of water—and a clown in tow. All she needed was to pitch a tent and she could call the whole thing a circus.

"This way, Lima," she called. She had finagled directions from Sam when he returned from delivering the Hummers to Rainbow Island. He didn't even ask why she was headed over there.

"I know how to get to Dead Man's Island," Lima shouted back, "and if you keep going that way, you're going to run into an oyster bar because it's nigh on low tide."

Sabrina was too tired to argue. She turned her kayak to follow Lima's.

She had not gotten to bed until late last night. By the time she asked Michael Siderius who bloodied his nose, and he took off without answering, it was close to eleven. Then she had to drive home and go through her nightly going-to-bed ritual, which took a good hour, so it was well after twelve by the time she got to bed.

Tired and lethargic was not the best way to start any day, but it grew worse after she encountered a tourist and local screaming at each other down in the Blue Cam Restaurant, and then saw Dennis Parker's determined young face on the front page of the newspaper.

How could they not tell her? They all must have known. No wonder everyone kept looking at her so funny when she said the news people were interested in Sophie. The model was small potatoes compared to famous basketball player Dennis Parker. She looked like a fool, and everyone must be laughing at her, thinking it was hilarious to keep such a secret from her.

But she was back on track now. She was convinced that the Hummers' private sessions were key. After all, the reason Sabrina became involved in this whole mess in the first place was because Gilbert and Michael were complaining that they needed more privacy for their sessions. And the reason that Gilbert was on Goat Island was because he was checking out the island for their sessions. Furthermore, none of the Hummers would talk about what went on at the sessions. There was something fishy there, and nothing was going to keep the truth from Sabrina this time.

A wake from a motor boat caught her off guard and almost flipped her into the water.

"Catch sharks right about here all the time," Lima yelled to her cheerfully. Now that he was away from Sam, his good mood had returned.

Rainbow Island, or Dead Man's Island as it had been called for a century, was not far from Goat Island, where Gilbert Kane met his fate. Sabrina glanced at her watch: almost ten-thirty. Sam had dropped the Hummers off at ten, and wasn't due to pick them back up until one, so she had plenty of time to scout around.

Another boat zoomed by, and Calvin shrieked as he gripped her shoulder with needle-sharp claws. Sabrina gritted her teeth and managed to hang onto her balance.

It was a beautiful day, which explained the number of boats on the water. Clear and calm, with enough of a breeze to keep the air limber and cool. The water was a flirty blue today, playfully flashing glimpses of sandbars and glimmering fish, and tossing small white waves up just for fun.

As they got closer, Rainbow Island revealed itself to be a run-of-the-mill spoil island, a strip of beach and grass circling a thick growth of bushes and trees. The underbrush looked more and more forbidding as they pulled their kayaks up onto the sand. An osprey circled, shrieking, and then dipped down to pick a stick off the beach and wing its way back toward its nest.

"Dang shrilly birds, always yelling about something. Well, we're here. Now what?" Lima, red wig askew and wearing only one shoe, had found a tree trunk on which to sit. Sabrina worried at the heaviness of his breathing; the kayak ride must have been too strenuous for him.

"Why don't you wait here? I'll go reconnoiter."

"You'll do what?"

"I'll go look around. Then I'll come back and get you." She said this with no particular sincerity, because if she had her way, Lima would get no farther than this patch of sand.

Lima waved her away without arguing, which, she thought later, should have been her sign, but she was too revved up to notice. She struck out through the underbrush, her skirt and shirt catching on every branch they came across. It felt like little hands were pulling her backward. But she persevered. Rustling in the undergrowth indicated that she was not alone, but she tried not to think about what kind of animal was producing the sounds. Something slithery and scaly, no doubt, and it was better not to think of such things.

The trees worked as an effective canopy, and the light was gloomy and dim. Already she had numerous bug bites and scratches, and she feared her outfit would never be the same. As for her decorative sandals, they'd been ruined pretty much after her first step.

It felt like she had been pushing her way through undergrowth for hours, and Sabrina was so turned around she wasn't even sure from which way she had come. It was a small island; surely by now she would have run across some sign of the Hummers? If she didn't hurry, they would pack up and leave and this whole journey would have been in vain. Now that she had calmed down, she was beginning to feel it wasn't such a good idea anyway.

A few minutes later, she heard the sound of a soft drum and low chanting, and Calvin chattered with delight. She must be getting close. She slowed down and tried to quiet the noise of her passage, but she still felt as if she was making about as much noise as a medium-sized bulldozer. Calvin, who was whistling at the butterflies, wasn't helping, but he was too excited to hush. He loved butterflies.

She reached the edge of a clearing, and for a moment she thought she had found the Hummers.

Instead she saw Lima.

He was in full military crawl, snaking through the tall grass toward a patch of trees. Judging from the sounds emanating from within, this was where the Hummers were performing their rituals.

She was about to go after Lima, who had popped his head up to look around and then resumed his belly-crawl, when she noticed that there was someone else standing in the trees nearby. He was staring at Lima in open-mouthed disbelief.

Sabrina glanced back at Lima and acknowledged that he was a sight to inspire disbelief in about anyone. It wasn't every day that you saw an eighty-year-old clown doing a passable imitation of a low-crawl through the weeds for no apparent reason. Lima was pretty good at it, and Sabrina reflected that it was possible he learned the technique in World War II. Either that, or he was imitating John Wayne again. Lima imitated John Wayne at every opportunity.

Sabrina looked at the stranger, and realized that she recognized him. He was the bald, burly man who had given her the cold shoulder at the bar and then run into her last night. He was holding a camera, but his instincts must have failed him, because otherwise he would have been taking a picture of Lima. How else would anyone ever believe his story later?

What was he doing? Was he a reporter? That was the only thing that made sense. How did he score a room at the Shell Lodge, though? All the other reporters were staying in town, Sabrina knew. This morning she received calls from two hotel owners complaining about them, and adding this new task to her to-do list almost toppled it.

Sabrina didn't know what to do. She was contemplating her options when Calvin caught sight of a large, colorful butterfly and broke out in enthusiastic comment about it. The burly man looked around and saw her. His eyes widened, and then he turned and disappeared into the woods.

Lima stood up, and the marsh grass he had stuck into his red wig for camouflage wilted. "Will you quieten that dang bird down, everyone will hear us!" he roared.

There was sudden silence from the trees, and then a murmur of voices and a crashing of underbrush indicating someone was coming in their direction.

"Come on!" She gestured to Lima to hurry, but he shook his head and pointed in the opposite direction.

"I don't know what fun, scenic route you took to get here, but I plan to take the shortest trail back to the boat." His hearing aid must have been malfunctioning again, because he was speaking in nothing less than a bellow.

The crashing was getting closer, and now someone was shouting. Sabrina abdicated her illusion of free will and bolted after Lima as he made for a nearby path. Unfortunately, with only one big shoe, Lima's gait was hampered and they were being overtaken.

"Hurry, hurry!" she panted, and Calvin chittered his agreement.

"Last one back to the dock is a rotten egg," Lima gasped as they reached the beach.

Sabrina shoved her kayak into the water. She jumped onto it, but missed her mark and ended up waist deep in the water, a swirling whirl of yellow feathers in her face as Calvin tried to climb her head. Lima had just mounted his kayak and was paddling frantically when she stood up right in front of him.

"Lima!"

Sabrina caught hold of the back of Lima's clown suit and hauled him out of the water. Calvin was shrieking in terror, but he managed to hang on.

"I'll be fine if you let up the death grip," Lima wheezed. "Where are the dern kayaks?"

They looked around for them, but the commotion from their struggle and the outgoing tide had floated the kayaks out of their reach. Sabrina turned to go after them when a voice caught her up short.

"Sabrina, what in the world are you doing?"

Sabrina and Lima turned to see a group of puzzled Hummers standing on the beach.

Chapter Twenty-seven

"Oh, fancy meeting you here," Sabrina said. Calvin was clamoring at the top of his lungs.

"What in God's name are you doing?" Michael Siderius shouted over the bird's squawks. He stood at the edge of the water with an enraged expression on his face, embellished by his red, swollen nose.

The rest of them were there as well. Patti, Sophie, and Dennis huddled together and stared at them in disbelief, Walter and Lance stood apart, looking irritated, and Joseph Siderius was inspecting a spot on the horizon.

"Lima and I were out for a nice kayak ride when we saw this beautiful beach. We decided to stop for a swim," Sabrina said, ignoring the fact that they were fully clothed, and that Lima was in a clown suit to boot. "If you'll excuse me, I need to go capture our kayaks."

She began wading after the kayaks, splashing water on her shoulders to show how much she was enjoying herself, and earning another strident reprimand from Calvin. When she got back with the kayaks in tow, Lima was saying, "It's an island tradition to dunk a clown at the start of the season. Sabrina didn't want to tell you she'd been picked for this singular honor, but it's true. We've ensured good luck for the island for the next year. Well, here she is with the kayaks. Ta-da!"

Sabrina and Lima got onto the kayaks and paddled off before anybody thought to say a word.

What could they say, anyway?

"Pssst! Hey you!"

Sabrina looked around, but the hall was empty except for the sounds of hammering. She was pretty sure she must have taken a wrong turn somewhere. She thought the Shell Lodge's laundry was down this hall, but the sound of hammering was discouraging, unless the laundress had taken to beating the dirt out of the hotel's sheets and towels.

Sabrina just wanted to find the laundry and exchange her wet clothes for a bathrobe. When Matt saw her come into the lobby soaking wet again, he shook his head in disbelief and mouthed "laundry" before turning back to a customer. That paled in comparison to Sam's reaction when she and Lima returned to the dock. He was still laughing as she and Lima made their way up to the parking lot where she handed over the keys to her station wagon to Lima.

At least Lima was on his way home—Sabrina didn't like how exhausted her friend had looked—taking Calvin with him. Lima would grumble about having to watch the tiny bird, but Sabrina knew he adored Calvin. She would pick Calvin and her car up on her way home, and check on Lima.

"Pssst! Hey! Come here!"

Sabrina looked around again, but didn't see anyone until a head, resembling a large brown-spotted egg, popped out from behind a nearby doorsill and a withered hand beckoned for her to come closer.

"Please?" Sabrina ventured a step toward the door, but the man had disappeared again. Sabrina sighed. Her clothes were starting to chafe as the cloth stiffened with drying salt, but she was unable to turn off her curiosity long enough to walk away. She went to the doorway and knocked on the half-open door. A hand shot out and pulled her inside a dark room, slamming the door shut.

"What—"

"Shush!"

Sabrina shut her mouth, wondering as she did so why she didn't feel threatened. Perhaps it was the one glimpse she had of the small, ancient man who had kidnapped her. It was hard to feel threatened by a person who looked like he would blow away if she sneezed.

A flashlight popped on and was directed into her eyes. "I need a witness. You'll do," said a crackling, whistling voice, and she felt a small hand clasp around her arm. She was pulled with surprising force across the dim room. Her eyes were adjusting now, and she could make out tables and chairs stacked against the wall, and shelves of what looked like table linen. Some sort of storeroom, then. What she couldn't make out, though, was why her kidnapper was pulling a small wooden cart as he led her toward the opposite side of the room.

"Almost there, almost there." Then he cursed as his cart got hung up on the leg of a chair.

"Would you mind telling me your name and what we are doing?" Sabrina stumbled over a large box, producing an ominous breaking noise. Dishes?

"I'm Guy Fredericks, but I don't particularly care who you are. I just need a witness."

"A witness to what?"

The cart came unstuck at last, and grumbling, Guy Fredericks dragged her toward a door outlined by bright light. He pushed it open a crack and peered through the opening, and then looked over his shoulder at Sabrina.

"Well? What are you waiting for?"

Sabrina maneuvered around the cart so she could see. She was looking into a large, empty ballroom. Arched, fanciful windows drew in abundant sunshine, which illuminated the polished wood floors and white walls patterned with small shell designs. Real shells adorned window frames and the massive fireplace at the end of the room.

"See? See?" Guy said, his breath whistling with excitement.

Sabrina saw, but failed to grasp its importance. There were two workmen on the opposite side of the room, working on what appeared to be a hole in the wall. One was reaching inside the wall, while the other one leaned forward for a closer look.

"They think they're going to get away with it!" Guy cackled. "But they're not, not with you here!"

Sabrina began to have a bad feeling about this whole thing.

The workman with his arm in the wall looked surprised and said something to his companion. Then he pulled out what looked like an oversized wooden drawer.

"Hee, hee, hee," squealed Guy.

Both of the men looked inside the drawer, and then the first one reached in and pulled out a bottle.

"Get him!" Guy shouted and pushed Sabrina through the door. "Don't let him get away with it!"

Sabrina fell through the door into the bright ballroom, wondering how in the world she got herself into these things.

"Stop," she called forcefully, "in the name of the Comico Island Ombudsman's office!"

Chapter Twenty-eight

"Grandpa Guy knows where every rum-running hole in the lodge is hidden. I'm always finding old bottles under his bed, but he won't tell me where he gets them. He must have seen the workmen today and thought they were trying to steal his stash in that secret drawer. Of course, they were just fixing some water damage, but Grandpa didn't know that." Matt Fredericks looked across at his grandfather, who was happily engaged in blowing up his enemy's boats in a rousing game of Battleship.

"He had me convinced they were stealing something," Sabrina said. She hoped the workmen wouldn't tell Matt how she came charging across the room, flashing her old movie rental card at them. It was gold, and she thought they might mistake it for a badge.

They hadn't.

"She stopped them, Matt my boy, stopped them from robbing the bank." Guy looked up from his game and nodded in appreciation at Sabrina.

That he had disappeared, leaving Sabrina to confront the workmen, did not help matters. It wasn't until Sabrina, clutching the evidence in the form of a prohibition-era liquor bottle, had marched the two protesting men down to the lobby that things became clearer. It took Matt only a few minutes to deduce that his grandfather was behind the whole fiasco. He apologized to the workmen and escorted Sabrina to Guy's room.

"Grandpa pretty much lives in the past now," Matt said. "Grandpa Guy, what year is it?"

"Nineteen twenty-eight," Guy said promptly. "You make sure you stay out of Mama's way. She's out there sticking shells into the steps and if you step on it and mess it up, she cries. She cries when Daddy doesn't come home at night too, and sometimes I see her sticking shells into the walls in the middle of the night. Don't like to see her cry." Guy turned moodily back to his game.

"For a while he was in the fifties, but he's been stuck in the twenties for a couple of years now. That's when the bottles started appearing."

Guy looked up from his game and wheezed a cackle. Sabrina had discovered that the small wooden cart Guy carted around was to hold his oxygen tank. He had emphysema, and Matt said he abandoned the fancy roller the oxygen tank had come with, in favor of a rickety, wooden garden cart.

"I went to work on one of William McCoy's ships a couple of times," Guy said, and paused to cough for what seemed like forever. "Out there behind the Rum Line, with nigh on $200,000 worth of liquor on board. Bill used to be a boat builder in Daytona, until he decided to start running rum, and it was him who came up with the idea of the rum rows. That way his ships were safe and secure behind the territorial line where the Coast Guard couldn't get to him, and the smaller boats ran back and forth between his boat and shore, avoiding the Coast Guard the best they could. I heard that up in New York, they'd have sixty or more boats on rum row, and some of them with banners out advertising their wares, and prostitutes on board to entice the buyers. We never had anything like that off Comico, but it was impressive enough, let me tell you.

"Dad thought it would be a good way for me to get to know the business, so he asked Bill McCoy if I could help load Johnny Walker Red and Bacardi onto the speedboats that would run for the shore. And those boats were something else, let me tell you! Some of them were fitted with aircraft engines, machine guns and armor plating, and they kept cans of oil handy to pour on the hot exhaust manifolds to create a smoke screen when the Coasties got too close. You had to be careful of the pirates, though. We caught one sneaky bastard who was waiting to signal his crew to come aboard and rob us blind, but we caught him and sent him on the next ship to Bermuda. Dad caught 'em sneaking around the lodge sometimes, too, and boy, he knew what to do with them. Nobody ever saw them again. Didn't pay to cross Dad.

"Those pirates, they could be anywhere. They're here now, you know, after my stash. Caught one sneaking around the other night. Scared him silly when he saw me."

"Grandpa, are you sure you didn't just catch the maid in your room again? Remember, I told you Rosie comes in every day to clean your room. I wish you wouldn't hide behind the door and jump out at her, or set booby traps. It took me forever to find a replacement when the last one quit." Matt looked beleaguered.

"And that man," Guy continued, ignoring Matt, "coming around and asking all those questions. Thinks I'm stupid, thinks I'm going to tell him everything I know about Dad's business, just because he played a game with me. I sunk all his battleships and showed him the door."

"Mr. Olgivie is just being nice, Grandpa. He's not going to want to play any more games with you if you're rude to him." Matt turned to Sabrina. "Walter Olgivie has been playing Battleship with Grandpa."

"Walter?" Sabrina tried to imagine the wealthy, self-absorbed businessman taking the time to play a game with a senile old man. "That doesn't sound like something Walter would do if you held a gun to his head."

Matt looked defensive. "I thought it was very nice of him."

"What do you two talk about, Guy?" Sabrina asked.

"Women and drink." Guy winked at Sabrina. "I told him about the house over in Waver Town where all you have to do is wave a few dollars in the window, and you can—"

"Go back to your game, Grandpa. I'll come by later and play with you." Matt steered Sabrina out of the room before she could ask any other questions. "We need to get you to the laundry. You may want to think about taking up another sport, Sabrina. You don't seem to be getting the hang of kayaking."

"I thought I was doing good!" Sabrina clamped her mouth shut, though, when she realized it was better to let Matt think her utterly incompetent at kayaking than try to explain what had gone on at Rainbow Island. She didn't relish running into the Hummers when they returned from the island, which should be soon.

"I'll skip the laundry, I think. My clothes are almost dry at this point." Wrinkled and stiff, perhaps, but pretty much dry.

"Perhaps I can lend you a comb?"

Sabrina didn't have the heart to tell him that a comb wouldn't do a lick of good at this point. She needed a hair transplant to remove the boisterous tangles from her curls.

"Why is Walter Olgivie pumping Guy for information? Don't you find that odd?"

As he walked, Matt was running his finger over a windowsill to check for dust. He looked up, startled. "I seriously doubt *that.* Believe me, Grandpa Guy has a very vivid imagination. Lately, he thinks everybody is after his stash, but you have to remember that he doesn't have a stash. He was still a kid when prohibition ended."

"But Guy knows something, or how else would he have known the workmen were about to run across that secret drawer today?"

The bottle the workmen had found was empty, just an illegal crud of dried 1920's liquor in the bottom of the bottle. But what else might be hidden in the lodge's various hiding holes? Something in which Walter Olgivie was interested, Sabrina suspected. Why else would he be playing Battleship with Guy? Not out of the generosity of that cold heart, that was for sure.

"Oh! So much has happened, I almost forgot. There's a man staying here, a big, bald man in the leather jacket. I saw him—"

Too late, Sabrina realized she was about to reveal what happened at Rainbow Island that morning. She suspected the truth would be out of the bag once the Hummers returned home, but she could hope, couldn't she? But she needed to warn Matt about the man.

Matt's look was quizzical. "Fred Young?"

"Is that his name? I saw him, er, sneaking around the Hummers last night. With what happened to Sophie, I thought it disturbing. You may want to keep an eye on him."

Matt frowned. "I will."

"I'm wondering if maybe he isn't a reporter."

"A reporter? But that doesn't make any sense. Fred Young's been here all week. How did he find out about—" He stopped suddenly.

"Dennis Parker? I take it you haven't seen the papers today. The secret is out of the bag. Everyone knows he's here."

Matt shook his head. "I told Michael and Dennis that it would be impossible to keep his presence here a secret, especially after what happened to Gilbert. But I promised to try."

"Well, you did a good job. I didn't know who he was." Sabrina tried to keep her voice dry and matter-of-fact.

They'd reached the lobby and Matt raised a distracted hand before making a beeline for the front desk.

She glanced at her watch and saw that the Hummers should be arriving back right about now. Though she cringed at the very thought of seeing them, she needed to get it over with.

On the way down the path to the marina, Sabrina tried out a few lines. One was, "Oh, you must have met my twin sister, Serena." Another was, "Sorry about the disturbance, the old man keeps escaping from the home." Blaming it all on Lima was very appealing, but Sabrina didn't think either idea was going to fly.

She was saved from any immediate excuse-making, because as she reached the marina she saw that she had missed the Hummers' return. They had already scattered to their rooms.

Except for one.

As she turned back up the path, she heard a man shouting. She followed his voice to a small gazebo overlooking the cove, where he stood with one imperious foot on a bench as he talked loud and fast into his minuscule cell phone.

"Tom, you tell them if they don't quit all this talk about plumbing and roof repair that I'm going to kick every last one of them out of the building. Maybe I'll tear down the whole damn building, how does that sound? Can't worry about a few bugs and rodents if you don't even have a roof over your head, now can you? You tell them that, Tom, do you hear me?"

Walter Olgivie looked up and saw Sabrina standing nearby. He clicked his phone shut.

"Now you've taken to eavesdropping, as well as spying, have you?"

Chapter Twenty-nine

"The others may like you, but I don't trust you as far as I can leverage you," Walter continued. His face, a marvel of modern medicine, stayed smooth despite his sneer of derision. "Always lurking around, asking questions, sneaking over to spy on us at our sessions."

"I was not! My friend and I went for a kayak ride and happened to stop on that island. We had no idea you were on it." It was amazing how easy it was to be indignant when you were in the wrong. Sabrina almost had herself believing her own story.

Walter snorted. His dark sunglasses made it difficult to read his expression, but there was no doubt of his disgust for her excuse, which only made Sabrina angrier. He didn't know *for sure* she was lying. It was possible she was just out for a kayak ride, now wasn't it?

"You may not trust anyone, Walter, but there are trustworthy people in this world." There, that sounded good. Not that it applied to her at the moment.

Walter snorted again, and stood staring at her for a moment while Sabrina tried not to squirm like a berated child. Sweat stains were drying on his expensive shirt, and dirt stains caked the knees of his slacks. Even his well-trained silver hair looked rumpled.

"Well? What did you see?"

"See?"

"When you were spying on us. What did you see?"

"I wasn't spying! And I didn't see anything." Though she really wished she had. What was going on at the Hummer sessions? "What I wanted to ask you was why you've been spending time with Guy Fredericks."

"Who?" Walter frowned. "Oh, the old man."

"He says you've been asking him questions about his father's rum-running days."

"Sure. It's interesting. He reminds me of my grandfather, who passed away when I was a kid."

Sabrina studied him, but she couldn't judge whether it was sincerity or bologna oozing through his pores. She was pretty sure she caught a whiff of processed meat.

"Are you sure you're not looking for information about something specific?"

Walter shrugged. "I'm a collector, I've not hidden that. A lot of times, these old guys have stuff hidden away that's worth a gold mine, and they don't even know it. If I sweet-talk them a little, they'll sell it to me for a song."

"And then you make a mint off their ignorance."

"How do you think I got to be wealthy? By being a nice guy?" Walter flashed big white dentures in an orca smile.

"So what of value are you hoping to find?" Sabrina tried to hide her distaste in the interest of garnering information.

"I'm just looking for things for my own collection. I'm always on the lookout for interesting collectibles and I keep an eye out everywhere I go. You find some mighty interesting things if you know where to look."

"Like X-rated driftwood?" It was a leap in the dark, but Missy had mentioned that a man driving a Jeep with a hotel logo, similar to the Shell Lodge's rental Jeeps, came to see her display two days before it was vandalized.

Walter looked amused. "Sure. Like that."

Was there a connection? Could Walter have broken into Missy's house to steal her driftwood? Sabrina couldn't imagine it. And what about the other break-ins? That seemed even more unlikely. Perhaps Walter was simply the bored, wealthy collector he portrayed himself.

"Have you had the Jeep all week?"

"I rented it when I got here. Why?"

"I don't suppose you drove into town Tuesday night? Someone almost ran me into the water." Sabrina had asked Matt who had access to the lodge's five rental Jeeps. Walter and Michael were the only ones who had rented a Jeep for the entire week. The rest of the guests were content to rent a Jeep for an hour or two as needed, and no one besides Walter and Michael had access to a Jeep late Tuesday night. At least officially. Sabrina couldn't help but notice how easy it would be for someone to swipe a pair of keys from behind the desk.

Walter looked irritated, an expression that seemed to perpetu - ally linger on his face. "Of course it wasn't me."

Of course it wasn't.

"I understand you're having trouble with your tenants." Sabrina gestured to the phone he still held in his hand.

"Has my personal life suddenly become your business? Someone should have sent me a memo."

With that, Walter strode away.

Sabrina decided to go check on Sophie. She wondered how the girl was holding up after the attack last night.

Patti opened the door of Sophie's little cottage.

"Sabrina!" Patti stood blocking the doorway, her arms crossed over her chest. "What are you doing here?"

"I came to check on Sophie. How is she doing?"

"She's had a rough morning. None of us were happy to be interrupted at our session. Why did you do it?"

In the face of Patti's hurt bewilderment, Sabrina abandoned any pretense. "I'm trying to help you, Patti, but no one will tell me anything. I was trying to figure out what was going on so I can help."

Patti's dark eyes were skeptical. "What we do at those sessions is private, Sabrina. If you want to help us, you'll give us our pri- vacy. It's very important to all of us to control this humming in our heads. These sessions are the only way to help. We only have a few more days, and if I can't get rid of this Hum by Saturday, I don't know what I'll do!"

"Patti, I'm sorry! I was trying to help, I really was." Sabrina rushed to give the other woman a hug, and Patti clasped her tight. When they let go, Sabrina saw there were tears in Patti's eyes.

"What's wrong, Patti?"

"I guess I'm wondering if my life will ever go back to normal. It seems like everything is falling apart, and I don't know how much longer I can take it. Enough about me, though. Can you sit with Sophie a few minutes while I take care of a few things? Dennis said he would be by in a little bit, so if he gets here before I do, you can leave her in his care." Patti winked.

"Of course, I'd be happy to."

Patti retrieved her purse and departed, leaving Sabrina to sit next to the sleeping Sophie. The girl's bruises looked much worse this afternoon, blooming dark and purple across her cheekbone.

After having suffered awful abuse from her boyfriend, she came to this peaceful island to face only more violence. Who would do this to her, and why?

"Oh, oh," Sophie moaned, turning her head from side to side. "No, please, don't!" She put her hands in front of her face. "Please don't hurt me anymore!"

"Sophie, wake up! You're having a nightmare. Wake up!" Sabrina shook the girl's shoulder, but at her touch, Sophie screamed with fright and curled up into a ball. "Sophie, you need to wake up. It's just a nightmare."

Sophie stiffened and stopped crying, though she kept her eyes squeezed shut.

"Calm down, it's only a nightmare." Sabrina patted the girl's back until she rolled over.

"Sabrina?"

"Yes, it's Sabrina. Patti went to run some errands so she asked me to sit with you." It was amazing how gratifying it was to hear Sophie call her by her real name.

"Oh." Sophie put her hands over her eyes. "Oh, it was awful! He was in my room, and he was punching me. All I could smell was fish when he was holding me down on the bed, and I was pleading with him to let me go, or at least tell me what he wanted, but he wouldn't say anything. Poor Dennis. I had a nightmare last night and he tried to hold me to calm me down, and I screamed and screamed. I don't think I ever want anyone to hold me again, isn't that awful? I think I'm going to tell Dennis that he needs to find someone else. Now that I know he's famous, I know he can find someone better than me. It's for his own sake, because I'm not going to be any good to anyone ever again." Sophie's shoulders heaved as she tried to contain her sobs.

"Sweetie, it's okay, it's okay," Sabrina murmured, patting Sophie's back. "You can't make any important decisions right now, not when you're feeling like this. When you're afraid, it's tempting to take the easy way out, but you have to believe things will get better."

"I just want to feel safe again. Things have gotten so bad these last few months, and now I can't think straight with this noise in my head. It feels like everything is going bad, and I can't seem to do anything to stop it." Sophie's voice was soft as she reached out to clutch Sabrina's hand. "I want this Hum in my head to stop, and then maybe I could figure out everything else."

"Let me show you something I do sometimes, when I'm feeling vulnerable. I visualize that I'm donning a coat of armor, you see..." In a hushed voice, Sabrina talked Sophie through the visualization, and the girl was beginning to look calmer when they heard a quiet knock on the door.

Sabrina went to let in a lovelorn and resolute Dennis Parker.

"How is she?" He brushed past Sabrina to rush to Sophie's side.

"Dennis!" Tears overflowed, and Dennis leaned his head close to the girl's, holding her hands and murmuring soundless words in her ear.

Sabrina watched them for a moment, feeling like a voyeur but unable to resist.

Then she left, closing the door softly so as not to disturb the young lovers.

Her conversation with Sophie had revealed one clue about the girl's attacker, one that Sophie did not mention the night before. It might or might not be important, but it reminded Sabrina of something else that she had been meaning to pursue. She turned down the path toward the marina.

With luck, Sam was engaged elsewhere.

Chapter Thirty

Sam Myers, as he was known here at Shell Lodge, came down the path from the main lodge and saw an apparition in orange and olive green with a mane of riotous blond curls standing beside his boat.

"Sam? Are you in there?"

Curious, because there was something furtive about her repeated glances over her shoulder, Sam stepped behind a tree to watch.

"Sam, I need to speak with you about…about…something I left on the kayak this morning. I left my shoes." She looked down at her white sandals. "I mean my purse." She shoved the purse she carried behind a nearby potted palm. "I left my purse on the kayak and I need to talk to you about it. Are you there? Sam?"

Seemingly satisfied that the boat was empty, she looked over her shoulder once more and stepped over the railing so she stood with one foot on the boat and the other on the dock. Not surprisingly, the boat chose that moment to strain outward against its lines, and Sabrina looked down with a horrified expression as the gap between vessel and dock widened. She made a desperate grab for the railing and swung her foot onto the boat.

Good form, Sam thought, watching her smooth out her skirt and step daintily down to the main hatch.

Cat jumped down from where he had been napping in the stowed sails and Sabrina shrieked. Cat jumped straight back up in the air and they gaped at each other in mutual terror and surprise before Cat shot off down the dock.

Sabrina stood, chest heaving, and put a hand to her wrist to time her pulse. Then she turned to study the locked hatch. She tugged on it, but it would not open.

Sam wondered how long it would take her to give up, but he underestimated her determination. Balanced precariously on the narrow walkway, she circled the cabin until she found the pop-up hatch at the front of the cabin. She pulled at it, and Sam groaned as he realized he forgot to latch it this morning. But it was impossible for a grown woman to get into unless—

Sabrina retreated off the boat long enough to retrieve something out of her purse. When she returned to the hatch, Sam saw that she was holding a screwdriver, which she used to unscrew the stabilizer bars. After a few moments, she was able to lay the hatch flat onto its back. It was still a tight fit for her, however, and Sam enjoyed watching her wriggle and gasp her way through the hatch. He was beginning to wonder what she would do if she got stuck when she popped out of sight like a cork shot from a champagne bottle.

What was she looking for? Everything was well hidden. He'd made sure of that after what happened last night. He still couldn't get the smell of fish out of his sheets. But what had made her suspicious of him? And what would she do when he caught her on his boat?

He intended to find out.

Sabrina dropped down onto a neatly made bunk, breathing hard from the exertion of squeezing through the hatch. It was touch and go there for a minute, and she hadn't let herself think about what she would do if she got stuck. Perhaps she needed to lose a few pounds after all. Thankfully, though, no one had observed her struggle.

There were several closed lockers in the sleeping cabin, and Sabrina hesitated for a moment before deciding against searching them just yet. Maybe if she had time. Right now, she wanted to see what was in the box under the table. Why had Sam stowed it so quickly when he heard her voice two nights ago? What was he hiding?

She intended to find out, especially now that Sophie revealed her attacker smelled like fish. Sam's windbreaker had smelled distinctly of fish. But why would Sam attack Sophie? Sabrina needed more information, and she simply refused to think about what happened the last time she went looking for more information. She'd decided to wipe the memory of Rainbow Island from her mind.

The box wasn't under the table.

Sabrina stood up, and surveyed the cabin in dismay. It wasn't that it was large. Actually, the cabin was quite compact, paneled with dark wood and containing a small galley and a dining booth upholstered in a serviceable tropical print. The problem was that there were lockers tucked everywhere. It would take hours to search all of them, and she still wouldn't be sure she found every one.

Well, perhaps she would get lucky. Sabrina was a big fan of luck, not that her enthusiasm for the lady had ever panned out.

Sabrina began opening lockers at random, finding cans and boxes of food, and other items that she labeled "boat stuff" in her mind. She had no idea what they were, but they looked like they belonged on a boat. She turned to find Sam standing behind her.

"Sabrina!"

She stopped screaming. "I—I was looking for you."

"It looks like you were looking for toilet paper."

Sabrina looked down at the roll she held in her hand and shoved it back into the locker. "I thought you might have some—I was looking for my...purse. I left my purse on the kayak." Ah, there was her cover story, remembered in the nick of time. Hopefully, he wouldn't remember that she wasn't carrying a purse when she got on the kayak this morning. She had the foresight to leave it at the front desk or it would have been dunked along with everything else.

"This one?"

She blinked at her purse. Where on earth…? "Yes, that's it. Thank you!"

With that she tried a breezy exit. It worked this morning on Rainbow Island, leaving her audience flummoxed. She saw no reason not to try it again.

She should have known Sam was made of sterner stuff. He moved to block her entrance up the stairs and, as she bounced off his chest, she noticed that he did not smell like fish. He smelled like clean soap and light sweat.

"You manage to pack a lot of stuff in this boat," she commented, as if he had not just aborted an escape attempt.

"At least I'm a better housekeeper than some ospreys I know. They love junk. I've seen nests with hula hoops, toy boats, fishing nets and even a Barbie doll. Of course, you can't overlook the bird's wings. I've seen the wings of both ducks and gulls lining an osprey's nest—just the wings, mind you." Sam put his arm against the wall and stared down at Sabrina with an annoying spark of amusement.

"That's pretty bloodthirsty." She threw a glance back over her shoulder at the sleeping cabin through which she had made her illicit entrance. Sam didn't know she had unscrewed the front hatch and let herself in. It was comforting to know that in an emergency she could make a dive for that exit. She refused to think about what would happen if she got stuck in the hatch.

"The fishing line is the worst, though. The osprey brings it back to the nest and soon it unravels, wrapping fine filament around the bird's body and legs until it can't move and eventually dies."

"I need to get going," Sabrina said, not caring if he heard the desperation in her voice. "Matt is expecting me, and he said, 'Sabrina, if you're not back in ten minutes, I'm going to come down to Sam's boat and fetch you.' We don't want to drag the big boss man from his important work, so…" She made a tentative run at him, but he stood firm, and she backed off. Now what? She certainly couldn't ask him if he was the one who attacked Sophie last night. Speaking of which, she was suddenly aware that in reality no one knew she was on this boat, and Sam *had* caught her snooping. What if he was the one to attack Sophie? What might he do to her?

Sabrina backed toward the sleeping cabin, trying to imagine a way to improve her chances of getting through the hatch quickly. Her glance flew around the galley. Perhaps some cooking oil? Pan spray?

"What are you looking for?" He had followed her as she backed up and was now standing only two feet away.

"Why, I was just noticing this beautiful African violet. It's gorgeous!" Moving so she didn't turn her back on him, which resulted in a small-stepped sideways shuffle, she went over to inspect the small plant sitting beside the sink. "I'm not very good with plants. The children in my class would bring them to me, but they never survived. I kept having to run out and buy plants to replace the ones that died so the children wouldn't know. I'm glad they didn't bring me any pets." She couldn't seem to stop babbling as she stroked the velvety leaves.

"African violets thrive on lots of attention." Sam's voice sounded odd as he moved closer to touch the only small blooming flower. "It's my sister's, so I need to take care of it."

"I'm sure she'll want it back in good shape."

"No, she won't be wanting it back at all. She's dead." His voice was flat.

"Sam, I'm sorry!" Sabrina turned to him, only to find that he was mere inches away. She jumped a little at the nearness of him, but continued her move to pat his arm. She recognized grief and was incapable of ignoring it, despite the fact that he might be a violent attacker. "When did she die?"

"Last year." So much pain in those two words.

Sam's tanned face was dark in the dim light, limned by the golden-white stubble over his cheekbones. His thin lips still bore a trace of the sardonic smile he always wore, but his blue eyes were bleak. Sabrina gazed up at him, unable to move. Even her patting had stopped.

He reached up and brushed a curl off her cheek and Sabrina closed her eyes for a moment.

"Perhaps you would have dinner with me some night?" Sam's voice was soft.

The words acted like a cattle prod, and Sabrina jumped away from him with the alacrity of a shocked calf.

"Is that Matt I hear? Matt! I'm in here!" Sabrina pushed past Sam and headed up the steps.

"Sabrina!"

"It was great to see you, thank you for holding onto my purse…" Sabrina paused as it belatedly occurred to her to wonder how Sam had gotten her purse, but she plowed on. "I'll be right out, Matt!" she called to the nonexistent voice.

"Sabrina."

She slowed her headlong rush. Now that she was safely out of his reach, she looked back over her shoulder.

"What were you really looking for?"

"Whatever do you mean? I'll see you later!" With that she dove out of the door.

It was only as she trotted up the long length of dock that she remembered the disabled front hatch. What would Sam think when he found it?

By the time he did, Sabrina intended to be far, far away.

Henry, the Shell Lodge's maintenance man, offered to drive her all the way to her apartment at the Blue Cam, but Sabrina assured him that she was in the mood to walk. Since she lent her station wagon to Lima, she was lucky to catch Henry leaving the lodge for the day and cadge a ride.

Henry dropped her off near his house on Lighthouse Road, and she started for home. She realized how late it was as her stomach rumbled in protest. She still needed to pick Calvin up from Lima's, and that would give her a chance to check on her friend. She had urged him to make an appointment with Doc Hailey for a check-up, but the old man was stubborn.

As she turned onto Tittletott Row, several cars passed her in quick succession, and then the road quieted. She was almost to the bridge over Down the Middle Creek, the small body of water that separated the fishing village of Waver Town from the more touristy Towner Town. This distinction between what outsiders would see as two halves of the same town did not show up on any map, but the differentiation was very real to the islanders. Up until very recently, feuds between the two groups were an everyday occurrence. For the moment, a truce had been called, in part because of what happened this past fall during the race for the Sanitary Concessionary position, and in part out of the necessity to face the burgeoning tourist threat unilaterally.

There were no streetlights down this stretch of Tittletott Row, except one lone light over the bridge. It produced a parsimonious pool on the pavement, which did not stretch even to the sluggish brown water directly below.

Sabrina stopped to look for cars and then stepped onto the bridge. She heard a car start nearby, and headlights flashed on, blinding her.

She put a hand in front of her face and quickened her step. There was a small parking area and picnic area on the far side of the bridge, for those who wished to fish the creek. It was too late for even the tardiest of picnickers, so the car must belong to a zealous fisherman. The bridge wasn't called the fishingest bridge in the world for nothing.

The car drove onto the bridge, and Sabrina moved closer to the railing. She wished the driver of the car would dim his lights, they were making it difficult for her to see. She put her hand back to her face, hoping the driver would get the message.

The car speeded up and Sabrina pressed herself to the rail. Even though there was plenty of room for the car to get by, she felt better giving him as much room as possible. She wished he would slow down, though. Didn't he see her?

Instead of slowing as it neared her, the car suddenly leapt forward. Sabrina stared in horror as it swerved onto her side of the road, coming right at her.

Chapter Thirty-one

The car's approach seemed surreal to Sabrina. She kept expecting it to slow down as she waved her arms and jumped up and down, but instead the driver stepped on the gas. It was in that horrifying instant she realized the driver fully intended to run her down.

Sabrina turned and began running back the way she had come, but she knew at once that this was futile. The car was speeding along at almost forty miles an hour by now, and there was no time to reach the safety of the woods at the end of the bridge. She looked back over her shoulder and then did the only thing she could.

She threw herself over the side of the bridge.

Her back slammed into the rail, and for a moment she didn't think she was going to make it over. She twisted her body around and shoved herself off the rail, just as the car sideswiped it. The fall seemed interminable, and she clenched every muscle in her body in preparation for the impact, knowing it was far better to relax but unable to convince her body to cooperate. She hoped it was high tide, and that the water was deeper than the mere couple of feet it stood at low tide. She hoped she did not land on anything with teeth. She hoped—

She landed with a resounding splash, sinking into five feet of water and sticky mud. The wind was knocked out of her and her lungs strove for air as she floundered in the ooze. She waved her arms and legs, trying for the surface, but even when she thrust her face above the water, she still could not breathe. Her lungs refused to work.

She sank again, and her struggles were a little weaker as she forced herself back to the surface. This time she managed to get her feet under her and could stand with her head out of the water. Her lungs unlocked enough to permit a thread of air to enter and she concentrated on this success, her chest heaving as she tried to draw in more breath.

Then, suddenly, she could breathe again, and she took in a great lungful of the fetid, river-soaked air. At that moment it smelled better than just-baked chocolate-chip cookies.

Where was the car? She looked up at the bridge, but it was dark except for the one paltry street light. The driver of the car could have stopped just off the bridge and be coming down the bank to see if he had gotten her. The only thing working to her advantage was that the moon had yet to rise, and the night was very dark. She might not be able to see her attacker, but he couldn't see her either.

A flashlight flicked on, and began playing over the slow-moving water.

Then again, maybe there was nothing working to her advantage.

The beam swept toward her and Sabrina ducked her head underwater and began swimming toward the bridge. The water should be muddy enough to shield her progress. She hoped. Her back prickled as she considered the possibility of a gun training on her.

But no shot came, and with a few discreet trips to the surface for air, she reached the relative safety of the rickety bridge pilings. Once there, however, she realized how skinny they were.

Still, she felt safer and risked standing up to see if she could see anything. The flashlight glow had disappeared, but that didn't mean someone wasn't still out there. Waiting.

Beginning to feel the various aches and bruises that permeated her body, and to wonder what type of animals might be lurking under the surface of the water, Sabrina settled in and prepared to do some waiting of her own.

Lima insisted on calling Doc Hailey. Sabrina was glad that he was old-fashioned enough not to automatically think of an ambulance. She didn't feel up to the noise and flashing lights right now.

Calvin ran up and down her arm, pecking at the numerous specks of partly dried dirt. He considered it his solemn duty to remove dirt and bugs from her skin, as he would if she were another bird, and in quieter moments this often included things like freckles and moles. In this case, however, he had plenty of dirt with which to work.

"You think a dad-gummed tourist ran you clean off the bridge? Is that what you really think?" Lima was agitated, pacing the small confines of his kitchen.

"I told you, Lima, there's no reason to think it was a tourist. I don't know who it was." She was beginning to wish she had not come to Lima's, but he would have worried if she had not come by to pick up Calvin.

Well, perhaps not, she thought, remembering that she found Lima fast asleep in his recliner, Calvin snuggled under his chin.

In a fog of weariness after she felt safe enough to crawl from beneath the bridge, she had not been thinking clearly. She managed to twist her ankle climbing up the embankment, and Lima's house seemed the nearest safe haven.

It was too late now to change her mind, and she closed her eyes and wished for a cup of hot tea and some Tylenol.

"But you think someone tried to run you down on purpose?" Lima sniffed, because somewhere along the line he seemed to have decided that the whole thing was an attack of her overactive imagination. He was still worried, yes, but more about her mental stability than her physical health. At another time, this would have worried Sabrina a lot. Right now, she could care less, as long as he stopped telling her that Elvis was telling him to eat another jelly doughnut, and was she hearing any voices in *her* head?

"You look like the ground floor tenant in a two story out-house, you know."

"Thank you, Lima."

"Why would someone try to run you down?"

Sabrina closed her eyes. "Maybe they mistook me for someone else, someone who deserved to be run down. Maybe they were drunk. But maybe it was because I've been asking a lot of questions lately. Maybe I've gotten close to something that someone doesn't want me to."

"You mean in that man's murder?"

"That, or the break-ins. I don't know which." Sabrina pushed Calvin aside so she could touch her ankle with her fingers. She was beginning to think it was broken, probably shattered. Her back ached—a possible ruptured disc?—and her left arm felt numb. That was bad, though a diagnosis didn't immediately present itself. Maybe she was having a heart attack?

A brisk knock on the door heralded the arrival of Doc Hailey, who limped into the house with a shake of his head.

"Lima, you know they pick up trash at the curb these days. No need to stash it in your yard."

"I was wondering what those people were doing, putting those cans out by the road. I'll have to think a spell on that." Lima got up to shake the doctor's hand, and said in what he clearly thought was a whisper, "She's not looking too good, Doc. I don't mean her hair and clothes, either, that's the way she normally looks, at least by the end of the day. She's not sounding right. You know, loopy. You gotta do something."

"I'll take good care of her," the doctor said in his wonderful, creamy, hot chocolate and brandy voice. Over Lima's shoulder he dropped Sabrina a wink. She smiled, despite her aches and pains.

"I hear you've had some excitement tonight." Doc Hailey sat down on the couch beside her and put his old-fashioned black doctor's bag on the coffee table. "And who is this?" To Calvin, who was chattering at him to stay back if he knew what was good for him.

"This is Calvin. He's feeling protective." She scooped Calvin off her lap and put him on her shoulder, where he continued to talk in between forays at the mud in Sabrina's ear. "I jumped off a bridge tonight, so I'm not feeling top-notch."

In her peripheral vision, she saw Lima tugging at his ear and nodding meaningfully at the doctor, who ignored him.

"And why did you jump off the bridge?" The doctor leaned forward, interested in hearing her answer. The doctor's entire body language conveyed his eagerness to understand, to comprehend what she was saying. She didn't at all feel that she was crazy to jump off a bridge, Lima's exaggerated gestures notwithstanding.

"Someone tried to run me over, and I had to jump off the bridge to avoid being hit. Then I had to stay in the water a while, because whoever it was came looking for me with a flashlight."

"How terrible for you. Have you called the police?" Without her even being aware of it, the doctor had begun his examination, running his fingers over the bruise beginning to bloom on her upper arm, the shallow cut on her leg, and bending close to examine her swollen ankle.

"Lima called Sergeant Jimmy, but he was on a call. After Jimmy made sure it wasn't an emergency, he said he'd be here as soon as he could."

"Does this hurt? This? And here?" The doctor continued his examination, and Sabrina found that his touch seemed to draw away the pain. Despite her earlier conviction that her injuries were quite serious, under the gentle brush of his fingers none of them seemed that bad. She even nodded in agreement when he pronounced her ankle twisted, not broken, and her back bruised, not ruptured.

"You need to try to stay off your ankle for a few days to give it time to heal. Since you're not going to do that, I'm going to bring some crutches by in the morning. Now, I think the best thing for you is to go home and sleep in your own bed. I would suggest staying here, but since Lima has an aversion to cleaning products, you'd probably be better off in your own home. I'll drive you."

As he helped Sabrina to the door, Lima was busy gesturing and winking at the doctor, so much so that he looked like an owl on crack. Finally, he resorted to saying in a loud voice, "Doc, I'd like for you to take a look at this bunion on my butt, if you could come in the other room for a minute."

Doc Hailey sighed. Sabrina nodded that she was fine, and he followed Lima into the other room. Sabrina could hear bits and pieces of the conversation, mostly Lima's half, which consisted of statements like, "What if she decides she's Wonder Woman and decides to levitate out her window?"

Whatever Doc Hailey said seemed to appease Lima, at least to the point where he came out and wished Sabrina a good night without sounding as if he was speaking to a person standing on a ledge.

"Lima, I mean it, I want to see you soon," Doc Hailey said as he helped Sabrina down Lima's front stairs, littered with newspapers, and oddly, a toaster. Lima grimaced and shut the door without answering.

"Do you believe me, Doc Hailey?" Sabrina said as soon as Lima was out of earshot. "Or do you think I imagined it all?"

Chapter Thirty-two

"Crackpot!" The woman's voice broke, and she coughed a little to clear her throat. "I'm sorry, but he is. All of them are. You can't understand how much they have damaged our image. Hummers International Incorporated is so public, so visible, that everybody thinks it's what the Hum is all about. But it's not, not at all. 'Voice of the universe' my foot!"

"Veronica, I really appreciate any information you can give me about Hummers International." Holding the phone to her ear with her shoulder, Sabrina unwound the ace bandage around her ankle and thrilled at the darkish blue pouffy lump her ankle had become overnight. Even Doc Hailey would whistle in appreciation when he came by with the crutches this morning.

"I have plenty to say about those two. Joseph Siderius defected, you know. He was a pioneer in the Hearer field, raising the alarm long before most of us knew what was afflicting us. It was because of him that I realized what was happening to me. I respected him, and his opinion, and then he went and started talking about this 'voice of the universe' junk." She snorted. "What a crock. While what we Hearers suffer may not be acoustic in nature—we believe it's a low-frequency, pulsed electrical signal—we *do* know it has an earthly source. We may not know exactly what's causing it, but the idea that it's some spiritual, alien voice is plain ridiculous. It belittles the pain and suffering thousands of us have been enduring for years."

"I understand that some of you disagree on where the Hum is coming from." She'd found Veronica Hillerman's phone number on the Internet, on one of the rare websites about the Hum which was not sponsored by Hummers International. Veronica was part of the Taos movement back in the early 1990's that petitioned U.S. Representative Bill Richardson to look into the Hum.

"That's our problem, I'm afraid." Veronica sounded a brisk, no-nonsense fifty-something, who had no patience for things not done in an efficient, time-effective manner. "If we could all get together and agree on even a few things, we could be a much more unified voice. People would *have* to listen to us. I'm afraid our heyday was back in the nineties, though. Ever since, we've been arguing and fragmenting. I was so delighted when Joseph Siderius started Hummers International. I was even a member for a while. A lot of us were. But over the years, Joseph first seemed to lose interest, and then he started issuing those ridiculous press releases. It was ludicrous."

"Do you know anything about Michael Siderius?"

"We never even knew Joseph had a son until he took over Hummers International a couple of years ago. And then he and that spokesman of his, Gilbert Kane, were all over the news. They seemed to want to make as big a splash as possible. They attracted a lot of members, but they lost a lot of old ones, people like me who didn't want anything to do with that mumbo jumbo. All that crap about communing with the universe and trying to understand what it's saying." Her snort was emphatic. "My goal is simple. I want to figure out what is causing this hum in my head, and I want it to stop. I had a good friend commit suicide to get away from it. She gave up hope that it would ever stop."

"How terrible!" Whatever they professed publicly, the Hummers had one thing in common: their desire to rid themselves of the Hum. Hummers International Incorporated might tout the Hum as a special gift, one that its recipients should revel in, but from what Sabrina had seen, the Hummers wanted nothing more than to silence the invasive noise.

"That's why—and I know this is not nice to say, but I can't help the way I feel—I wasn't sorry to hear Gilbert Kane was dead. He helped put our movement back ten years, and I'd be happy if Michael and Joseph followed him!"

And desperation, Sabrina thought. That was another trait the Hummers all shared. She wondered if she should ask where Veronica Hillerman was Monday night when Gilbert was murdered. Instead, she asked, "What do you know about Gilbert Kane?"

"He and Michael showed up on the Hummers International scene about the same time. My thought is that Gilbert encouraged Michael to take over Hummers International when Joseph started getting senile. I think Gilbert was the brains behind the whole thing. Michael's not a go-getter. The most significant thing he's ever done was to try to make the Olympic gymnastics team, but he choked during the trials. Ever since he's floated from one lackluster job to another, never amounting to much.

"Gilbert was another story, though. Fifteen years ago, he was in charge of publicity for an investment firm and he hired Michael out of college. They both resigned over some sort of scandal involving hiring a PI firm to spy on a rival firm's executives. Gilbert went on to be the spokesperson for a big medical research and development firm. He was fired from there as well, accused of stealing company secrets. That's when Gilbert and Michael hooked back up again at Hummers International.

"I know all this because we did some research on them when we saw what was happening with the group. Gilbert was always brilliant, but unstable, as far as I can tell. He went to Harvard on scholarship, but he took off a semester his sophomore year, reportedly because he was depressed, and then he had to drop out his senior year after he was accused of blackmailing another student to write papers for him. It was like he did it for fun, because he was smart enough to write those papers himself. He did it because he could."

Sabrina mulled this over for a moment. "Can you think of anyone who would actually kill Gilbert?"

Veronica laughed, an ironical huff of breath. "I know twenty people offhand who wouldn't swerve if he stepped out in the road in front of their car." Sabrina winced as Veronica continued, oblivious. "He and Hummers International have drastically decreased the chance that the rest of us will ever be taken seriously again, and that means we'll be stuck with this Hum for life. At times, the thought is almost unbearable." Her voice was bleak. "As far as whether any of them would travel to some isolated island I've never heard of to do it…no. It would take a rare hatred to do that."

"Can you tell me anything else about the Hummers? Anything I can use to help the poor people who seem to be caught up in this Hummers International web?"

"I do feel sorry for them, you know, even though I hate that their misguided actions are hurting our cause. But I know what that desperation feels like, and before you figure out ways to cope, you'll do almost anything to try to stop the Hum. I wish I could help."

"Do you know anything about their retreats? What do they do in their sessions, do you know?"

"No one I know has ever been invited to one of those special retreats. They hold them three or four times a year, but it's by invitation only. I've never wanted to attend, but I know people who still think maybe Joseph Siderius can teach them to control the Hum. They've petitioned Hummers International to attend a retreat, but they're turned down every time. I don't have any idea how they pick who's going to attend."

"Are the retreats inordinately expensive?" Time and time again, Sabrina had asked this question. "Follow the money" was the old adage. If Hummers International was a scam, where was the money? It had not escaped her notice that three of the five Hummers, Walter, Dennis, and Sophie, were most likely wealthy, but what about Lance and Patti? They seemed comfortable, but certainly not rich.

Veronica confirmed what Sabrina already suspected. "The price isn't cheap, but it's reasonable, I suppose."

Sabrina tried another tack. "Have you ever heard any rumors, then, about what goes on at the retreats?"

"No, the people who attend the retreats are very quiet afterward. They never talk about what goes on. I'm sorry I can't do more. The biggest help you can be to those poor people is to convince them to get away from Hummers International. There's something else worth thinking about, as well. Those of us who suffer the effects of the Hum might very well be the miner's canary for the rest of you. We may be the only ones to 'hear' the Hum, but it undoubtedly affects all of us."

After she hung up the phone, Sabrina sat and contemplated what she had learned. When she was done with that, she contemplated her aching body and impressive bruises. She wondered if Sergeant Jimmy had any luck finding the car or truck that tried to run her down. Of course, Sabrina wasn't even sure whether it *was* a car or truck, much less the color, the license number, or the gender of the person driving it. Last night, Jimmy shook his head and told her to go back to sleep and keep her doors locked. The only good thing was he didn't express an opinion one way or another about her sanity, or lack thereof.

Sabrina struggled to her feet and hopped into the kitchen to warm up her hot tea. Calvin was waiting for her by the microwave. He had a premonitory instinct about when she was about to use the machine, delighting in repeating the sounds the buttons made when pushed.

And speaking of extrasensory perception, Sabrina was not at all surprised to hear Sally's voice the next time the phone rang.

"Honey, what in all that's holy is going on down there?" bellowed her best friend from Cincinnati. Sally wasn't even pretending not to know that something had happened. Where did she get her information? By this time of the morning, the entire island knew about Sabrina's near-miss the night before. Anyone could have called Sally, but who was the squealer? Sally would never admit how she came by her information.

"Good morning, Sally. How are you doing this morning?"

"A lot better than you, from what I hear! What happened?" Sally was opinionated, nosy, frequently insensitive, civic-minded to a fault, and Sabrina's very best friend in the whole world.

Sabrina swirled her cup on the table, and Calvin darted after the tag from the tea bag as it fluttered over the side. He was keeping a close eye on her this morning. "Somebody tried to run me over last night. I'm banged up pretty good, but nothing is broken."

"Don't sound so disappointed."

"Of course I'm not!" Though a sneaking part of her thought if her ankle was going to hurt this much, it might as well give her the satisfaction of being able to say it was broken.

"I'm not going to feed into your hypochondriacal fantasies by asking you to detail your injuries to me. I trust you will survive." The only way Sally would be this blasé about her friend's health was because she knew that Sabrina was basically intact. She had other fish to fry. "Who tried to run you down?"

"I have no idea. The police are out looking for the person, but as far as I know they haven't found him or her yet." And the chances they would find the perpetrator on a description of the slight yellowness of the headlights were pretty slim.

"Yes, but who would want to run you down, Sabrina? When you lived in Cincinnati, nobody even knew you were alive, much less wanted to kill you."

Sabrina thought about that for a moment. Was it worth having people know she was alive, if that knowledge made them want to kill her? It reminded her of the old puzzle about the tree in the forest. Would the tree rather have stayed alive and upright, rather than prove its existence by falling so someone could hear it?

Sally was finishing up with "…sure you don't want to come back to Cincinnati? At least you could walk the streets in safety. Well, unless you decided to wear a 'I hate Parrotheads' tee-shirt just before Jimmy Buffett is scheduled to perform at Riverbend Music Center, but then you'd just be an idiot. Honey, the only thing you had to live for before was that horrible, drunken mother of yours, and when she died you were lost. Then you found the lump in your breast. I'm not sure quitting your job here and moving to that godforsaken island was the best medicine for you."

"I'm doing fine, Sally. I think this is a good sign. It means I'm doing my job. I must be getting close to something, or why else would someone be trying to shut me up?" Sabrina looked down at her ankle, seeing it in a new light. Now it seemed to shine with the virtuous glow of an injury received in the line of duty.

"Sabrina, really, how are you doing?" Sally's tone dropped to a solicitous, you-can-tell-me-anything tone. "Are you still having to visualize your armor every day?"

"No, I haven't had to do that for a day or two. I've been too busy to think about it." Actually, having to jump off a bridge and swim for her life made her feel pretty strong. She wondered if she could remember how she felt as she soared off that bridge the next time she was feeling vulnerable. Wasn't saving yourself from a determined killer the act of a brave person? She wished now she had done a swan dive, or maybe a cannonball.

"And you have no idea who it could have been?"

"I've been thinking about that…" And she had, all last night as she tossed and turned, starting at every creak and groan in her apartment. Who would want to kill her? And why now? The fact that she was scaring someone was good, but not if she had no idea how.

"I don't understand how you could have made someone so mad that they tried to run you down. What in the world are you doing on that godforsaken island? Do I need to come and knock some heads together?"

"I'd love to see you, Sally, you're welcome anytime. Calvin misses you."

"You're changing the subject," Sally grumbled. "Have you gone out on a date yet? Honey, you know you're not going out on any dates because you don't have any confidence in yourself. How are you ever going to—"

"It was good talking to you, Sally, but I've got to go. Bye!"

Chapter Thirty-three

Bicycle Bob was humming "Singin' in the Rain" as Sabrina maneuvered herself off of the bright blue moped and undid the bungee cords holding her crutches strapped to the sides.

"Where in the heck did you get that?" Lima sounded irritable. Rain made his joints ache.

Ignoring the raindrops that kept falling on her head, Sabrina arranged the crutches under her arms. Did she have them backward? *Was* there a front and back? "The moped? I borrowed it from May at the Blue Cam this morning."

Lima and Bicycle watched her in fascination as she tried to climb the stairs on the crutches. It took three tries and a near-fall backward before she gained the porch and sank into a rocking chair beside Lima.

"It's raining, you're hurt, and you're running around on a moped?"

"I had things I needed to do."

"What was so important you had to get out in this mess?"

In truth, it wasn't much of a rain. All morning, low clouds had wept a melancholy dribble that was more mist than rain. The rose-colored light reflected through the clouds made the grass appear a glowing emerald and the sky a strange bruised green.

"I had work to do," Sabrina said in a lofty tone. "I decided to revisit the victims of the recent break-ins and see how they were doing." And ask if any noticed the smell of fish on their burglar. It was slim, but it was all she had. Now she had nothing, however, because none of them had noticed a fishy smell.

"And what did you find out?"

"Not much. I went by Hill Mitchell's first, since his was the first break-in. At first he pretended he wasn't home, but he finally let me in."

Lima massaged his knee. "It's a shame what's become of that boy. Both his dad and granddad were such pistols. His grand-dad was sheriff of Teach County back during prohibition, you know. So how does Hill turn out to be as soft as a bag of wet kittens? Makes no sense."

"Then I went to see Maggie Fromlin. Remember, she was staying at the rental cottage and saw the burglar? But she couldn't remember anything else. They're having so much fun that they've decided to stay on a couple of extra days. Then, I tracked Missy Garrison down at the Tittletott House. She was waiting tables and angry because several of her tourist customers were being rude. Of course, she was wearing her 'If you don't live here, go home' tee-shirt, so that might have contributed to their hostility, but who knows."

"I don't know, things are getting pretty ugly." Lima rubbed at a scab on his elbow. "Jimmy came by and he looked pretty tired. He'd been out all night breaking up fights at the bars between the tourists and locals. Oh, and he told me to tell you he didn't have any luck finding your attacker yet, but he was still working on it. Bye, Bicycle."

Sabrina looked up to see that Bicycle Bob had risen and was wheeling his bike down the road, weaving unsteadily. He was too drunk even to mount the bike.

"He always gets worse this time of year," Lima said, watching his friend go with a sad shake of his head. "One year we closed down the liquor store for these couple of days, thinking it might help, but he rode his bike onto the ferry and went to the mainland. As far as I know, that's the only time he's left the island for twenty years."

Sabrina frowned. "What—"

"Oh no, you gotta go. There's Mary, and she's been on the warpath for you all morning. Go, go, go!"

Sabrina looked down the street and saw the rotund, determined shape of Mary Garrison Tubbs rounding the corner by the ferry docks. For a moment, with the memory of her flight off the bridge the night before shining like a newly minted badge of courage, she thought about staying and facing the woman. But she'd never been one of those people to say no to Novocain when having dental work done, so she struggled to her feet and grabbed her crutches. She swung over to the edge of the steps, and then stared down in dismay at the precipice before her.

"Sabrina!" The sound of her name being called in that irate, self-satisfied voice spurred her on. She half-hopped, half-fell down the stairs and swung her leg across the seat of the moped. It took her a moment to remember how to get the thing started, and by the time she did, she could feel the hot flames of Mary's breath practically on her neck. But now she had the roar of the engine to account for her sudden attack of deafness, and without bothering to secure her crutches, she took off with a spurt of gravel.

"See you later, Lima!" she called without looking back.

"*Sabrina!*" The enraged shout followed her down the street as she pinged the stop sign with her crutch at the corner of Tittletott Row, and almost took out an elderly gentleman taking pictures of the lofty mansions.

When her station wagon refused to start this morning, she agreed to accept the moped from May. It was coming in handy, even if she couldn't figure out how she kept activating the horn, or how to turn off the left turn signal.

Sabrina looked around to see that she had somehow ended up in battered, worn Waver Town. She thought about stopping by Nettie's Candy Shop for a blueberry muffin, but decided that she needed to get over to the Shell Lodge. Just as she was looking for a place to turn around on the narrow, pothole-infested street, she caught sight of a bright yellow bike being pushed by an erratic Bicycle Bob. He weaved his way through someone's yard, knocked over a pile of crab pots, and disappeared.

Sabrina hesitated, but concern for the drunken man won out. It looked as if he was headed for home, but she better follow and make sure he got there. Bicycle Bob was never sober, but this degree of meandering inebriation was unusual. She would have to remember to ask Lima why this time of year was worse for Bicycle.

The narrow road that led to Bicycle Bob's house was tucked between two dilapidated houses. The road didn't look like much more than a path into someone's backyard, but she had been this way before, so with confidence she drove through the carport and around the swing set. In the heavy woods beyond the houses, the road twisted and turned through heavy overgrowth, marked here and there by driveways that led to invisible houses. Long after the road seemed to peter out, she kept going, looking for the paths around logs and even wading through a small stream. She'd lost sight of Bicycle, but she knew that he could traverse this road quicker than she with his eyes closed. Double or even triple vision wouldn't slow him down one bit.

Finally, she reached the ramshackle, neon-colored structure that Bicycle called home. The first time she visited Bicycle, she was amazed at the colorful, incoherent murals that swirled over the broken, warped boards of his siding. Psychedelic fish fashioned out of coconuts swam in a sea of net across the front porch, and less identifiable objects made from beer cans marched up the front steps.

As Sabrina negotiated the steps, she called, "Bicycle! It's Sabrina Dunsweeney!"

She knew he was here, as his yellow beach bike was parked near the stairs. She made it onto the porch and ducked under the net, swinging with coconut fish and brightly painted sea shells, to knock on the screen door. A moment later, Bicycle appeared and wordlessly held the door open in invitation.

Some instinctive gene for neatness must have been rooted in Bicycle's subconscious, because with the exception of a work table piled with paint supplies and beer cans on the counter in various stags of dissection, the house was clean and straight. She knew that Bicycle's mother and brother, Sergeant Jimmy, stopped by often to bring him food and paint supplies, but she didn't think they were obsessively cleaning his house. That was all Bicycle.

Even in the last stages of drunkenness, Bicycle was a different person in his own home. He still did not speak, but he swung a hand for Sabrina to sit and opened the refrigerator in silent inquiry. Since the only beverages in sight were alcoholic, Sabrina shook her head with a smile. As she turned to the small living room, she stopped in shock.

Joseph Siderius sat on the couch, and vivid red stains splattered his hands and clothes.

Chapter Thirty-four

After a moment, Sabrina saw that what she first took to be blood on Joseph Siderius was actually red paint. Several cans of it were spread across newspapers on the coffee table in front of him, and he was concentrating on painting designs on a piece of driftwood. Though there were cans of blue, green and yellow paint as well, he ignored them in favor of various shades of crimson and orange.

"Hello, Joseph. I didn't know you knew Bicycle."

Joseph looked up, and it took a moment for his eyes to focus on her. Then his gaze sharpened and he smiled gently as he nodded in greeting.

Sabrina looked around and saw that Bicycle was working on a beer can, using a knife to peel the aluminum into layers which he was arranging into a shape only he could see.

"How long have you two known each other?" She didn't expect an answer, and was not surprised by a burst of loquaciousness from either of the taciturn men. In fact, they had gone back to work on their various projects and did not seem aware of her presence.

Sabrina remembered Michael complaining that Joseph had started disappearing ever since arriving on the island. Was this where Joseph had been? How in the world did Bicycle Bob and Joseph meet? Though after watching them for a few minutes, she saw there was a natural affinity between the two silent men. Both were locked in an inner place, their own reality preferable to the real world.

Sabrina went to sit next to Joseph on the couch and he shifted his weight to give her room. She watched him hesitate between a bright stop-sign red and a darker, rust red before settling on the second color. He dipped the brush into the paint and bent close to the driftwood. As he concentrated on his work, she realized what she had taken for careful squiggles were equations of some sort. Even if she had been mathematically literate, it would be impossible to read them, however, as he had painted hundreds of them across the surface of the wood, overlapping this way and that.

At one point Joseph looked up at her and smiled, and he reached a hand out to lay on Sabrina's wrist. Sabrina clasped it with her own hand, and smiled back. She wondered how this benign man had produced a son like Michael. On second thought, from all accounts, Joseph used to be a different person. How had he metamorphosed from a driven scientist, determined to discover the source of the Hum, into this quiet man who was content to observe the contents of his soul? How could he be teaching anyone how to control the Hum when, as far as she could tell, he didn't speak?

At that moment, she became aware of a vague thrumming sound that gradually grew louder. She looked around to see if Bicycle's refrigerator had cycled on, but the sound was now singing through her head, billowing and falling, throbbing along her nerve endings until all she could do was close her eyes. She felt as if she was falling, swirling down a rushing, humming drain.

Then it was gone, and Sabrina looked up to find that Joseph had removed his hand and gone back to painting his indecipherable equations on the piece of wave-washed wood.

Sabrina was still a little dazed as she drove the moped toward the Shell Lodge. What had happened to her? Was that the Hum? Did Joseph somehow tap her into it, or did she have a particularly nasty panic attack, complete with vertigo and the sound of blood rushing in her ears?

She wasn't sure, but she still didn't feel right.

Sam was pulling in when she arrived at the Shell Lodge. Several police cars were taking up prime parking spots, so he parked the Lodge's Jeep in the loading zone and hopped out.

"I would turn around and go back the way I came, if I were you," he said amiably as he watched her maneuver herself off the moped. "You're persona non grata around here today. By the way, you look like you got hit by a car. What happened this time?"

Sabrina regarded him for a moment, and then shook away her suspicions. After talking to everyone else involved in the break-ins and not finding anyone else who noticed a fishy smell, she was inclined to think Sophie was imagining it.

"What do you mean, turn around and go back the way I came?" She fitted the crutches under her arms, wincing at the raw spots. Her head was still buzzing, and it was difficult to think.

"Matt has been looking for you, and he sounds pretty pissed. He asked if I let you borrow a kayak yesterday."

Sabrina paused. So Michael told Matt about the incident at Rainbow Island. Well, it was embarrassing, but she had expected it.

"That Michael Siderius came around too. Said he noticed the two of us were chummy, and that I better not let you take out any more kayaks if I knew what was good for me. Oooh. I was shaking in my boots."

They both looked down at his leather sandals.

"What have you done to get everybody's panties in a bunch?" Sam had finished unloading the Jeep and stood looking at her with a pile of boxes in his arms.

"It's a long story. I wanted to ask you a question. I saw you looking through a box the other night and it looked like a box of bottles. What was it?" The thrum in her head was making her reckless, but she felt as if she was close, though she wasn't sure to what. The box was something she wanted to cross off her list because she was convinced it was unrelated to what was going on. Sam's expression went blank and her confident assumption of his innocence collapsed.

"When did you see the box?" His voice was neutral, but he couldn't hide his agitation.

"I don't know. The other night." She was being evasive, but she didn't like what she was seeing. She backed up as best as she could on the crutches. "You seem upset."

"My sister was a glassblower. After she died, I kept some of her favorite pieces. I take them out and look at them every once in a while. The other night, someone broke into my boat and smashed them and a lot of other things. They dumped over the cooler of fresh chum and left my fridge wide open so everything stank by the time I got home."

"Somebody broke into your boat? When was this?" Sabrina stared at Sam in incredulity. Here was another break-in she hadn't heard about.

"It was my night off, Wednesday. I usually take the Mako and spend the night out fishing. I didn't get back until early Thursday morning, and by that time everybody was so excited about the attack on Ms. Sophie, I didn't even bother to mention it." He shifted the boxes in his arms, grimacing at the weight of them.

"It's possible that someone ransacked your boat, got splattered with chum, and then went on to Sophie's cottage. That's why she smelled fish on her attacker!" Sabrina was suffused with excitement. It was another piece of the puzzle, and though she wasn't at all sure how it fit, the fact that there were more pieces on the table was encouraging. And besides, she found that she believed Sam's story, which relieved her. She hadn't realized how much she was hoping he wasn't guilty of the vicious attack on Sophie.

Sergeant Jimmy came up the path from the marina and stopped when he saw them.

"Jimmy, I have something to tell you!" Sabrina cried, and Sam slowly turned around. The sergeant and the dock master regarded each other for a long moment, and some sort of understanding seemed to pass between them.

"Sabrina, I need you to step back, please. Nicholas Samuel Myers? Could you please put down those boxes?"

Sabrina looked at Sam. His face was clean of expression as he lowered the boxes to the ground. Several more police officers were coming up the path, and they all stopped when they saw Sam. One put his hand to his gun.

"Jimmy, what—?"

"Sabrina, please get behind my car and stay out of the way. He could be dangerous." Sergeant Jimmy was circling around toward Sabrina, and Sam watched him with hollow eyes.

One of the other police officers said, "Nicholas Myers, I am placing you under arrest for the murder of Gilbert Kane. You have the right to—"

Chapter Thirty-five

Sabrina watched in shock as Sam was handcuffed and put in the back of a police car. He did not look at her as he was driven away.

"What in the world is going on? Sam didn't kill Gilbert! I've found out all sorts of things. You need to listen, Jimmy!"

"Sabrina, please calm down. We don't arrest people unless we're sure we have the right guy."

"But you don't!" Sam couldn't be a murderer!

"Sabrina, I know you liked the man, but you need to calm down and listen to me. Can we please go inside out of the rain?"

Sabrina followed Jimmy toward the lodge's back door, her mind reeling with questions. It made no sense! Why would Sam kill Gilbert? Because Gilbert kicked his cat?

Sergeant Jimmy took her crutches and handed her into a seat near an open window inside the empty restaurant. Sabrina noticed that rain was splattering on the inside windowsill, but made no move to close the window.

"Sabrina, it looks like he did it. His arrest wasn't my decision to make, but I probably would have done it too. The evidence is pretty damning."

"What evidence?"

"We just searched his boat and found Gilbert Kane's camera hidden away, the one we know Kane took to the island in his duffel bag. There are bloodstains on the camera."

"Bloodstains?"

"We haven't tested it yet, but it's a pretty good bet it's the victim's blood. And that's not all we found on the suspect's boat. He had an entire file on the Hummers International organization, and specifically Gilbert Kane and Michael Siderius."

Sabrina stared at Jimmy in shock. Why in the world would Sam have amassed a file on the Hummers?

"You know I'm telling you this in complete confidence, right?"

Sabrina nodded, unable to speak.

"By his own admission, Myers was the last one to see Kane alive, and the kayak with the victim's blood on it had Myers' fingerprints all over it."

"Well, of course they were!" Sabrina felt on safer ground. "He was the dock master."

Jimmy shrugged. "Sure, if it wasn't for everything else. There's more, you know. We know why he did it."

"Why?" She felt like covering her ears with her hands. She didn't want to hear this.

"The suspect's sister committed suicide last year. He blamed Hummers International for her death. She attended one of their retreats, and as soon as she came back she took an entire bottle of Xanax. Myers was convinced that the Hummers drove her to kill herself, but there wasn't any proof of this. She was involved in a bad divorce and her husband wouldn't leave her alone, despite several restraining orders. The conclusion was that she killed herself to get away from him."

"How awful!"

"It gets worse. The husband came after Myers, broke into his house a few nights after the sister killed herself. Myers shot him to death. There were some who thought he might have set up his sister's husband so he could kill him. They looked at Myers long and hard, but eventually cleared him."

Sabrina remembered Sam's flippant comment soon after she first met him: *I was afraid you were going to grill me until I confessed that I cheated on a math test in the fourth grade and killed a man last year.* She'd assumed he was being facetious.

He wasn't.

It made a horrible kind of sense. She had heard the depth of pain in Sam's voice as he talked about his sister. If he thought Hummers International was responsible for her suicide, it was almost believable that he might come after Gilbert. Were Michael and Joseph next on his list?

"But why did he blame Hummers International for her suicide?"

Jimmy shook his head. "I don't know all the details, but the officials in Atlanta didn't find it creditable."

Sabrina shook her head, trying to suppress the tears welling in her eyes. It was silly for her to cry over Sam, but somehow she felt so sorry for him, tortured this long year over his beloved sister's death.

"I'm sorry, Sabrina, but it doesn't look good. It's not a coincidence he's here using an assumed name and posing as a dock master. He's taken indefinite leave from his university, so he must have been planning this for a while."

"His university?"

"He's a professor, or at least that's what he used to be."

"Sabrina!" A frowning Matt Fredericks came toward their table.

"I've got things to do." Despite his bulk, Jimmy rose gracefully to his feet and tipped his hat at Matt as he made his way out into the rain.

"Sabrina, I need to talk to you."

"Matt, did you hear they arrested Sam for Gilbert's murder?"

"They did?" Matt shook his head. "I wondered why they were asking for Sam's employment records." He stared after Jimmy, and then turned back to Sabrina with a stern look. "I've been looking for you. I heard about what you and Lima Lowry did yesterday on Rainbow Island. How could you? The whole reason you were here was because the Hummers were complaining about their lack of privacy! And then you go and interrupt them yourself? It makes no sense."

"I know." Perhaps the trip to the island wasn't such a good idea after all.

"Now, Michael Siderius is insisting that I ban you from the lodge until they leave, and I'm inclined to agree. You've caused more problems than you've solved, Sabrina. I think you should leave now."

Sabrina had nothing to say. She got to her feet and reached for her crutches. Matt's face was determined but regretful as he held the screen door for her. It was his responsible, general manager face, the one he used when he had to fire an unsatisfactory employee. And *she* was the unsatisfactory employee.

"I've spoken with Mary Garrison Tubbs, just so you know."

Sabrina nodded without looking back. Of course he had. Could things get any worse?

"You're fired, Sabrina."

Mary Garrison Tubbs had found her sitting on the front porch of the general store. This time there was no escape.

"What are you talking about, Mary?" Lima glared at Mary, but the woman didn't even blink at his hostile tone.

"I'm saying Sabrina is fired. I've been trying to find her all day, but as usual, she's been off gallivanting instead of doing her job. The council voted last night to remove her from the ombudsman position due to gross negligence." Mary shook her head in disgust. "I can't believe how badly you've messed this up, Sabrina. I didn't have high hopes for you in the first place, but I never thought you'd make things worse, rather than better. You've let us all down."

Sabrina stared fixedly at her hands. Nothing like this had ever happened to her before. She'd always received glowing commendations when she was a teacher.

"Sabrina has been doing her best," Lima said huffily. "She's done a lot of good things."

"Like what? The problem between the tourists and locals has gotten much worse since she started, you know, and Vicki

Carroway is still one step ahead of us. Both Matt Fredericks and Michael Siderius, the two people she was supposed to help resolve their differences, have come to a consensus on only one item: they want Sabrina fired. For goodness' sake, the whole reason she was at the lodge was to help ensure that group's privacy, and then she goes and interrupts them herself. I've heard you had a hand in that as well, Lima. You should be ashamed of yourself." Mary's face was as scarlet as her hair as she stamped one sneakered foot. "It's intolerable!"

"*You're* intolerable, Mary!"

"I understand," Sabrina said, interrupting the face-off between Lima and Mary before it got any more acrimonious. "You're right, Mary, I've let down the entire island and I'm sorry. Of course you are right to fire me. I would fire me, too. I should have quit days ago." She got to her feet. She had to get out of here, now. She felt like she was disintegrating.

"Sabrina…" Lima said.

She shook her head and made her way down the stairs to the moped.

"I'll be out by Monday," Sabrina told Vicki Carroway. "I'll pay this month's rent, but I'll be leaving right away."

The property manager nodded, her eyes bright with malice. Her long silver hair was piled on top of her head, and she was wearing a smart coral suit that made Sabrina realize how wet and bedraggled she was. It was amazing how little she cared.

"Couldn't hack it, could you, Sabrina? Ha! I'm not surprised. I'll be keeping your security deposit, you know, don't even bother asking for that back."

"I wasn't." Sabrina turned to leave.

"By the way, I've got a new group booked to arrive in a few weeks. It's 'Pedophiles Anonymous.' What do you think about that?"

Sabrina hesitated a moment, but it wasn't her job any longer. She shook her head and left without saying a word.

Then she went home to pack.

Chapter Thirty-six

Lima cleared his throat outside Sabrina's door. His throat didn't clear, so he tried again. And again.

The door swung open and Sabrina stood staring at him wide-eyed. "Lima, are you all right? It sounded like someone was trying to start a chain saw out here."

"I'm fine, I'm fine," Lima mumbled, and shoved the bottle of whisky into Sabrina's hands as he entered her apartment. He'd never seen her *drink* whisky, but it had been ingrained in him by his mother that whisky was what a body needed in a crisis. And this was a crisis, Lima saw, as soon as he looked around the small living room.

Calvin was hopping from one suitcase to another, chattering in a worried frenzy. Drawers and cabinets stood open, and piles of knickknacks and clothes littered every available surface.

"Sabrina, what are you doing?" He took the bottle back from her and went to the kitchen to pour himself a shot. He gulped it down, and then poured another in the same glass and handed it to Sabrina.

"I'm packing, Lima."

"I might have been born eighty-something years ago, but I'm not stupid. I can see that. What I want to know is why?" He took the still full glass from her hand and swallowed down the whisky. It did nothing to ease the pain in his chest.

"I'm going back to Cincinnati." She said the words with simple certainty, and turned back to folding a scarlet blouse.

As she was about to put it in the suitcase, she paused, and then dropped it into a box marked "Goodwill."

Lima shook his head and sat in a chair, ignoring the clatter of tins that hit the floor. He should have come earlier. He'd been telling himself for the past two hours that he needed to get off his lard butt and come, but with the way he was feeling and...well, he really didn't want to. He liked Sabrina, he did, but he didn't like dealing with emotional women, and he'd had a feeling that going to talk to Sabrina was going to be like talking a howling cat down from a tree.

He'd been wrong. And late. Sabrina wasn't upset or panicked. She was calm and resigned as she moved around her apartment, discarding her bright wardrobe in the Goodwill box and placing Calvin's toys in a suitcase. He was carrying them out again as soon as her back was turned.

"Why are you leaving, Sabrina? Could you please stop that gosh-dern fiddling and sit down for a minute?"

Sabrina looked up, and though her expression was calm, her eyes were barren. "It's over, Lima," she said, and sat down. "You know what I saw on my way back from Vicki Carroway's office? I saw a sign on the bait shop down by the harbor that read 'Tourist Roast this Sunday.' I heard a vacationing family talking about packing up and going home early because they were so miserable here on the island. Everywhere I looked I saw unhappy vacationers and grumbling locals. It's like a rot is eating away at the fabric of the island, and now it's all falling apart." Sabrina was looking right at Lima as she spoke these words, trying to make him understand what she had seen. Lima didn't need to understand, he'd seen it for himself. On his way here, a man had jumped out of his car and punched another man who had jaywalked in front of his car.

"Sabrina, you can't blame yourself for what's going on. You did the best you could."

"I was right all along, you know," she said, and now her gaze was over his shoulder somewhere, and he felt like he was watching someone on TV. He could watch, but he couldn't break through that smooth wall of impassivity. "I didn't want to take the job. I knew I'd let everybody down."

"Sabrina…" He was helpless. He hated this type of thing, he never knew what to say and he was left feeling dumber than a headlit rabbit.

"I never should have come here at all. I thought everything would change if I moved here. There seemed to be a magic about the place, a special shine that I thought would wear off on me if I lived here. But it didn't work that way. I need to go back to my old house in Cincinnati, and my old job. At least I felt safe there."

"I want to tell you about Bicycle Bob," Lima said, before he even knew what he was going to say, just to shut her up before she said any more irretrievable things. He stopped, and thought a moment, but the interest in Sabrina's eyes convinced him this was the right thing to do.

"Bicycle?" She leaned forward. "Is he okay?"

Lima leaned back in his chair, satisfied with what he was seeing. She wasn't completely frozen inside, no matter how hard she was trying to turn down the thermostat.

"Bob McCall was the kid we all knew was going to leave the island, almost before he could even talk. Some kids are like that. They aren't cut out for this place, more and more of 'em, really. His brother Jimmy, now, he left for a spell and went to ride Harleys in Californ-ee-ah, but he came back and settled down like we all knew he would. Bob, though, he was different. He had that restless look about him, that look that said he wanted to DO something with his life, and those were some big ole' capital letters. He meant it, and right after high school he joined the Peace Corps and went off to Africa or Australia, or one of them beleaguered countries, to help the starving children. Then he did the college thing and went to work at one of those places, the ones that put the ads on TV about how you can save a kid for the price of a cup of coffee a day. He was a lawyer, and his specialty was suing these big companies that tell everybody they're helping the poor, hungry children, and then dump a few rotten apples on them and pocket the rest of the money.

"He got married, and he brought his wife to the island every Christmas, and she was a sight to behold. One of the sweetest, most fragile-looking things you ever did see. Bob adored her, you could see that plain as day. That last Christmas, she was expecting, and I've never seen two people so happy."

Lima found that the clog was back in his throat, and he leaned forward and poured himself a belt of whisky to clear it. Then another, to ease the growing pressure in his chest. He'd pound his fingers with a hammer if he caught a tear in his eye. That would give him something to cry about.

"Then we heard the news. It was a car accident, and Bob's wife was in a coma. They knew right off she wasn't going to make it, but they kept her alive for a while to try to save the baby, but it didn't work. They both died, and Josie McCall held a nice memorial service on the island, though they buried them up north. Bob didn't come. We heard that he quit his job, and Josie didn't hear from him for a long time. No one did. A couple of years later we started hearing rumors about someone living at the old McCall homestead in the woods. It had been abandoned for years after the McCalls decided to move to town. Then we saw Bob. He would come to town for his liquor, and it looked like he hadn't drawn a sober breath for the past two years. We thought he'd snap out of it. We waited for a while, and then Josie started holding little interventions for him, got all of us together to confront him. He was still talking then, and after a while he told us to leave him alone, that he was trying to survive. Did we want to see him dead? That was what got us. He swore if we messed with him in any way, tried to put him in one of those dry-out places like some were talking about, that he would kill himself. We left him alone after that, and he's been like this for twenty years. Tomorrow or the next day is the anniversary of his wife's death, and he always gets worse around then. Then he goes back to being the same old Bicycle, painting his coconuts and riding his bike. He gave up, you see, just didn't want to try no more."

Lima felt very tired as he leaned back in his chair. He felt kind of sick, actually.

Sabrina was silent, her big blue eyes welling with dismay and sympathy. She started to say something, and then stopped.

Lima stood up. He was afraid if he didn't leave now he was going to be sick. "You think on that tonight, and I'll be back tomorrow," he said with as much dignity as he could muster with vomit hovering in the back of his throat.

"Lima, are you all right?"

"My nephew, Kealy, the one I told you got an envelope full of cash? He got another one, and he's going to treat me to dinner at the Pub tonight, so I need to be moving along." Lima felt as if he was on one of those rides at the carnival, the one where they stand you up against the wall and close the door, and the next thing you know you're going around so fast that you're stuck to the wall.

"Your nephew got another envelope full of cash? What in the world is going on?"

"I don't know, but if there's anyone who deserves it, it's him. That side of the family has had bad luck ever since Gerry Lowry committed suicide back in the twenties. Kealy's the only one left now, because the rest of them have either drunk themselves to death or died young some other way."

"Did you say Gerry Lowry? I've been thinking about that note, the one the burglar dropped at the rental cottage. You know, the one that said, 'Mit,' 'Har,' 'Gar,' and 'Fred.' I think I know what it means. And now that you've said that your nephew is Gerry Lowry's only surviving relative, I can't help but wonder—Lima?"

Lima felt an explosion of pain in his chest, and he put out his hand to brace himself on the table, but the table wasn't there and he felt himself toppling in slow motion toward the floor.

"Lima!"

His last memory before darkness closed in was the sound of Sabrina saying "I know I have an aspirin in here somewhere" and "Dammit, is it two breaths and fifteen chest compressions or the other way around?"

Chapter Thirty-seven

Lima Lowry looked old, and that was something Mary Garrison Tubbs did not like to see, because it meant she was old, too. Of course, nobody looked their best laid out on a hospital bed in a paper-thin gown with tubes stuck up their nose. But still…Lima didn't look capable of swatting a fly right now, much less burping the national anthem, which he was known to do on the Fourth of July.

"I have Sara Lowry coming in at four this afternoon, Josie McCall at eight, and Nettie Wrightly has offered to do the midnight shift."

Sabrina Dunsweeney smiled without looking up from where she sat beside Lima's bed, holding his hand.

Mary huffed in annoyance and said, "I happen to love cute little birds, especially in good gravy. How about you?"

Sabrina nodded with the same absent-minded enthusiasm. She'd been like this since Mary arrived this morning, smiling and nodding when spoken to, answering direct questions if necessary, but for the most part saying nothing as she held onto Lima's hand with single-minded determination. At first Mary thought Sabrina had the sulkies, paying Mary back for firing her yesterday, but Sabrina barely seemed to notice that Mary was in the room.

The old man having a heart attack was no surprise. Mary had been after him for years to get himself checked out, but it was like arguing with a stop sign. Couldn't get him to do anything you said. Thinking back on it, Mary should have told him to go kill himself, sure as anything that would have sent him straight to Doc Hailey for a check-up.

Long ago, Mary adopted a sensible diet and an exercise plan, and look at her, her heart was as strong and fit as any eighteen-year-old's. Lima should have listened to her advice, but then, Mary didn't understand why everybody didn't do what she told them to do. She was always right, wasn't she? People might squawk about the way she did things, but they always appreciated the results. She had no patience for people who were too squeamish to get the job done. Take Mayor Hill, for example. Mary didn't understand why the islanders wouldn't elect her mayor—it was just plain stupidity, that's what—but she could have moped about and watched the island go to helius in a handbasket.

Instead, she'd done the island a favor. Hill was a council member for many years while he was florist, before he retired and got strange. With prodding—well, okay, and the judicious use of a little blackmail—Mary got him to run for mayor. It was mainly due to voter apathy that he triumphed. The other candidate was Hoopla McCall, who was running on a one-plank platform to keep the bars open another two hours every night. Hill did what Mary told him to do, and everybody was happy. A perfect case of the end justifying the means.

Hill had squawked a bit when Mary told him it was time to fire Sabrina. For a minute during the emergency council meeting, it looked as if he were going to vote with Nettie and Sondra against her and Bill Large, in favor of keeping Sabrina on. But in the end, Mary had prevailed, as she knew she would. She was only doing what was best for everybody, even if they were too stupid to see it just now.

Mary looked down at her list of things to do: putting together a group of girls to go clean Lima's house, contacting his brother, and making sure Matt Fredericks worked out a way to put up the Hummer group a couple more nights to accommodate the ongoing police investigation. Who else would think to do these very necessary things?

Sabrina was now gazing out the window at the parking lot. Mary didn't understand the woman, she really didn't. Suggesting the ombudsman job for Sabrina was the right thing to do. It needed to be done, Sabrina needed a job, and it seemed like something she could handle. Mary didn't care for the woman much, but Sabrina was part of this community now, and as such, she had to be looked after like everyone else.

The fact that Sabrina screwed up in such a spectacular manner confirmed Mary's basic distrust of the woman's character. But now…Mary didn't know what to think, and she wasn't afraid to admit it. It was hard not to have a little respect for the woman after she saved Lima Lowry's life. Mary heard Sabrina performed CPR for the twenty minutes it took to get an ambulance on the scene—Mary would make sure Hill addressed *that* tardiness at the next council meeting—and then followed the ambulance to the hospital. She hadn't left the man's side since.

"Sabrina, go home and get some sleep. I've got things under control." It wasn't the first time Mary had issued the order, but she was surprised when Sabrina looked up and met her eyes for the first time that day. Almost against her will, Mary softened her voice. "You heard them say he's going to be fine. You did good. Now it's just a matter of time. Go on home."

"That sounds like a good idea. Thank you, Mary." With that, Sabrina leaned forward, touched Lima's cheek, and then got up. She hesitated at the door, and looked back.

"Go on," Mary said, already moving to the seat Sabrina had vacated. "You look like a stray dog someone forgot to feed."

That sweet, preoccupied smile, and then she was gone.

Head librarian Iris Hillkins heard the front door open and glanced at her watch to see that it wasn't quite closing time. Not that she would have turned the person away, as long as he or she had legitimate business in the library. Lucas passed away five years ago, and Iris didn't have any pressing reason to be rushing home, even on a Saturday night.

It was Sabrina Dunsweeney, and she looked like she just stepped out of a wind tunnel. Sabrina often looked some variation on this theme, but the wrinkled clothes, flyaway hair and lines around her eyes were more pronounced tonight than usual. Iris liked Sabrina's energy and spunk, and like any good librarian, she knew more about the woman than she would ever share. You can't help but notice what sort of books a person checks out, and wonder about the questions your patrons ask.

Tonight, Sabrina looked tired, but at the same time jazzed, as if she just gulped a large shot of espresso. She had a long night, Iris knew. She must have come straight from the hospital on the mainland.

"Hi, Iris. Is there a computer free?"

"Nobody here this evening. Help yourself. How is Lima doing?"

Sabrina signed the clipboard. "They say he's out of the woods."

"It's a wonderful thing you did for him." Iris wished someone could have been there for Lucas, but he was fishing by himself when the stroke hit.

For the next two hours, Iris read quietly while Sabrina Dunsweeney worked her way from the computer to the microfiche machine to the original document section, where she asked permission to look through several old diaries. Iris helped when she was needed and stayed out of Sabrina's way the rest of the time. She wasn't sure what Sabrina was up to, but she recognized that it was important to the woman, so important that Sabrina didn't even realize that closing time had come and gone. Iris wasn't about to mention it. In her eyes, Sabrina was a hero.

Iris did think it was interesting that prohibition on the island had become such a hot topic lately. She couldn't remember any time in the past fifty years that some of these books and microfiches had been requested, and here they were being perused twice in the same month. Of course, Iris prided herself on not letting herself think too much on the items her patrons requested.

More, she would never betray the inherent confidences they placed in her discretion.

Iris was thinking about calling to see if the Pub would deliver her some dinner when Sabrina leaned back from the table and smiled with deep satisfaction.

"Ah. So *that's* what it's all about."

Chapter Thirty-eight

All day Sunday, Comico Island was abuzz with rumors and speculation. The frenetic energy gripping the island was not unlike the dreadful, excited animation that preceded a hurricane's approach. Every piece of news, no matter how insignificant, was vital, every rumor was amplified, and every person was eager to talk.

There was so much going on! It wasn't every week that a murder occurred on the island, and not just any murder either. The news teams made it clear that if the death of Gilbert Kane wasn't important enough to rate national news, basketball player Dennis Parker's involvement certainly did. Throwing in a strange cult and a comely model made the story all the more fascinating. It was true, it would have been more interesting if Dennis Parker was guilty of the murder (perhaps in cahoots with his model girlfriend?), but now that someone had been arrested, the media were circling like vultures over road kill.

The news teams were asking locals and vacationers alike their reaction to the news that Nicholas Samuel Myers had been arrested for the murder of Gilbert Kane. The fact that the people they interviewed did not know the victim, or the suspect, did not stop the journalists. It was not easy to find the dumbest person on the island to interview for national news, but, as usual, the news crews took up the challenge with relish.

Most of the islanders affected indifference to the media, though many of them had taken to dressing in their finest clothes and finding various reasons to walk by the plastic-faced men and women brandishing microphones.

Lima's heart attack and the new island ombudsman's abrupt termination were also good for a minute or two of gossip currency. Another tidbit kept cropping up as well, though no one knew where it came from, or why everyone else was so interested in it. The Shell Lodge was infested with termites, it seemed, and major demolition was going to start tomorrow.

This piece of news was tacked on to the bigger stories of the day, so as one person stopped another in the street, the conversation might go something like this:

"Sure glad the rain stopped. How things going for you?"

"I've been interviewed by three different news crews this morning. You?"

"Just the one, but that was CNN, so I guess that counts for something. Did you hear the news about Sabrina Dunsweeney?"

"No, what happened?"

"The town council fired her. Saved Lima Lowry's life last night, you know. They should be giving her a medal, not firing her."

"I don't know her well, but she always has a smile for me when she goes by. I think it's a darn shame they fired her. How about the Shell Lodge? Did you hear about the termites? Going to tear it down tomorrow, I hear."

"No! Really?"

And so on and so on and so on. Around six o'clock, the news about the termites at the Shell Lodge hit the ears of someone who actually cared.

Chapter Thirty-nine

Even in the middle of the night, discreet spotlights played across the thousands of whelk shells embedded in the walls of the lodge, imbuing them with a wavering mobility they never possessed in life.

The back doors to the lodge were locked. No surprise there. The front door was open, but that avenue led past a sleepy desk clerk watching an infomercial on kitchen knives that were sharp enough to slice concrete and move onto steel beams for dessert.

There were several guards to avoid, but this proved easy. Despite the lights, there were plenty of rustling shadows in which to duck in a hurry, and really, just standing still as the flat-footed guard leisured past with his flashlight trained on the ground was good enough.

The problem of how to get in the lodge was a little more difficult. All the doors were locked, but that wasn't any surprise. With all that had been going on at the Shell Lodge, it would have been surprising if the doors *weren't* locked.

However, it was a nice night, and there were several windows open to admit the brisk night breeze. Most of these windows led into sleeping rooms, which would not work, but one window in the dining room had been left open, barred only by a thick screen. Perfect.

Wait for the guard to pass, and then slide up the screen as quietly as possible. There. Now it was a simple matter to shimmy in through the window and close the screen so as not to attract any unwanted attention.

Creeping through the halls on bare feet, keeping a sharp eye out for the old man. Last time he jumped out from behind a door, screaming bloody murder. The decision to wait for a while on the second attempt was an easy one after that. There was no hurry.

But hearing the news about the termite damage, and more importantly, the demolition work that was supposed to begin tomorrow, put an urgent spin on things. It had to be tonight, or never. And never wasn't an option.

Reading about something in a book in the comfortable, well-lit library, however, was a far cry from trying to find it in the dark, sleeping hotel. Where to start? The lounge seemed like a good bet. Unlike the cottages and the west wing, the lounge was part of the original hotel, and used to be Kenneth Fredericks' office in the twenties. That seemed an obvious place for Fredericks to hide something, so that would be first.

Thankfully, the lounge doors were not locked. For a moment, fleeting doubt—why weren't the doors locked?—but excitement won out over discretion.

That excitement was soon extinguished at the flare of overhead lights, which revealed an array of people sitting at bar tables.

Marilee Howard stood blinking in astonishment at this turn of events.

Chapter Forty

"Right before his heart attack, Lima mentioned that his nephew Kealy received another anonymous envelope of cash. Kealy was the only direct descendent of Gerry Lowry, who supposedly committed suicide back in the twenties. His death has been the subject of rampant rumors over the years. Many people think he was killed because he had a falling out with his smuggling partners." Sabrina looked around the Shell Lodge's lounge and saw she had everyone's complete attention. Good. Marilee took her sweet time showing up, and Sabrina had to talk fast to keep everyone sitting in the darkened lounge.

Marilee Howard, dressed in black jeans and shirt with her long red hair tucked beneath a dark baseball hat, sat at the bar with an untouched soda in front of her. The young girl listened without speaking as Sabrina recounted the events that led up to Marilee's unmasking as the serial burglar.

"Then Lima had his heart attack, and I didn't think about anything else for a while. Yesterday evening, though, I went to the library and discovered some interesting coincidences. Most of the good stuff was in private diaries, not in the news accounts, but it was all there if you knew where to look."

"Sabrina, it's three in the morning, and I don't understand how this connects with Marilee breaking into houses. You should be ashamed of yourself, girl, trying to mess with my driftwood collection!" Missy Garrison glared at Marilee. She had needed no persuading to come this evening once Sabrina promised her the identity of the burglar would be revealed.

Sabrina had a harder time convincing the other two victims of the break-ins to attend this overnight vigil, but both Mayor Hill Mitchell and Maggie Fromlin sat on either side of Missy. This trio of accusers did not seem to faze a defiant Marilee.

"She wasn't trying to mess with your driftwood collection, Missy. She was looking for rum-runner hiding places. That's why she needed the handsaw. It was possible she would have to cut in the wall to find what she was looking for."

"And what was she looking for?" Walter Olgivie had an avaricious gleam in his eye. This was why he was here. After Sabrina came to him with questions about what kind of valuables could still be hidden in forgotten rum-runner hiding holes, he enlisted himself in the operation.

"I don't know what she was looking for exactly. I'm sure she will be happy to tell us." They all looked at Marilee, who showed no signs of happiness or that she intended to tell them the time of day.

"What I want to know is how you knew she would break into the lodge tonight, and what she planned to do." Matt Fredericks looked weary. Only Sabrina's abundant confidence that the Shell Lodge would be burglarized in the near future if he did not cooperate in the sting tonight had convinced him to participate. Sabrina wasn't on his top ten list of favorite people at the moment, but he was too good a businessman not to realize what a messy burglary would do to the hotel's image at this point. The Shell Lodge's reputation was already in tatters after an employee had been arrested for the murder of one of its guests.

"I'm getting to that." Sabrina felt a wave of exhaustion hit and barely suppressed a yawn. She could feel two nights of no sleep catching up with her. "It's pretty simple. Besides Booker Howard, Marilee's great-grandfather, there were four men rumored to be involved in Gerry Lowry's alleged murder, all deeply involved in the smuggling business on Comico Island. Those four men were:

Sheriff Fitz Mitchell, David Harrington, Foster Garrison, and—"
Sabrina paused for dramatic effect—"Kenneth Fredericks."

There was a deafening silence, not at all the reaction Sabrina
was expecting.

"I'm sure it's because we're outsiders and don't recognize the
names, Sabrina," Patti said tactfully. "Perhaps you could explain
further?" She looked tired, but kept stealing pleased glances at
Sophie's rapt expression. When Sabrina had confided in Patti
her plans for the evening, neither were aware that Sophie was
listening. But the plan seemed to tickle the girl so much that
neither had the heart to say no when she pleaded to be included.
Of course, Sophie told Dennis, so there he sat yawning and
trying to look interested.

The last member of their "unveiling the villain" party was
Lance Mayhew. Sabrina wasn't sure who told him about the
plan, or why he was interested, or even that he did not come
upon them accidentally in the lounge while looking for an after-
hours drink. In any case, he sat in the back as always, soaking
up every word uttered.

"Don't you understand?" Sabrina fumbled through her
fatigued memory. Didn't she say it plain as day? Evidently
not. "Did I mention that Maggie's first rental cottage, the one
called Seas the Day, was built by David Harrington, a friend of
Kenneth Fredericks, who constructed the house to be used as a
rum-running depot? Sue Harrington, his great granddaughter,
still owns it.

"All of the houses that were broken into thus far, Hill
Mitchell's, Sue Harrington's, and Missy Garrison's—I'm not
counting the unrelated break-ins that happened here on Shell
Island—were connected in some way to the alleged cover-up of
Gerry Lowry's murder over eighty years ago. Hill is Sheriff Fitz
Mitchell's grandson, Maggie was staying in David Harrington's
old house and—"

"Foster Garrison was my great-grandfather," Missy said.
"I'm living in the house he built. Are you saying that Marilee
was breaking into houses looking for rum-running treasure?"

Her pique had disappeared now that she realized Marilee wasn't interested in her driftwood collection.

Again, they all looked at Marilee, who affected intense interest in the bar napkin soaking up condensation from her glass.

"It looks that way. That's why I hoped Marilee would come tonight. I suspected that she was the guilty party—there were other possibilities, but Marilee made the most sense—but I knew I had no proof, so the only solution was to catch her red-handed. She dropped a note at the rental cottage. I think it must have been her list for the houses she had targeted. 'Mit,' 'Har,' 'Gar,' and 'Fred.' Do you see? It's shorthand. Hill Mitchell's was the first house, Sue Harrington's the second, then Missy Garrison's, and finally—"

"Fredericks. The Shell Inn," Matt Fredericks said.

"Exactly." Sabrina felt light-headed. She'd been on such an emotional roller coaster ride the last couple of days that she wasn't sure how to describe the way she was feeling. Numb was probably the best word for it. Numb, but the Novocain was wearing off.

"Can you please explain again about this Gerry Lowry's suicide, or murder, or whatever it was? You ran it by me last night, but you were talking so quick I didn't understand half of it." Matt ran his fingers through his hair and then looked at his fingers as if baffled about the whereabouts of the rest of his hair.

"There isn't much to tell. Seventeen-year-old Booker Howard found Gerry Lowry dead with a gun in his hand. Sheriff Mitchell held an inquest and they ruled it a suicide. In the news reports it seems pretty cut and dried. But the newspapers don't reveal the whole story, not by a long shot. Like the names of the men supposedly involved in a Comico Island rum-running ring, or the fact that Gerry was rumored to have been cheating his rum-running partners, or that Booker got a job with the sheriff's department soon after Gerry's death."

"How did you set this up? How did you know she would be here tonight?" Sophie leaned forward, her hands clasped in front of her as she watched and listened with intense delight. She could have been watching a movie, or the opera, and Sabrina wondered if she was expected to sing.

"With the help of a couple of people, I spread the rumor that the Shell Lodge was infested with termites, and that demolition started tomorrow." She pretended not to notice Matt wince. This was the part of the plan he disliked the most. "Who knew what the demolition crew would discover? From something Matt's grandfather said, I suspected that the burglar had tried the lodge once already, and that this news would spur her into action. It did."

Marilee waved as they all turned once again to look at her. "Okay, Miss Dunsweeney, you got me, though I wish you would have come to me first, instead of setting me up like this. You've been so nice, helping me with college and everything. Were you doing that so you could get information?"

It was the first words she had spoken since being caught.

"I'm sorry, Marilee, I really am. And no, I didn't suspect you until last night. I've been assisting with your college admissions because I wanted to help you. Would you have confessed to all of this if I had come to you with no proof?"

"Probably not." Marilee took off her hat and ran her fingers through her gleaming red hair. "But you caught me fair and square, so I suppose I'll come clean. You've heard the official version of Gerry Lowry's suicide. Let me tell you the story my Granddad Booker told on his deathbed."

Chapter Forty-one

Booker had lived with guilt his whole life. It was a drink he took every night before bed, an acidic elixir that ensured insomnia and nightmares. No matter how much time passed, and as Booker lived into ripe old age, it was quite a long time indeed, he could not rid himself of that festering, putrid regret.

He told himself that he couldn't blame himself, that he was young when it happened, that they had hoodwinked him. This was a lie, though, a soul bulwark that crumbled nightly with the onset of the dreams. Yes, he'd been young, but he had not been stupid. In some deep recess of his mind, he knew even then what was going on, but was so eager to please that he didn't stand up for himself. He didn't do the right thing.

And certainly later he knew the truth, or at least enough of it to know he had committed a mortal sin. He could have assuaged his guilt, cleansed his conscience, but by that time he was in too deep himself. If he brought them down, he would bring himself down as well.

He turned to drink, and when that wouldn't drown the nightmares, he turned to the Bible. The Bible only confirmed what he already knew, that he was going to hell. And as the cancer ate away at his pancreas, the nightmares ate away at his soul.

So Booker turned to his sixteen-year-old great-granddaughter, Marilee, for redemption.

◇◇◇

It all started one summer day in 1925, when seventeen-year-old Booker decided to go fishing. Even at five o'clock in the afternoon, it was so hot the whole island was hiding away in the shade. It was a good time to get out on the water, and his mother, busy with a colicky baby, was glad to see him go. He stopped by one of the area fish houses to tell the caretaker, Gerry Lowry, he'd be coming by in the morning, hopefully with a mess of fish.

Gerry Lowry was a big man who didn't believe in baths and liked to cry when he got drunk. That afternoon he was crying, big swollen tears running down his flabby cheeks.

"I don't much care what you do," he said to Booker. "I plan to be gone on the run boat tomorrow morning." He took another swig of his drink, and then gestured for Booker to help himself to the bottle sitting next to his elbow. Since Gerry wasn't given to displays of generosity, Booker was quick to obey before the fat man changed his mind. The only glass was the one Gerry was using, so Booker tipped back the bottle. He was expecting Orgadent, which was a moonshine popular on the island, but was surprised by the smooth, expensive taste of the liquor. He took two more quick gulps while Gerry was looking out the window, liking the way the whisky slid down his throat like liquid flame.

"Where you going?" Booker asked, putting the bottle back down as Gerry looked around.

"I don't know. Somewhere. Anywhere." Now Gerry was crying in earnest, his face red. "I haven't been this scared since I fought at Argonne Forest in 1918. Boy, have I told you about Argonne Forest? I was a hero, a pure hero, is what I was." Gerry toyed with his ring. It was gold set with a gaudy blue stone, with a German inscription on the underside. Booker knew Gerry took it from a German soldier with whom he fought hand to hand for three hours. He also knew if he didn't get out of here fast, he'd have to hear the whole story again.

So he left, and didn't think much about Gerry all that night. Gerry said stuff all the time when he was drunk; sometimes it was necessary for him to dig deep for a reason to blubber. Booker caught a bunch of fish, wishing the whole time he had a bottle of that liquor Gerry was drinking, or at least some Orgadent. Fishing and drinking went together like fig jelly and hot biscuits. You could have one without the other, but why would you want to?

Around nine o'clock the next morning, he decided to call it quits and headed back over to Gerry's fish house to sell the fish and go home for a couple hours of sleep. He tied his boat to the dock and went to the back door. Inside he could hear Gerry's snores, wet, slippery exhalations, and Booker thought if the fat man intended to leave on the run boat, he'd better hurry because it was almost here. Not that Booker ever thought Gerry would, anyhow. Booker called out, but didn't put a dent in that massive racket. He tried the door, but it was tied with a rope from the inside. He went around to the front of the house, staring in curiosity at a tin wind-up speedboat sitting on the bottom step of the stairs. He wondered what kid had left the toy there, and if anyone would notice if he took it. Georgie, his little brother, would love it.

The front door was open, and Booker pushed his way inside, saying, "Gerry, you old so-and-so, I got those fish like I told you," and then he stopped, because there was something wrong about the way Gerry was breathing. Up close, it sounded wet and ragged and labored. Booker stepped closer, noticing the empty bottle on the table and the two glasses, but more interested in why old Gerry was making those strange sounds as he lay on his cot. Then he saw that Gerry's brain was running out both sides of his head.

Booker got right back on his boat and went looking for Sheriff Fitz Mitchell. It was unusual for the sheriff of Teach County to live on Comico Island, but folks said he had to live somewhere in the sprawling, sparsely populated county, so why not Comico Island? Others, more quietly, said he wanted to be closer to the rum-running, but most of the time they said this in voices too quiet to be heard. Both rum and the sheriff were hugely popular on Comico Island.

Sheriff Mitchell did not seem surprised by his story, just wiped the sweat off his face and said, "Go fetch the doctor, will you, Booker?"

Booker went to fetch the doctor from the mainland, and when he got back he found the sheriff and the run boat captain sitting on Gerry's front porch, sharing a pint of something or another. They didn't offer any to Booker as the doctor went inside to look at Gerry. After a while the doctor came back outside. He shrugged as he sat down and accepted the bottle from the sheriff.

Then they waited for Gerry to die. Every now and then the doctor would go back in and check on the man, and around four o'clock that afternoon he finally died. Booker knew it was wrong, but by that time he was wishing the fish master would just stop breathing so he could go home and sleep.

The sheriff had asked Booker a bunch of questions, and Booker answered them the best he could. When the sheriff asked him if he noticed the gun on the floor beside Gerry's cot, at first he said no, that Gerry was so afraid of guns that he cried the last time someone shot one close to his fish shack. The sheriff kept asking, though, and after a while Booker said maybe he had, because by that time he was so tired he couldn't think straight. He knew he didn't notice the gun before, but now he could see it plain as day through Gerry's open front door, lying under the cot, so it must have been there all along.

The sheriff got six people together, including Booker and the run boat captain, and held an inquest. That Booker was only seventeen and couldn't legally serve at an inquest didn't seem to bother anyone. After some discussion, the six men agreed on a verdict of suicide. Much was made of the fact that the back door was tied from the inside (no one mentioned that the front door was unlocked), and that the gun was found exactly where it would have been dropped by Gerry if he shot himself. Everyone agreed that Gerry had been an unstable soul since returning from the war, prone to hysterics and crying, and most likely killed himself in a drunken impulse. No one mentioned how much Gerry disliked guns.

The verdict was made, and Booker went home to sleep. The next day Sheriff Mitchell came by his house and offered him a job as a deputy, and his mother and father were so thrilled they offered to move his little brother back in their room so he could have his old room all to himself again.

He was paid twenty dollars a week, but before long the extra envelopes of twenties started coming in, and he couldn't find it in himself to say no. After all, the islanders' predominant sentiment toward prohibition was resounding disgust. Oftentimes, on principle alone, regular citizens would help smugglers evade capture.

He bought a nice car and built a room on his parents' house and hung out at the Shell Lodge with Sheriff Mitchell and the high rollers from the mainland. All for the price of being absent on a certain day, or looking the other way when told to do so. Another islander, Foster Garrison, was whooping it up in the gaming room, riding high on his profits as a smuggler captain. Booker was on first-name basis with Kenneth Fredericks, the owner of the Shell Lodge, and his buddy David Harrington. People looked at him with respect and he liked it.

All the while, he knew it was wrong. He could never quite shake that feeling, no matter how much he enjoyed the attention and the money. He took to drinking a lot, and gambling. His parents heard the rumors of what he was doing, and encouraged him to quit. His father gave him a Bible one liquor-soaked morning and told him he needed to reacquaint himself with Matthew, specifically the part where the devil tried to bribe Jesus with all the kingdoms of the world.

One night, he and Sheriff Fitz Mitchell stayed up all night playing poker and drinking expensive French champagne. When the sun came up over the Shell Lodge, Booker turned to Fitz and asked the question that had been haunting him: "Did Gerry Lowry really kill himself?"

Fitz kicked his chair back and propped his feet up on the rail. Down on the dock, vacationing fishermen were crowding around the local guides, eager to start their day of fishing. Many

of them had been up until all hours of the night at the Shell
Lodge's gaming tables, but wouldn't let something like lack of
sleep and a hangover interfere with their sport.

"You don't want to be thinking on that, Booker. Trust me on
this." Fitz Mitchell was a big man, not given to much introspec-
tion or thought. This was all he had to say on the subject as far
as he was concerned.

"But I have to know," Booker pressed on, the champagne
singing in his head, spurring him into a recklessness he normally
avoided. "I *need* to know."

"There are very few things you need to know in this world,
and most of them are destined to disappoint. Haven't you learned
that yet, boy?" Fitz looked over at Booker's earnest, young face
and sighed. "Let me ask you a question. The day you found Gerry
Lowry with his brains coming out his head, did you notice he
wasn't wearing that ring of his, the one he was always bragging
he took off a German soldier? It was his proudest possession,
you'll recall, one he wouldn't part with unless it was pried off
his cold, dead finger."

Booker tipped his bottle up, guzzling at the sweet champagne
while he thought. He put the bottle down and stared at Fitz.
"No, I don't reckon I saw it on his hand."

"Well, I'll tell you something. I've seen it since. He keeps it
in one of his rum holes, and he takes it out sometimes when he
gets drunk. That, and some other souvenirs he keeps in there.
He plays with it, and there's a look in his eye, like a shark gets
right before he comes up after that fish splashing around on your
line. I'm telling you, boy, I have no intention of crossing him,
and you shouldn't either. That's what Gerry Lowry did. Gerry
crossed him on just a couple bottles of liquor and now Gerry's
dead. When I looked at that man at the poker table tonight, I
got chills thinking about what he's done. You like your life, don't
you, Booker? You don't want to lose everything, the money, the
prestige, do you? And don't forget your parents and brothers.
He wouldn't stop at anything if he felt threatened, trust me, I
know."

With that, Fitz propped his hat over his eyes and promptly fell asleep, leaving Booker alone with his thoughts. He had never seen Fitz scared before, but there was fear in his voice tonight. Booker wasn't stupid enough to disregard what he heard.

He never mentioned Gerry Lowry's name again. After a couple of months, he quit the police force and went back to fishing. It took a while before he stopped looking over his shoulder when he was out on the water late at night by himself.

The problem was, he never knew exactly who he was looking for. Fitz didn't mention a name, and Booker was left to wonder which of their poker partners was a cold-blooded killer.

Besides Fitz and Booker, there were three men at the table that night: Kenneth Fredericks, David Harrington, and Foster Garrison.

Chapter Forty-two

"Granddad Booker said he was going to hell for what he did, but he wanted to die knowing that he tried to set things right. That's what he wanted me to do, set things right for him." Marilee's smile was heartbreaking. "It was the least I could do after all he'd done for me. I knew that all of them were dead, that they could no longer be punished, but Granddad said the truth needed to come out. He said Gerry's kin should know the truth.

"But I didn't have any idea how to go about it. Granddad didn't know who killed Gerry Lowry, but he knew it was one of three men. I thought if I found the ring, I would have found the killer. From what the sheriff said, the killer had hidden it away in one of his rum-running hiding holes. I thought it was possible it was still there, but I didn't know where to start.

"I did know that Kealy Lowry was Gerry's great-grandson, so I took the big jar of change Granddad left me and went over to the mainland and cashed it in. I sent that money to Kealy, hoping it would make a start on the debt my family owed his. Then I went to the library to do some research."

"I suspect you looked through some of the same things I did," Sabrina said. "I noticed the boxes of microfiche had fresh fingerprints in the dust. While I understand how you picked the houses to break into, I'm still curious how you knew where to look."

Marilee's eyes sparkled with enjoyment. She had enjoyed her task. "Granddad told me about the hiding places he knew about.

I did those first. Even though I knew Sheriff Fitz Mitchell wasn't the killer, I thought maybe he kept a diary or journal, so I went to Hill's house first. Granddad told me the sheriff's hiding hole was in the floor in the master bedroom." She glanced at Hill Mitchell, but he would not meet her eyes, so she continued her story. "Granddad also told me where David Harrington's secret hiding place was in the Harrington rental cottage, so I went there next. I didn't want to go in when there were people at the house, but when I found out the house was booked through December, I took a chance. It was the middle of the night, and I didn't figure anyone would see me if I snuck in the closet and checked the hiding place real quick. It was empty, too."

"I thought you were bigger," Maggie Fromlin said. "I see I would make a horrible eye witness. But why were you bare-foot?"

"Bare feet are quieter." Marilee shrugged. "Besides, I only wear shoes when I have to."

It was a typical island child foible, Sabrina thought.

"Then I went into Missy's house," Marilee continued. "I didn't have any idea where the hiding place was in her house, so I needed her out of the way for a while. I got a friend to call and act like he was a tourist on the mainland who needed a ride. I couldn't find the rum hole in her house, though. I was still looking when she came back. I'm sorry, Missy, I didn't mean to mess with your collection. It's pretty cool, by the way."

Missy beamed. "Isn't it? You'll have to come by for a more formal tour one of these days."

"That'd be great! Oh, and before Missy's house, I came in here. That was a total joke, though. First I ran into the guy sneaking around carrying a duffel bag, and then that old geezer jumped out at me screaming. I didn't get a chance to—"

"Aha!" yelled the old geezer, popping out of the closet. "Freeze, sucker, I've caught you!"

"Grandpa, we've already caught her. Haven't I told you about hiding in closets?" Matt got up to help his diminutive grandfather roll his cart out of the closet. "What are you doing up?"

Guy wheezed for a minute as he looked around at them with bright eyes, his tiny bald head flushed with excitement. "I bet you'd like to know where the hidey hole is, wouldn't you?"

"Yes!" Sabrina cried. "Can you show us?" They had searched unsuccessfully for it before Marilee arrived. It only made sense that the hiding place would be in the lounge, which, Sabrina had discovered in her research last night, was the room Kenneth Fredericks used as his office in the twenties.

"No, I cannot. It's gone." Guy grinned evilly at their obvious disappointment. "You all should have stayed in bed and done something illegal in thirty-two states, instead of traipsing out here to bother good, sleeping citizens."

Matt was patient. "What do you mean, it's gone, Grandpa? Where did it go?"

"It used to be in the baseboard where the bar is now. It's not there anymore, though, so don't you bother looking." He sat there, all false teeth and big ears, his little hands crossed over the top of his oxygen tank, and he looked like nothing more than a malevolent little Yoda.

"Was there anything in the hole, Guy? Like a ring, maybe?" Sabrina had to give it a try.

"No, the ring wasn't in the hole. Dad gave it to me right before he died, along with some other important mementos. I have it in my room. Do you want to see it?" He struggled to his feet and rolled his cart out without another word.

"That means Kenneth Fredericks is the killer," Marilee said. "He killed Gerry Lowry!"

Matt Fredericks groaned. "This is the last time I listen to you, Sabrina. I agreed to this because I thought it would be better than having someone break in any time they felt like it. Now you're telling me my great-grandfather was a murderer? Wonderful, just wonderful."

"Just think, Matt, of all the publicity this will bring the Shell Lodge. They say any publicity is good publicity, you know." Sabrina nodded as if she knew what she was talking about. "You could advertise the Shell Lodge as a prohibition-era showplace.

You already know a lot of stories, and with Guy's help, you could come up with smuggling tours and flapper parties, and who knows what else. It would be a lot of fun, and you could charge a lot of money for it."

"Flapper parties?" Matt looked thoughtful.

"Here it is!" Guy trundled back into the room, holding up a ring. "You can look, but you can't touch."

By unspoken consent, they all let Marilee approach the old man first. He held it close to his chest, in a half-clenched fist, but after a moment Marilee nodded. "It's got the inscription on it. It belonged to Gerry Lowry."

"I'll be happy to buy that ring off you," Walter Olgivie offered in a hearty voice. "Sight unseen, I'll give you twenty dollars."

Guy gave him a disdainful look. "You play a lousy game of Battleship."

"Guy, did your father tell you where he got the ring?"

"He took it off that man he killed. I was there, you know. I was sitting outside the fish house playing with my new wind-up speedboat, like the ones the smugglers used, when I heard the shot. Daddy came out kind of quick, and he said we needed to go talk to the sheriff. Later he told me not to tell anyone we were there, so of course I didn't, and before he died he gave me this ring. Isn't it pretty?"

"It's very nice, Guy," Sabrina managed, because no one else seemed to know what to say.

"Well, what do we do now, Sabrina?" Matt looked at Sabrina wearily. "We can't very well have Sergeant Jimmy take the killer into custody. He's been dead forty years."

"Marilee, what do you want to do?"

Marilee looked startled by Sabrina's question. "I hadn't really thought it through," she said, "but I guess I need to tell Kealy Lowry the truth about his great-granddad Gerry, that Gerry didn't kill himself."

"Maybe that'll take the burden of bad luck off him," Hill offered, and immediately looked around as if to see who had spoken.

"That sounds fine," Sabrina said.

"But what about her?" Matt indicated Marilee. "Should we call Jimmy to come get her?"

"I have SATs next Saturday," Marilee said in a stricken voice. "I don't have time to be arrested!"

"I'm sure we can work that out tomorrow." Sabrina remained seated, however, and the two or three people who had half-risen from their seats sat back down again.

"Now what?" Matt groaned.

"It was something Marilee said right before Guy came in. What night did you try to break into the Shell Lodge the first time?"

"Monday night." Marilee seemed much more light-hearted now, more like the kid she was, than the adult she wasn't.

"That was the night Gilbert was killed. Didn't you say you saw someone sneaking around with a duffel bag?"

Marilee looked around and then pointed to the back of the room at Lance Mayhew. "I'm pretty sure it was him. Why? Does it matter?"

Chapter Forty-three

Everyone turned to stare at Lance. Most of them had no idea why they were doing so.

Lance did, however. He stood and left the room without a word.

"Oh no, you don't." Sabrina was up in an instant, hurrying after the man. By the time she got to the door, he was halfway down the hall. He wasn't running, but he wasn't walking slowly, either. "Lance, was that Gilbert Kane's duffel bag you were carrying?" she called after his retreating back.

Behind her there was an interested murmur and then people began pouring out of the room as Sabrina set off after Lance.

"Sabrina, why would Lance be sneaking around with Gilbert's bag?" asked Sophie in a high, excited voice.

"And if Gilbert was dead, how did Lance get his bag? Do we know for sure it *was* Gilbert's bag?" This from Patti. "Lance, you better stop and answer some of these questions."

Lance sent a harried look over his hunched shoulder and kept walking.

"Wait for me, wait for me!" screeched Guy, who was bringing up the very rear as he struggled with his cart. Dennis Parker went back, picked up the little man, put him in the cart with his tank and sprinted him down the hall. "Wheee!"

"Please, people, can we try to be more quiet?" Matt pleaded as several guests opened their doors to see what all the commotion was about. "Sabrina, I hold you responsible for this!"

Sabrina was not far behind Lance as he turned the corner at the end of the hall.

"Lance," she said in clear, ringing tones. "What do you know about Gilbert's murder? Why did you have his bag?" She rushed to follow Lance out the glass doors onto the pool deck.

Dawn was just arriving, cool, foggy and pearlescent as it slid across the hushed sky.

Lance stopped and turned around at the edge of the pool. People kept piling out through the door and then came to a shoving, whispering halt when they saw him. No one knew what to do.

"It would be easier if you told us what you were doing, Lance." Sabrina stood closest to him, and she could see the dew drops of sweat beading his brow.

"I don't want to be like the man in her story," he said at last, and his words were so quiet that it was almost necessary to stop breathing to hear him.

"What man?" Sabrina had no idea what he was talking about.

"Speak up, buster, I'm in the balcony back here," Guy called.

"Her great-grandfather," Lance said, "the one who lived his whole life consumed by guilt. It's *already* eating away at me, and I don't think I can stand it. But if I tell you, I might lose my kids." His gray eyes were wild with indecision.

"What kind of father will you be with something like this on your conscience?" Sabrina had no idea what *this* was, but it seemed to work. Lance groaned and turned away. For a moment, she thought he was going to walk away again, but then he turned back around.

"I went after Gilbert that afternoon. I overheard him," Lance nodded at Matt, "telling the dock guy to take Gilbert over to Goat Island and leave him for a while. I looked at the big map of all the islands in the bar, and I saw where Goat Island was. I waited until I saw them leave on the motorboat, and then I took one of the kayaks. I got really lost, so it took me a while, but then I saw Gilbert lying on the beach. Just...lying there. I pulled the kayak up on the beach and went over to him, but it was too late. He was already dead. There was a bottle of wine overturned next to him, and a corkscrew covered with blood lying beside him. There was nothing I could do." He looked around as if someone had disputed this statement.

"How did you come by his duffel bag?"

"It was there, beside him. I thought it might have…things in it, so I took it. It was sitting right next to Gilbert, so it was covered with blood, and it got the kayak all bloody as well. I looked through it when I got back to my room, and that night, when the girl saw me, I was on my way to get rid of it. I took another kayak and dropped it overboard. I knew what the police would think if they found me with it."

"Did you search Gilbert's room that night?" Sabrina asked the question in as non-threatening a tone as possible. Behind her, it sounded as if the group had its collective breath held.

"Yes. I did. It turned out it didn't matter, but I didn't know that then." Lance's voice was bitter. "At the time I thought I was free, but I wanted to make sure Gilbert didn't have anything else hidden away in his room."

"What kind of things were you looking for?"

Lance looked up and seemed to notice the group for the first time in several minutes. "I was trying to save all of us Hummers, you know," he said to them. "Not just myself. But I guess you don't even know what I mean, do you? You're being blackmailed, every one of you, and you don't even know it."

Chapter Forty-four

There was a moment of stunned silence, and then everyone started talking at once. Sabrina raised a hand for quiet.

"Please continue," she said.

Lance nodded, and then swallowed hard. There was a long pause before he started speaking again. When he did, he addressed his fellow Hummers directly. "They photograph us at our sessions."

"Fred Young," Sabrina said. "The big, bald man in the leather jacket. That explains what he was doing on Rainbow Island with a camera."

Horrified expressions crossed the Hummers' faces.

"Normally you wouldn't find out until later," Lance continued. "When you left the retreat, the Hum would be gone, but there would be an envelope full of pictures waiting for you when you got home. Pictures of you. Doing what they made us do in our sessions." He paused meaningfully, and Sabrina glanced around to see shock and panic.

"What did they make you do?" Guy called out. "Did I miss something?"

Lance waved away the question, and Sabrina could see the relief on the faces of the Hummers. "It's not important. Suffice it to say we were desperate, and truly thought these...rituals would help."

"I suppose they want money to keep quiet about these pictures?" Here was the money, Sabrina thought, it had been there all along.

But Lance surprised her.

"No, they don't ask for a dime. There's always a request, but it's seldom for money. You see, it's more complicated than that. We're not picked randomly. Someone in our life has nominated us for this torture. In my case, it was my ex-wife. She heard about this...service through a friend. Word of mouth is the only advertising for this type of thing, but it can be very effective. My ex-wife paid a lot of money to Hummers International to set me up." He took a deep breath and looked around at his fellow victims. "They come in the middle of the night and knock us out. Then they use a hypodermic needle to insert two miniature electrodes into our backs. The electrodes are so small that they are almost undetectable by most medical diagnostic procedures. Gilbert stole the plans for the electrodes from a biomedical research firm where he worked before coming to Hummers International, and then paid someone to adapt them for his purposes.

"These electrodes feed sound waves through our skin, which to us sound like a refrigerator running, or a diesel motor idling. No one else can hear it. It gets louder and louder as time goes on, and we get more and more desperate. Doctors are useless, because the electrodes don't show up on their tests."

"They insert the electrodes in your *back*? I would suspect most doctors would be concentrating on your head and ears. But how do they work?" Sabrina involuntarily put her hand to her back, and noticed that many of the Hummers were doing the same.

"The technology is based on a recent invention that helps deaf people hear through their skin, instead of through their ears. The noise sounds like it is coming from inside your head." Lance grimaced. "We become willing to do almost anything to get rid of it. Most of us turn to the Internet, and most of us discover Hummers International. When we contact them for help, they set us up on these retreats. Once we're here, they make us believe that we have to do these...things to get rid of the Hum. And they're waiting there with the camera. They deliberately do this outside, you know, just to make it more humiliating, and the photos more shocking."

"But surely this doesn't work on everyone? What if a person refused to perform at these sessions? Or what if they never find Hummers International in the first place, or sign up for the retreat?" Sabrina was trying to grasp the enormity of this blackmail scheme.

"Of course there are failures. The blackmailer pays a hefty fee even if the victim doesn't cooperate, though they would get the bulk of their money back."

"But this doesn't account for the thousands of people around the world who suffer from this Hum. That's been going on for years. The government even funded an investigation into it."

Lance shrugged. "Michael and Gilbert have been doing this for a couple of years. I don't know about all those other people, the ones who aren't hearing the Hum through the electrodes. I suppose they're hearing something, though I don't know what."

"Master Joseph hears it for real, I know that," Sophie said, her voice firm with certainty.

Sabrina nodded. Whatever shenanigans Hummers International Incorporated had going on, she did not doubt that Joseph Siderius' Hum was genuine.

"How did you find out all this?" Patti asked, her voice hard with anger.

"The second day we were here, I went by Gilbert's room to clear up a question he had about my payment for the retreat. Isn't that nice, by the way? We have to pay for the privilege of being set up for blackmail. He wasn't there. The door was locked, but he hadn't pulled it all the way shut. When I knocked on it, the door swung open. I figured I would go in and wait for him. I saw pictures lying on his desk and others displayed on his laptop. They were…they were horrible. I was too stunned to think, at first. I just left.

"I went down for a drink and saw Gilbert in the bar. He looked like he was going to be there for a while. By this time, I had recovered my wits. I went back up and copied his hard drive onto my laptop. Then I went through it. All of it's in there. He must have been getting sloppy, to leave that laptop out of its locked briefcase."

Sabrina remembered the first time she met Gilbert, and Michael Siderius saying: *You're getting sloppy, you know that? You've been acting like a chicken with its head cut off ever since we got here.* Something was weighing on Gilbert's mind, enough to make him careless when he should have been most on his guard.

"I found him that night in the restaurant and confronted him with what I knew. Gilbert laughed—he was quite drunk—and he said he'd make me a deal. He wouldn't give my session pictures to my ex-wife to use against me in our upcoming custody hearing, if I would keep my mouth shut. I didn't know what to say, I was so pissed. We were in public, and I left after a few heated words. When I heard he was going to be on the island by himself, it seemed like a perfect opportunity to talk to him in private. That's why I went, but when I saw he was dead, I took the duffel bag in case there were pictures in it. Good thing I did, because there was a bunch of them in there, plus a lot of other information about the blackmailing scheme. That night I broke into Gilbert's room, took his laptop, and searched for any other incriminating evidence. After that, I thought I was safe. I thought we were all safe from them."

Lance shook his head. "Little did I know, Michael Siderius had another file with all the same information. Gilbert had told him that I knew about them, and after Gilbert died, Michael confronted me, accusing me of killing Gilbert. We had a little altercation and I punched him. But I kept my mouth shut, anyway, because I couldn't bear to lose my kids. I couldn't bear for them to ever see those pictures." Lance's voice broke and he dropped his head into his hands.

Sabrina looked around to see that the Hummers had closed ranks. "Did any of you know this was going on?"

They all shook their heads.

"I know who's doing it to me, though," Patti said. "I'm being sued by this woman who has hated me since we were in high school. She has tons of money ever since her husband died, but now she wants my coffee shop, too. She must've planned to use the pictures to put me out of business, and who knows what else."

"It's Shane, I know it is," Sophie murmured, and Dennis held her hands tightly. "He'll do anything to get me back."

"I don't know who would do this to me," Dennis said, looking around. "I can't think of anyone who hates me."

It was Matt who answered. "It could be anyone," he said. "You're a big basketball star. Any number of people would love to have something on you so they could control whether you win or lose your games."

Dennis looked stricken. "Someone could use those pictures to make me blow a game whenever they wanted me to! I wouldn't do it, though, I'd quit first."

"I, on the other hand, can think of about a dozen people right off hand who would pay lots of money to get me by the…ahem." Walter laughed, but it was weak, wavering sound.

"My ex-wife won the lottery," Lance said. "I wondered what she'd do with the money. Now I know."

"I wondered where the money came into this," Sabrina said. "Not all of you are rich, but all of you have rich enemies. Matt, you better call the police to come get Michael Siderius." She felt incredibly tired all of a sudden.

"He was just here," Sophie said. "I saw him come out of his room and follow us. He was listening to everything Lance said."

They looked around, but Michael had disappeared.

Chapter Forty-five

Vicki Carroway was locking the front door of Paradise Vacations when she saw Sabrina Dunsweeney limping up the front steps. Vicki turned, putting a hand in her purse for her stun gun. She'd been attacked before by unhappy customers.

Sabrina stopped at the top of the stairs and regarded Vicki without speaking. Her blond curls were smashed flat on one side of her head, as if she just woke up and didn't think to run a comb through them before leaving the house, and her clothes looked as if she hadn't changed them in days.

Vicki smiled. This would be fun.

"I've got something I want to say to you." Sabrina's voice was calm, and for the first time, Vicki noticed the bird sitting on her shoulder. Vicki tried to take a step back, but the door was behind her. She wondered if stun guns worked on birds.

"I know you're not here in an official capacity. I heard you got fired. So, what do you want?" The bird was looking at her. Just staring with those beady little eyes. Vicki wanted to wring its tiny neck. Her father used to make her spend the night in the chicken coop as punishment for everything from talking back to bringing ice cream cones to her convalescent mother. Ever since, she hadn't been able to stand their musty smells, their feathers, or those chirpy noises they made.

"No, I'm here as a private citizen. I wanted to tell you good-bye. You've caused enough havoc on this island, and I think it's time for you to leave."

Oh, this was rich, rich, rich! Was the woman serious? "*You* think it's time for *me* to go? The last I heard, you were the one without a job or a home. I think it's time for *you* to leave." Vicki went to step around the lunatic, but couldn't bring herself to come any closer to the bird, so she acted like she had put her leg out to inspect her hose for runs.

"The game's up, Vicki. No one wants you here. If you don't leave voluntarily, I'm going to personally make sure your life is miserable until you do."

"Oh, yeah? I'm quivering in my boots." Vicki smirked, but her hands were shaking just a little bit. Why was the woman freaking her out? She seemed different, somehow. Vicki reached for bravado. "I plan to be around for a long, long time, Sabrina, you mark my words."

The battle lines had been drawn.

Sabrina's voice was soft. "It's time for you to leave."

Vicki found she had nothing to say.

Sabrina turned and walked down the stairs into the gathering shadows.

Chapter Forty-six

After leaving Vicki, Sabrina steered the moped down the gravel road beside the harbor. She should be going the other way, toward her apartment and her packing, but she had unfinished business at Boathouse Alley.

The small nap she stole after returning from the hospital on the mainland was just a drop in the empty reservoir of her sleep deficit. She felt as if she could sleep for days, but when she was finally done with the police out at Shell Lodge, the choice had been either lying down to sleep or visiting Lima.

Lima was asleep, but still Sabrina told him everything that had happened. She hoped the story would relieve the boredom that abundant unconsciousness must be bringing him. Mary Garrison Tubbs listened in open-mouthed astonishment

"And he got away? They let him get away?" Mary pounded her fist on a nearby machine, making it sound an alarm. Nurses came running.

Amid the scrambling nurses, Sabrina nodded. "Michael must have heard Lance tell his story. By the time the police arrived, he and his father had left, and they found Michael's rental Jeep at the ferry docks. Cindy at the ticket booth said Michael bought a walk-aboard ticket, but by the time they got things organized on the mainland, the ferry had docked and Michael was gone."

"Was Cindy sober when she saw him?"

"It was seven o'clock in the morning," Sabrina protested.

"You didn't answer my question." Mary tapped her foot.

"Anyway, it looks like he left his father on the island. The Hummers agree, though, that Joseph never uttered a word in their sessions. It looks like Michael was using him as a puppet, so the police have named Joseph a person of interest for his own safety. They still haven't found him." Sabrina had not told them where to look. She wasn't sure why, but it somehow seemed a betrayal of both Joseph and Bicycle.

"And the Hummers, they're all here at the hospital getting those electrodes taken out?"

"I'm sure they're done by now. With the help of the files from Gilbert's computer, the doctors knew exactly where to look." Sabrina gazed down at Lima. He looked so fragile, his cheeks drooping with age spots, his eyelids bruised and brittle. He would hate it if he knew he looked vulnerable.

Now, as she drove the moped down Hurricane Harbor Circle, she saw Sergeant Jimmy watching her, shaking his head.

"Where in the world did you get that contraption?" he asked as she pulled up in front of him. "Never mind. They've been questioning Lance Mayhew all day, but he's sticking to his story."

"He could have killed Gilbert easily," Sabrina mused as Calvin woke up and chirped at Jimmy. He liked the sergeant's beard. "And he had a very good reason to do so."

"I'm not convinced he didn't go to Goat Island with the intention of killing the victim. Why didn't he sign out the kayak? Why weren't his fingerprints on it? By his own admission he was the last to see Gilbert. Whether he did it or not is anyone's guess. We're still sorting through the ramifications of this blackmailing scam. Of course, this just introduces a bunch more people who had very good reasons to want the man dead. I wish we knew where the murder weapon—the corkscrew—went. That bugs me, that the killer came back for it after Lance Mayhew saw the victim dead on the beach. I'm not sure what to think, but I have my money on Michael Siderius."

"I think he was jealous of Gilbert." Sabrina tried to keep the moped balanced with one good leg. "If Gilbert was gone, Michael would have complete control of the organization."

Jimmy nodded. "Makes sense to me. I've got him figured for the attack on the model, and the ransacking of Myers' boat, at the very least. I think he must have figured out what Myers was up to and sacked his boat as a kind of warning."

"Then he went on to attack Sophie. I wonder why?"

"He may have been looking for something, or he may have just felt like taking a go at her. She is a beautiful woman, and Siderius doesn't strike me as the type to control his impulses."

"What about Sam? What happens to him?"

"Officially, he's still our guy, but we've widened the investigation. A judge set his bail this morning, and some group out of Taos raised it by this afternoon. We told him not to leave the island, and since we impounded his boat, he's staying down at Boathouse Alley."

Sabrina didn't mention that she had already heard this piece of information through the island grapevine, or that Boathouse Alley was where she was headed now. She was in Jimmy's good graces at the moment, and she did so hate to ruin that.

"What about Marilee and the break-ins? What will happen to her?"

"Nobody wants to press charges, not even the absent owner of the rental cottage, once I explained the circumstances. I think Marilee's learned her lesson, and Matt Fredericks has apparently decided to capitalize on the whole thing. He's hired Marilee to be some sort of part-time prohibition tour guide at his lodge. Isn't that something?"

"It sure is," Sabrina agreed, but her eyes were on a tall man limping down the street toward them.

"It's good to have Doc Hailey back in town." Jimmy had followed the direction of her gaze.

The doctor approached the two of them and tipped his head in a cordial nod. "Sergeant, Sabrina. I trust you are doing well?"

"Have you heard anything about the Hummers, doctor?" Sabrina asked. He had coordinated the five Hummers' visit to the hospital on the mainland to remove the electrodes.

"The whole thing is very interesting," he said. "These electrodes are based on the principle of transmitting sound through the skin, bones, and liquids of our body, which in theory allows people to hear without using their ears. I really would like to do some more research on the whole matter. Perhaps after my next trip."

"The Hummers are back from the mainland, and we've asked that they stay around a while longer," Jimmy said. "This whole thing is still up in the air."

"However, they are all so happy to be rid of the electrodes and the resultant hum that they are treating these extra days as a sort of vacation," Doc Hailey said with a smile that lit up his irregular face.

"I guess I can't help but wonder about all the other people out there who are hearing the Hum," Sabrina said. "They aren't connected with Hummers International and their blackmailing scheme, so what's causing their Hum?"

"I looked into it after I heard Joseph Siderius speak all those years ago. It seems clear that there are thousands of people who are suffering but, because their symptoms are so ephemeral, it's hard to get anyone to pay attention to them. It's a shame really, because these people may very well be tuning into something that is affecting all of us, and we don't even realize it."

"Sounds pretty deep," Jimmy said.

"I'll be going now," Doc Hailey said. "Sabrina, please feel free to come see me if your injuries should trouble you. As a matter of fact," he hesitated, the first time Sabrina had seen him show anything but complete confidence, "perhaps we could have dinner one night?"

Calvin trilled in delight as she sped toward Boathouse Alley. Well, sped was not quite the word for it. Calvin enjoyed the wind through his feathers, but he considered anything over ten miles an hour too fast. That's why Sabrina was leading a parade of impatiently honking cars around Hurricane Harbor Circle toward the ferry docks. She understood their agitation as the ferry's horn blew, announcing the last departure for the evening. She pulled off the road and watched the cars barrel past her, only to brake at the roadblock set up in front of the entrance to the ferry.

The police weren't taking any chances. Sabrina nodded in approval and waved at the police officers manning the blockade. The public beach was empty this cloudy, windy evening, except for a few diehards who were searching the sand for shells. The sound looked dark and unsettled as the wind pushed at it fitfully, and thick clouds were drawn over the sky.

Ahead was the hulking row of two-story boathouses. The old dames of Comico Island, made up in bright colors for their last birthday party, were considered one of the island's historic landmarks. Sabrina couldn't imagine the waterfront without them. They were moored on the old ferry docks, which were damaged in a long-ago hurricane. Beyond the boathouses, behind a fence, were the ruins of the rest of the docks. It was a large complex, as the Navy had built onto the existing docks to use as a supply depot during World War II. The military soon abandoned the docks to move to a newly built base on the other end of the island.

Every year someone would start kicking up a fuss about tearing down the docks because they were an eyesore and a danger to the fisherman who snuck past the padlocked gates. Every year the initiative failed out of inertia. There wasn't enough money to tear them down, and besides, no one really cared.

Sabrina got off the moped and limped toward the Boathouse Alley office, which was a small shack perched on the edge of the docks. An old golf cart, with "Boathouse Alley" painted across the side, was parked out front. The boathouses were rented out weekly and monthly, and a few of them had year-round inhabitants. Right now they were rocking and creaking in the freshening gale, straining against the massive ropes that held them in place.

Sabrina stared down the row of boathouses, wondering how she was going to find Sam. Most of the boathouses contained two apartments, and it looked as if some of them were occupied. However, there was no clue as to which might house Sam Myers. For all Sabrina knew, he was watching her out the window right now.

Her only warning was a startled chirp from Calvin before an arm came down across her windpipe, and Sabrina was dragged backward into the shadows beside the empty office. Sabrina choked and clawed at the arm holding her, but it felt like a sinewy piece of board across her neck. She couldn't breathe, and all of her exertion was not improving her oxygen supply. She could hear Calvin shrieking and hoped her attacker would not harm him as well.

She began jabbing her elbows into her attacker's abdomen, and kicking her heels back into sensitive shin and ankle bones, wincing as her own sore ankle protested this treatment. Just as Sabrina felt the edges of her vision turn black, her assailant yelped and let go. She stumbled forward a few steps, drawing in great gasping breaths of air, and then forced herself to keep going. Her moped was only a few steps away, but her attacker wasn't down for the count. Footsteps were already staggering behind her in pursuit.

Her ankle was sending sharp, stabbing signals up her leg, and she knew she couldn't rely on it much longer. Calvin was tangled in her hair, beating his wings against the back of her neck and screeching for help for all he was worth. Sabrina hoped someone heard him, because she didn't have the breath for screaming right now.

She reached her moped and threw herself on it. She started the engine and felt a hand come down on her arm just before she took off with a peel of rubber past the row of boathouses.

Here the dock was concrete and about as wide as a one-lane road. That was the good news. The bad news was that there was a fence up ahead, blocking the entrance to the ruined docks beyond. She should never have gone this way, but that was well and good to think now. At the time, there was no choice but to accelerate whichever way the moped was pointed.

A glance behind showed that any hope that her attacker had abandoned the chase was misguided. A golf cart—it must have been the one that had been parked in front of the office—was headed in her direction. It was already past the boathouses and was accelerating along the cracked concrete toward her. She still could not make out the person's face.

A trill of alarm had her looking around to see the rusty gate looming in front of her. She slammed on the brakes, skidding the last few inches so the front tire of the moped crashed into the gate. The rusty chain holding it together snapped, and the gate swung open in creaky invitation.

With no other choice, Sabrina revved the moped through the gate. She slowed, wondering if she should try to bar the gate in some fashion, but the sound of shrieking metal told her it was already too late. A glance over her shoulder confirmed her suspicion. The golf cart was right behind her.

And now she could see the face of her assailant.

Chapter Forty-seven

Michael Siderius was smiling.

Sabrina had to look twice to make sure she was seeing correctly. She was. Michael seemed to be enjoying himself as he steered the golf cart around debris on the dock, so much so that a gleeful grin played across his handsome face.

Sabrina turned back around just in time to see that she was about to become airborne. At some point in the last couple of years, kids had snuck past the gate and built a makeshift skateboard park. The first ramped jump sent her flying two feet into the air at fifteen miles an hour, her legs flying out from beneath her as she clutched at the handles. Calvin whooped as they hit the ground with a jarring thump and she managed to regain her feet on the footrests enough to continue forward.

A quick look revealed that Michael had tried to avoid the jump, though he was only partially successful. Two tires hit the ramp, lifting them off the ground. For a moment it looked as if maybe the cart would tip over, but then the airborne tires came crashing down with a sparking jolt.

She thought she was better prepared for the next jump, but it proved higher than the first, and she hung in the air, fighting to keep her grip on handles and pedals while trying to ignore the hard concrete sliding beneath her. If she landed the wrong way, the results would be at the least very painful, and possibly fatal. Her moped hit the ground on the back tire and she felt like an inept cousin of Evel Kneivel as she roared along in classic wheelie presentation. She leaned all her weight forward and finally the front tire came down with a teeth-knocking thud.

The last jump she managed to avoid altogether, and as she accelerated past it, she saw that it was a good thing, too, as the jump was almost five feet tall. She couldn't even imagine children launching their fragile little bodies off it.

Michael had avoided the last two jumps, but was having trouble steering his larger vehicle around the trash and crumpled concrete that littered the docks. She wondered why he had come back to the island, and then realized he had never left. Cindy was mistaken about the identity of the buyer of the walk-aboard ticket.

Michael must have arrived at the docks after the first ferry sailed, but the police showed up soon after that and he was forced to leave on foot. Remembering the die-hard beach-goers she saw as she passed the public beach, she thought it was likely that Michael had hung out on the beach all day, watching for his chance to board the ferry. Clearly, that opportunity never arose. He must have seen her pass on the moped and stop at the boathouse office, though what he wanted with her was anyone's guess. What did Jimmy say? *Siderius doesn't strike me as the type to control his impulses.* Perhaps he was coming after her out of sheer anger that she helped unmask his blackmail scheme and engineered the fall of the Hummers International empire.

Whatever his reasons, he showed no signs of giving up. Sabrina concentrated on the seamed, trash-strewn pavement before her. She refused to think about what she would do when she reached the end of the long dock. She briefly considered the wooden finger piers that jutted off the main concrete pier, but they were rickety and marked with strident "Keep out" signs. Her only choice was to continue the way she was going until she reached the end of the line. But then what?

On the face of it, Sabrina and the moped should have won the race to the end of the pier hands down. Her moped was faster and more maneuverable than Michael's golf cart, which seemed to top out at about fifteen miles an hour. This equation, however, did not take Calvin into consideration. He had somehow made it to the top of her head, and was perched there precariously, his claws dug into her scalp for balance. Whenever she tried to push the moped faster than ten or fifteen miles an hour, he yelped as his grip on her head loosened. The thought of him flying off her head like a yellow feather duster and landing in the path of the golf cart kept her speed down. He'd never survive. Like a turtle following the sloth, she and Michael continued their slow motion race toward the end of the pier.

Sabrina tried to reach up and rescue Calvin from his dangerous perch, but as soon as her hand left the handle, a loose rock sent the moped's front tire jittering sideways. For a moment she thought she was going to lose control, and she fought to keep the moped from falling over on its side. She regained control, but Michael pulled his golf cart up beside her and began edging her toward the edge of the pier and the fifteen-foot dropoff into the water. Sabrina tried to accelerate, but Calvin screeched in alarm as his grip loosened. As the edge neared, she did the only thing she could, and slammed on the brakes. Then she dodged behind the golf cart and did a slow crawl past it on the other side. Michael looked around at her, his face twisted with frustration, and in that moment his vehicle slammed into a piling.

The golf cart bounced backward, two of its tires scrabbling for purchase on the concrete, the other two hanging in air. Michael slid out the passenger side of the cart as the vehicle slipped off the pier into the rough, hungry water.

There was no time to gloat over this victory, however, because the end of the pier was upon her. Sabrina reached it, slid the moped into a U-turn, and charged back the way she had come. She hoped to take Michael off guard and swoop by him before he knew what was happening, and for a moment it looked like it was going to work. At the last moment he took a charging leap across the concrete and grabbed the edge of her shirt. He lost his grip almost immediately, but she was thrown off balance. The moped wobbled back and forth as she fought for control, and then almost apologetically laid down on its side. Sabrina found herself sliding across the concrete, her hands over her head to protect Calvin.

When she sat up, she saw she had been jettisoned down one of the older wooden finger piers. Michael was coming toward her, and there would be no opportunity this time to get by him. Sabrina had no choice but to limp away from him, trying not to trip over loose and missing boards.

In front of her was new orange plastic fencing, and an old rusted sign that said "Keep out." Sabrina grabbed the top of the flexible fencing and pulled it down enough so she could climb over it. Her ankle was throbbing now, as were several other newer injuries.

Beyond the fencing, the dock continued for ten more feet, and then petered out into horizontal girder boards connected to pilings. The dock slats had long since disappeared. The wind was blowing viciously, kicking up whale spouts of salt spray.

Sabrina threw a glance back over her shoulder to see Michael clambering over the orange fencing, ripping it in the process. Calvin chittered in fear, huddling against the back of her neck. Sabrina looked around for a weapon, but all the loose boards had been taken or fallen into the water below. Michael was almost upon her.

Sabrina stepped out onto the nearest girder. The board was only an inch and a half wide, and slippery with salt spray, but she was desperate. She shuffled sideways until she reached the first piling and clung onto it for dear life. She looked up to see Michael kicking his shoes off and laughing.

"I almost went to the Olympics, Sabrina, did you know that?" he called over the sound of pounding waves and cawing seagulls.

With a capsized feeling, Sabrina remembered. Michael's sport was gymnastics. She had made a horrific mistake. "Why are you doing this?" she called back. "Hurting me won't help you in any way."

"Sure it will. It'll make *me* feel better. You've ruined everything, you know." As he talked he stepped out onto the girder. He smiled as he spun around on one foot and then moved easily toward her. Sabrina turned and looked at the next girder, but she couldn't bring herself to go any farther. What was the point? He would just follow her. Her options were gone. Below the angry water swirled around large rocks. If she fell off now, it would be almost impossible to miss one of those rocks. And even if she did, they were a long way from shore, and the waves were rough.

She looked up to see Michael doing a handstand. He brought his feet down and stood, smiling at her. He was like a wild puppy off its leash, and had been ever since Gilbert died. Gilbert had been Michael's restraining influence, Sabrina saw now. Without him, Michael was free to give in to his every dangerous inclination.

"Did you try to run me over the other night?" she asked, the only thing that occurred to her.

"Sure did. Fred said you saw him taking pictures of the morons at their rituals. Then I saw you talking to Myers on his sailboat. I knew who Myers was, and I figured you and him were plotting against me. I followed you after you left the lodge. Once I saw you were headed for the bridge, I went around the long way and parked on the other side to wait for you."

"You almost killed me!" Calvin added a shriek of indignation and Michael laughed.

"I didn't figure I'd kill you, though I wasn't sure, really. I just wanted to get you out of the way for a couple of days until we left. You don't scare easy, that's for sure. Did you even notice how close I came to running you off the road that night on the causeway?"

"That was you? I thought it was just some drunk. And what about Gilbert? Why did you kill Gilbert?"

"Gilbert? I didn't touch a hair on his head, as much as I might have wanted to. I've never killed anyone before, though I had some fun roughing up the model. Now that I see how easy it is to do and not get caught, I think I'll start. With you." His smile was wide.

"If you didn't kill Gilbert, who did?"

"You're asking me? I thought it was Lance. I was going to give the guy a medal but he punched me in the nose instead. Gilbert was losing it, he really was. Someone needed to put him out of his misery." Michael raised his arms over his head and leaned backward until he touched the girder with the palms of his hands.

"What about your father? Where's he?" For the first time it occurred to her that Michael could have harmed Joseph.

"He wasn't in his room when I left, not that I would have taken him anyway. The old man has no idea what's going on. He would sit there and look wise while I intoned all this bogus crap. He's in his own world, has been since he started getting all mystical and then stopped talking. I think he started believing all his own hype about the Hum, can you believe it?" Michael laughed.

"That's when you and Gilbert stepped in and took over Hummers International."

"My father didn't know what to do with what he had. He put together this organization of rubes, and then he squandered the gold mine. Gilbert and I saw the potential, and we did what needed to be done."

"By blackmailing people?"

"It was a great scheme. It was. It's all over now, of course, but I have a new idea that will be even better. This time I can do it the way *I* want, with no Gilbert to ruin the fun. It'll be great." Michael smiled with genuine pleasure. "I'd love to do a back flip," he said, almost to himself.

"A back flip?" Sabrina stared at him in astonishment.

"A back flip is the only thing that kept me from winning Olympic gold, you know." Michael bounced up and down on the balls of his feet.

"I bet you couldn't do one here." Sabrina's hand slipped on bird excrement, and she threw both of her arms around the piling to keep her balance. The light was fading fast.

"That Olympics thing, it was a fluke. I'd've won gold if my foot hadn't slipped." Michael was growing agitated, gripping and ungripping the girder with his bare toes.

"I bet you were never any good. Nothing I've seen you do looks very impressive to me." Calvin was muttering miserably and Sabrina was beginning to shiver as the combination of spray and wind leached away her body heat.

Michael glared at her. "Not impressive? This from the woman clutching a piling covered with bird crap? Not so high and mighty now, are you?"

"I'm saying I don't think you're very good, that's all. In fact, you look pretty lousy to me." Sabrina's teeth chattered as she said this. It was all or nothing. Either Michael would come after her, and that would be the end, or—

Michael took a step forward and then did the back flip. He executed it perfectly, coming down on both feet. He started to raise his arms triumphantly, but his foot slipped, and he fell forward. His head collided with the girder with a brain-smashing thud and he lay still, his arms and legs draped on either side of the girder.

◇◇◇

A half an hour later, a battered and bruised Sabrina rode her hiccuping moped back down the pier. It had been no easy task getting to safety past an unconscious Michael Siderius. She had to clamber over him, praying he wouldn't fall onto the rocks below and take her with him.

But in the end, she managed that and more, as she pulled his insensate body the few feet to the relative safety of the dock. He now lay wrapped in flexible orange fencing. She had no illusions it would hold him for long after he woke, but she hoped it would be good enough until the police arrived.

Sam Myers was coming out of one of the boathouses as she rode up.

"Sabrina! Are you okay?"

Sabrina pulled her moped to a weary stop. Without asking any other questions, Sam helped her into the boathouse and called 9-1-1. Then he listened as she recounted her tale. Sirens were approaching as she finished.

"Your sister," Sabrina said. "How did you know that the Hummers were involved in her suicide?"

"I found one of the pictures. This was after the police cleared me for the death of her ex-husband. I could have taken it to them, but...I couldn't do that to her. I burned it, but it put me on the right track. I hooked up with a group in Taos, New Mexico, who steered me in the right direction. I heard Hummers International planned to bring their next retreat to Comico Island, so I took a leave of absence from the university and got a job here as dock master a couple of months ago. Then I waited for my chance to avenge my sister."

"Did you kill Gilbert?" Sabrina was too tired to be anything other than blunt.

"Did you know a beetle is capable of—"

"Sam. Stop. Tell me the truth, please."

Sam leaned forward to brush dirt off her face. "No. I didn't. I wanted to, but I didn't. My only thought was to catch Michael or Gilbert doing something illegal so I could go to the police."

"So why did you have Gilbert's camera? With his blood on it?"

"He bled on it when we were on the boat on the way to Goat Island. He caught his hand in the zipper of the duffel bag. And then...I took the camera when his back was turned. After finding that picture of my sister, I wanted to see what kind of pictures he had on his camera."

Sabrina believed him.

With blaring sirens and blazing lights, the police cars pulled up outside. Sabrina leaned on Sam's arm as she limped out to face them.

Chapter Forty-eight

Like a blowtorch heating metal until it glowed red and orange and flowed liquid silver, the setting sun burned a brilliant path across the mercurial water.

Sabrina dipped her paddle in the water and continued on.

She was sore, but most of the damage was just aching muscles and a pretty good case of road rash. The paddling seemed to be loosening her up, and she shrugged out of her jacket as her muscles warmed and stretched like pulled taffy.

Up ahead was Goat Island, and she stopped rowing as she neared the island. She had no intention of stepping foot on the sand where Gilbert Kane met his demise. Above, a seagull circled, his body bathed a rich orange from the setting sun. His foot hung oddly, as if maybe it was broken.

She felt calm and rested as she watched the serene water ignite in an explosion of color. The seagull circled endlessly, his raucous call lonely and cheerless. An osprey shrieked back from her large nest high in a tree. A second osprey in a nearby tree added to the racket.

Michael Siderius maintained his innocence in Gilbert Kane's death, as did Lance Mayhew and Sam Myers. With Lance's help, the police had retrieved Gilbert's duffel bag from the sound. The papers were soggy and unreadable, but there were two interesting things about the bag, one in its presence, the other in its absence.

There was no corkscrew. The weapon used to kill Gilbert was still unaccounted for, which left the police baffled.

The second seemed so insignificant that Lance had not thought to mention it. There was another item in the bag beside the papers.

A rope.

Sabrina's gaze swept over Goat Island, taking in the few trees that grew straight up without any reachable lower branches. The rest of the vegetation on the island was tangled undergrowth no higher than a man's head. It would have been impossible for Gilbert to use the rope. Was that when he started eyeing the corkscrew?

Today she had gone to Bicycle Bob's house. Bicycle was passed out on the couch, clutching a picture frame to his chest. Joseph sat on the couch, painting his indecipherable symbols onto a piece of driftwood. He didn't look up as she came in.

"Your son has been arrested," she told him. "They know what he's been doing to those people. It's all over now."

Joseph did not look up as she left, either, but there were tears rolling down his wrinkled cheeks.

She thought about Joseph's touch the other day, the one that had made her head buzz and rational thought impossible. She thought about how much Joseph must hate Gilbert for what he'd done to Hummers International and his life's work, not to mention his son.

Gilbert Kane had been acting strangely the last week of his life, distracted and forgetful. He kept clutching his head. She couldn't forget the expression on Gilbert's face when Joseph touched him that first day in the meeting room. Was Joseph somehow able to tap Gilbert into the Hum? Gilbert must have been under a lot of strain those last few days, and the Hum would have only compounded it. Lance was threatening to go to the police, and Gilbert knew Sam Myers was camped on his doorstep, just waiting for a misstep. It was enough to drive a man to drink.

Or to suicide.

The osprey called again, a shrill piercing sound that made Sabrina want to clap her hands over her ears. She looked up at the massive nest in the top of the pine tree, thinking about the ospreys' compulsive junk collecting.

Was there a bloody corkscrew buried in that mass of twigs somewhere? Was Joseph Siderius crying because his long nightmare was finally over, or because he had done the unforgivable, and driven an unstable man over the edge?

To the west, the sun was being submerged in a puddle of incandescent light. The edges of the salmon clouds were turning dark, like the golden glory of an orange turning black with age and time.

Sabrina glanced at her watch. If she didn't hurry, she was going to be late. She might not have a job or a home, or any idea what she was going to do next, but she did have something.

A date.

Sabrina picked up her paddle and turned back toward Comico Island.

Author's Note

Comico Island is fictional, created from a conglomeration of traditions and lore from some of my favorite islands. This time, I utilized two books by Elaine Blohm Jordan, *Tales of Pine Island* and *Pine Island, the Forgotten Island,* to lend verisimilitude to my Comico stories.

In the forensics department, I would like to extend thanks to D. P. Lyle, MD, for answering my admittedly bloody questions about corkscrews and their effect on the human brain. Any mistakes are my own.

The Hummers, or Hearers, are real, though Hummers International is not. If you are interested in more information about the Hum phenomenon, please go to my website, www.wendyhowellmills.com, for links to some interesting Hum-related sites.

I would like to thank Momma, A.J., and Alan for putting aside everything and reading this manuscript in its early stages. They understood the urgency: the baby is coming, the baby is coming!

Finally, I would like to thank you, my readers. Without you, Comico Island would just be a figment of my imagination. You make it real.

To receive a free catalog of Poisoned Pen Press titles, please contact us in one of the following ways:

Phone: 1-800-421-3976
Facsimile: 1-480-949-1707
Email: info@poisonedpenpress.com
Website: www.poisonedpenpress.com

Poisoned Pen Press
6962 E. First Ave. Ste. 103
Scottsdale, AZ 85251